D0149503

ADVANCE PRAISE FOR

PREMONITION

"A psycho-thriller roller coaster ride that probes the dark corners of one woman's seemingly overwhelming paranoia…or is it? From a crime and justice expert, *Premonition* nails every detail of the criminal mind, the hunter and the hunted. *Premonition* is full of twists and surprises…*I love it!* Bravo!"

—NANCY GRACE, Founder, CrimeOnline.com, Host of *Crime Stories* on Fox Nation, Sirius XM, and *NYT* Bestselling Author

"Chilling and original, *Premonition* is a brilliant debut thriller from Wendy Whitman, an insider whose deep knowledge of crime and the law has created a platform for suspenseful storytelling. Taut and fast-paced, Whitman's tale, and her unique central character, combine to create a riveting plot that drives the story to its stunning conclusion."

—JACK FORD, Emmy and Peabody Award–Winning Journalist and Bestselling Author of *Chariot on the Mountain*

"A unique psychological thriller that weaves true crime into a plot that keeps the reader captivated from the very first page. A bold, heartfelt debut novel from an author who has created one of the most complex and provocative heroines in recent memory. A perfect read sure to keep you up at night."

—RITA COSBY, Emmy-Winning TV Host and Bestselling Author of *Quiet Hero*

"My friend and colleague at Court TV, Wendy Whitman, has created a compelling psychological thriller filled with shocking twists that captivate the reader to the very end…. Whitman weaves plot, personality, and prose in a high-octane suspense that will give you paper cuts as you quickly turn the pages. *Premonition* offers a gripping storyline…and a chilling chase to an ending that you never expected."

—GREGG JARRETT, Network Legal Analyst and Bestselling Author

"If there is anyone best suited to write a book about the reality of evil in this crazy world we live in, it's Whitman. Her book is unique because although fiction, it so mirrors reality that each page hits home more and more. Having been in the criminal law arena for fifty-five years and having dealt with two notorious serial killer cases, Whitman's novel captures all aspects of the utter insanity of the criminal mind."

—GERALD P. BOYLE, Attorney, Represented Serial Killer Jeffrey Dahmer

"The decades of Wendy Whitman's focus and dedication to the crime and justice genre shine through each page, as she spins the yarn in this gripping crime tale. Speaking from experience that has imbued her with personal knowledge of the inner workings of hundreds of criminal minds, she is an authoritative voice in telling crime stories...because she has lived through reporting some of the most disturbing ones in American history. Brava, Wendy!"

—ASHLEIGH BANFIELD, Court TV Special Contributor
and Host of *Judgment with Ashleigh Banfield*

"All of those cases on Court TV certainly permeated the mind of producer Wendy Whitman. Her book is a truly breathless thriller through every twist and turn. A stellar debut novel with a terrific female heroine!"

—RIKKI KLIEMAN, Attorney and CBS News Legal Analyst

"Wendy Whitman's debut novel is more than a crime story. Readers will identify with some of her protagonist's obsessions including food choices ('borderline vegan') and her love for animals. Peppered throughout the book are safety tips drawn from actual cases Whitman learned from years covering criminal trials at Court TV where she rose from a producer to a programming executive. There's something for everyone in *Premonition*."

—BETH KARAS, Former Prosecutor and Host
of Oxygen's *Snapped: Notorious*

PREMONITION

PREMONITION

WENDY WHITMAN

Post Hill
PRESS

A POST HILL PRESS BOOK

Premonition
© 2021 by Wendy Whitman
All Rights Reserved

ISBN: 978-1-64293-822-7
ISBN (eBook): 978-1-64293-823-4

Cover art by Cody Corcoran
Interior design and composition by Greg Johnson, Textbook Perfect

Post Hill Press
New York • Nashville
posthillpress.com

Published in the United States of America
1 2 3 4 5 6 7 8 9 10

For Obelus,
Grief is the final stage of love...

ONE

Cary knew she wasn't going to get much sleep. It was nearly one o'clock in the morning, and the sound of the wind continued to creep through the guesthouse. Cary had been living back in Connecticut near her sister since she lost her job, occasionally picking up a freelance gig. But twenty years of covering crime on television had taken a toll on her. And although the bulk of Cary's career was now behind her, she couldn't shake the gruesome details of a few of the particularly heinous murders she had covered. Each creaky noise jarred her and made rest of any kind virtually impossible. But the memories of various trials Cary had produced weren't actually the cause of her paranoia. In her mind, they just validated it. She had come to trust no one, to misread people at every turn. Whether Cary picked up the wrong vibe from someone she was interested in romantically, or got her signals crossed with someone she had trusted at work, she found herself constantly reevaluating her judgment of people. Cary lived her life obsessed over the statistically remote possibility that she could be the next murder victim, that it could happen to her.

This all-consuming phobia, however, was nothing new. It had been an integral part of Cary's psyche for as long as she could remember. The profound belief that one awful day she would join the ranks of the murdered controlled Cary's every move. As she tossed and turned, Cary regretted having done a Google search right before bed of one of the more gruesome cases she had become obsessed with. As Cary lay still, watching the clock, waiting anxiously for the next seemingly unexplained noise to spook her, she tried to combat the anxiety being alone in the dark caused. As much as she tried to fight it, there was nothing Cary could picture better than what it would be like to be confronted by a crazed intruder in the middle of the night. The very thought engendered such an intense fear that Cary couldn't imagine being alive in the morning.

* * *

When Cary woke up, she realized she had finally nodded off just before dawn. She had beaten the night—*again*. After jumping in the shower, Cary decided to run out and grab a hot chocolate. As she sat in the drive-through lane at the nearby Starbucks waiting to pay, Cary took out her wallet. Fumbling for her Amex card, Cary couldn't help but glance at her driver's license stuck in the little plastic window on the left side. *Carole Mackin*, it read. Every time she saw her given name in print, it bugged the shit out of her. Cary was so much better, and, as a bonus, it pissed off her mother.

As Cary drove away, she sipped slowly on the chocolate drink. She prided herself on being able to drive a stick shift with one hand while holding her drink of choice in the other. The lack of sleep last night, however, had left Cary exhausted and not in the best of moods. It also made it harder for her to process what she had seen the other night. Cary never ceased to be amazed at the cruelty people were capable of.

She had assumed it was a man, but Cary didn't actually get a good enough look to be sure. Still, Cary knew she should have called the police. But she couldn't identify the car, license plate, or whoever was inside and didn't think she would have been of any real help. Or at least that's what she told herself. In reality, all those years of covering one horrendous murder after another had made Cary paranoid to the point of going under fake names on social media. Her latest alias was her name spelled backward. Cary thought it was pure genius.

And so, contacting the police and getting involved in whatever was going on that night was out of the question, even though Cary knew it was the right thing to do. But why did *he* do it? That was the real question. *I mean, it had to be a man, right?* If there was one thing Cary had learned from her years of covering crime, it was that more than 80 percent of violent acts are committed by men. And the minority done by women are most often against their abusers or, sadly, their own children.

* * *

The night in question had started innocently enough. Cary had been having one of her late-night sugar attacks, so she had hopped into her Jeep Wrangler, clad only in her pajamas, to get a fix. Her conundrum: should she settle for a pint of Ben & Jerry's or find a place that might have Tim Tams, which, in Cary's opinion, were Australia's greatest contribution to the world? Cary had developed an addiction for the biscuits on her latest trip down under, and they finally were available in the United States.

At that hour, Cary decided that she might have to settle for gas station convenience store ice cream after all. As she was sitting in the parking lot of several closed stores, figuring out where to go next, Cary spotted an automobile heading toward a deer crossing the street. Just as the doe made it safely to the other side, the vehicle came to an abrupt halt. Two fawns waited hesitantly by the side of the pavement, uncertain if it was safe to follow their mother. That was when the headlights suddenly went off, and the car sat idly in the dark in the middle of the road.

At first, Cary couldn't figure out what was going on. Then it dawned on her: maybe the driver thought another vehicle might come along and hit the baby deer, so if he just turned off the lights and waited a minute, they would think that the danger had passed and would join their mother on the other side. What a clever way to lead the deer to safety. And then, just as they went for it, Cary heard a loud screech as the car accelerated, and blood was everywhere. Cary couldn't help but think, *Killers cut their teeth on animals.*

* * *

The man waited for the automobile to drive away before following at a safe distance. The sound of the engine starting up had surprised him. He hadn't noticed the other vehicle until it was too late, though he had sensed lights coming from that direction. He would need to pull over to check the damage to his own. Parts of the deer had to have gotten stuck to his car. Hell, one might even be pinned underneath. He wasn't sure if the woman in the other car had seen him, but he had seen her, if just enough to make out that it was indeed a woman. Better to be safe than sorry. She was a *threat*. The man decided he could check his car when he got home. Right now, he couldn't lose sight of the woman. Those night goggles were the best investment he had made in a long time.

* * *

Since Cary had lost her beloved job, it had been rough going. It had been her passion, her friends, her livelihood, and, most importantly, her identity, all wrapped into one. It defined her and everything she had ever aspired to, but in a dark way that her coworkers never really understood. How could she tell them? All they thought was that she had a passion for victims' rights, but the true reason remained hidden from them. They never knew *why*.

The final months at CrimeTV were very difficult for Cary and her coworkers. But once the deal was done, there was nothing any of them could do about it. The powers that be had decided they could squeeze more money out of the network by turning it into fluff. And so, although Cary had a good run, it came to an abrupt and disappointing end. Even so, if Cary thought about it, she had managed to stay busy over the past several years. The experience had made her bitter and resentful, and yet, somehow, she was pushing through it all.

* * *

Cary woke up wondering if what she had seen the other night was real. She couldn't get the image of the fawns and the sound of the impact out of her head. The car must have been damaged from the blow. There was still time to go to the police and tell them what she witnessed. But several days had passed, so it wouldn't look good for her. The authorities would wonder why she had waited so long, and her account of what happened would be shaky at best. *I mean, it was really dark, and it was late, and I was tired, and so on.* They would ask her, "What kind of car was it?" And she would say, "I couldn't really see." It would go downhill from there. No, she had made a split-second decision to do the *wrong* thing, so best stick with that, at least for the time being. But the look of horror on the deer's face as her babies went flying into the air would haunt Cary for the foreseeable future.

Anyway, today Cary was running late for work. She had to go into the city, and she had a bad feeling Eve would put her on tonight, which meant she would need to brush up on the facts of the case. The horror story of the day would be…God only knew. Cary didn't want to think about it. After being laid off and running through her severance and unemployment, Eve had come to her rescue and given Cary intermittent freelance work on her show at LNN: the Legal News Network. It was a lot of pressure and stress, but at least she was still covering crime and hopefully could eke out a few more years in television. And while Eve Arora had saved Cary's ass more than once, Cary was beginning to get the feeling that her days on Eve's show were numbered. They weren't really using her that much anymore as Cary was about to max out her allowable hours as a freelancer. But she didn't want to think about that right now either.

As she was driving to the train station, Cary passed a young girl, maybe fifteen years old, jogging by herself along one of Wooster's notoriously deserted streets. The town, an hour train ride from New York and made up of only about ten thousand people, was a lovely respite from the frenetic pace of the city. As always, Cary had to resist the urge to put down her window and strongly advise the young woman not to go jogging alone. She couldn't help but think about that poor teacher in Montana, the victim of a thrill kill by two twisted guys. If she had only had a dog with her, a friend, maybe things would have turned out differently. But the girl would only think she was crazy, so Cary drove on. She wanted to protect the world, but Cary wasn't even sure she could protect herself.

Cary cherished her morning naps on the train. The hour ride into the city gave her the time she needed to adjust to the outside world. She was not a morning person, and it was the perfect buffer to what lay ahead. Well, it would've been perfect had there been enough time to stop for her favorite hot chocolate when she got to New York's Grand Central Terminal, but Cary knew there wouldn't be.

After taking the subway to the Upper West Side, Cary settled into her cubicle at work. The staff was buzzing. A local story, something that happened in Connecticut, her neck of the woods, literally, might make the cut for tonight's lead story. As Cary read the facts of the case, her face went white, and she felt a nauseous feeling creep into her throat. Two sixteen-year-old girls had been mowed down and killed by a car not far from where Cary had spotted the deer killer the other night.

As Cary tried to make sense of what she had just discovered, her head started spinning. It had to be a coincidence, right? The two incidents couldn't be related. Or could they? Was the killer practicing on the deer? *Or am I just being a little paranoid?* Cary felt sick and headed for the bathroom.

After collecting herself, Cary went back to her desk to get her marching orders from Gene MacMaster, the executive producer of the show. MacMaster's fuse was as short as his height, so Cary knew she was in for a long day. And yes, just as she had suspected, Eve wanted her to go on air for the story, especially since it happened in her own backyard. Panic seized Cary like a vise. Should she tell Gene and Eve about what she saw the other night? But she knew she couldn't because she hadn't gone to the police straight away. She hadn't gone at all. Nothing had been reported, at least not by her. As she tried to assess her options, Cary began listing the facts of the girls' deaths as she knew them to be from the Associated Press articles distributed to the staff, which served as the holy grail for the show.

As she tried to organize her thoughts, Cary couldn't help but think about some notorious crimes that had taken place in Connecticut, a state many think of as a peaceful escape from New York. The Petit family murders, as well as the massacre in Newtown, were at odds with this assessment.

Fact One: Both girls were sophomores at Wooster High School and appeared to be good students and best friends.

Fact Two: No eyewitnesses have come forward so far, and there may not be any.

Fact Three: Although police and accident reconstructionists are attempting to lift tire marks off the road, it was rainy and muddy that night, and such attempts so far have proved futile.

Fact Four: Police don't have the make and model of the car.

Fact Five: There are no immediate suspects.

Fact Six: The families are not talking at this time.

Fact Seven: No one seems to know why the girls were out so late at night.

Fact, etc., etc., etc.

Not much to go on, Cary thought. What the hell is Eve going to ask her about tonight?

* * *

As Cary tried to get some sleep on her way home on the train, she thought the night could've gone a lot worse. With so little to go on, Eve and Gene did the story as a *Breaking News* segment, which meant they only spent about five minutes on it, teasing, "We will bring you the latest developments as they unfold." Cary was only asked a couple of basic questions, and then they went on to another story and she was paroled, off the hook, and the show, for the rest of the night. She needed a drink, and it wasn't hot chocolate.

TWO

Obsessive-compulsive disorder had plagued Cary in recent years, but she couldn't really remember when it had started. The only thing she knew was it definitely was getting worse. Her mother had shredded her self-esteem at an early age, but Cary wasn't sure the two issues were related. The way Cary figured it, she had several strikes going against her from birth. It didn't help that she was a twin, albeit fraternal, which brought its own set of problems, or that she was confused about her sexual identity.

Although the world saw her as gay, and although she had identified herself that way at work, Cary knew it was a lot more complicated. But branding herself with that label meant she wouldn't have to go through all the nuances and the "it's a sliding scale" bullshit that people talk about but don't really understand. So to the people Cary felt comfortable enough to come out to, she was gay, but inside, she tried to be more honest with herself. It was a slow process.

One thing Cary was pretty sure of, however, was that although she could be attracted to men sexually and even notice a man here or there, emotionally she needed to be with a woman. And, yes, the attraction was there as well, and more intense. So, Cary decided she was bisexual, but the scales tilted toward women, emotionally and physically. Although some of her best fantasies involved sex with men, she didn't think she ever could and never had fallen in love with one. Sometimes, Cary thought she needed her own special Kinsey scale.

But Cary's sexual identity aside, it was the foreboding feeling—dating as far back as she could remember—that something terrible would happen to her, that she would be *murdered*, that had dictated her entire life. It was something she couldn't verbalize to anyone, and it terrified her. It was *always* there. Her life was *centered* around preventing it even though, logically speaking, the odds were clearly in her favor. And so, Cary decided she was a bit of a mental mess. But most people were pretty fucked up, so why shouldn't she be? She had just taken it to a different level.

* * *

The next incident wasn't to happen for nearly a month. Cary had almost, almost, been able to forget about the night she encountered the "Deer Killer," as she had come to call him. She was supposed to meet her mother and sister for dinner but decided against it. Eve and Gene hadn't called her back to work since the night they broke the story of the two Connecticut girls, now being referred to as the "Hit-and-Run BFFs." But Cary knew there was a good possibility it was a lot more sinister than that. The case had fizzled in the news since the police seemed unable to develop any credible leads and the funerals and memorial gatherings for the unfortunate girls were now in the past. In any event, she didn't want to give her mother another opportunity to gleefully critique her failing career.

* * *

As Cary pulled out of her driveway that morning, she waited patiently as always for the garage door to close—she learned that trick from the "Tree Killer" case in Ohio. Matthew Hoffman had gained entry to Tina Herrmann's house by waiting for her to leave in a pickup truck and then sliding in under the garage door, which didn't close completely as it was broken and in need of repair. From every heinous story the network had covered, Cary tried to glean a safety tip that might have made all the difference. But this morning, Cary didn't want to think about the gruesome details of that case. She didn't want to think about Matthew Hoffman. She just wanted today to be normal. As it turned out, that would be a tall order.

In lieu of family dinner plans, Cary decided to stop by her sister's office and grab a quick lunch. Dr. Gayle Mackin was a dermatologist. Indeed, Cary came from a family of doctors, but she had always considered herself too squeamish to even consider going into the field. But murder, somehow that she could deal with. It was her former therapist who pointed out the hypocrisy.

Arthur Ross, MS M-whatever, was the only person she had ever told about her murder phobia. In turn, he posited that most people stay as far away as possible from their fears, irrational or not, and sought an explanation as to why, if Cary had this intense dread of being murdered, she would choose a career in exactly that. Cary had no answer, but she never looked at the autopsy photos at least. They tended, however, to be a big hit, perverse as it may be, with the staff.

Lunch was fine, if quick. Her sister was always in a hurry, lived at a frantic pace, and took on more than any reasonable person could handle. But Cary was convinced that's what she thrived on. They decided to go around the corner from her sister's office and dine at Eat No Evil, a borderline-vegan restaurant, where the veggie burgers were cleverly disguised as congealed globs of clay. For a fleeting minute, Cary considered confiding in her sister about what had happened, but in the end, she decided it was a bad idea. It would just be a burden to her, information she was better off without, and God knows her sister already had enough on her plate. Yes, she should be able to tell her twin anything—but *not* this. She had already fucked it all up.

Her sister paid the bill, as usual. And as they made their way to the car, a chaotic scene was unfolding in the parking lot. A woman, holding her lifeless puppy, was sobbing uncontrollably and speaking in an almost inaudible manner. All Cary could make out was something along the lines of, "I know I left the windows cracked...so hot out...don't understand," and so on. Cary instinctively got a pit in her stomach, but the police seemed to be handling the situation, and her sister was already likely backed up with patients for the afternoon, so they left.

But it was what Cary found out later that evening that didn't sit right with her. Just several hours after the dog died of heatstroke in the woman's car, a frazzled father a few towns over had called 911 to report that his baby daughter had met a similar fate: the car was found in the driveway, with the engine running, the windows closed, and the keys locked inside.

THREE

Cary's mother, Felicia Mackin, named her after the actress Carole Lombard, who had met a tragic fate, dying in a plane crash in the prime of her life. Cary never forgot her mother's dramatic recounting of how Lombard's husband, actor Clark Gable, heroically tried to search for her. Cary guessed her mother saw tragedy in her future—or wished for it.

* * *

As far as Cary knew, she was the only eyewitness to a disturbing event—the fawns—that, in her mind, *could* be connected to the recent killings of the sixteen-year-old girls. She was still rattled from witnessing the scene with the puppy. And while that incident might have nothing to do with what happened to the baby—from all reports, the father insisted that he left the car unlocked—something didn't *feel* right. But Cary couldn't figure out exactly what.

So, she thought the best way to proceed might be to get Eve to profile the baby story on her show. That way, Cary could find out more details without calling attention to herself. Maybe she could pitch the case to Gene, but he'd likely turn it down, citing the show's coverage of too many "baked baby" cases and their low ratings. And, yes, every case got a nickname. If Cary and her cohorts were good at anything, it was taking black humor to a new low.

* * *

Cary hadn't seen Vito Loggia since he handled her sister's divorce several years ago, but he was considered to be the number one private detective in the state and, if anyone could help her, it was him. She would have to be careful, though, to tread lightly, at least at first, and watch what she told him, because he was also the most ethical. Despite his name, Vito was only a quarter Italian, and he had more of a waspy look than anything else. Still, as far as Cary could tell, he identified that way, and his taste in food confirmed it.

They had decided to meet at his favorite restaurant, around the corner from his office in Stamford, but when Vito walked in, Cary hardly recognized him. He had always been this larger-than-life character, but the man walking toward her now was anything but. He was both shorter and thinner than she remembered and appeared to be walking with a limp. Unsure of how to greet him, Cary awkwardly put out her hand, but Vito brushed it aside and gave her his signature bear hug. Cary guessed he hadn't changed as much as she thought.

"Thank you so much for meeting me, Vito. It's so good to see you."

If Cary was anything, it was loyal, and Vito had really stood by her sister, so she had a soft spot for him.

"For you, anything," he said, in his own uniquely charming way.

Cary knew he thought she was straight, and although he was upward of twenty years her senior, he couldn't help but flirt with her a bit. She let him have his fantasy.

"The food here is wonderful. I've been looking forward to lunch all morning," Vito said with his usual grin.

But he also got right down to business. "So, Cary, what's going on?"

Uncertain how to approach the subject, Cary tried to steer the conversation away from why she contacted him in the first place and to the menu, which was food porn on drugs. Cary had always been a huge fan of Italian food, and this place had the best.

"Everything looks so good. I'll never be able to decide what to have," Cary mused. But her favorite pasta was pappardelle with pesto, so she already knew what she was going to order; she was just buying time, or at least trying to. Luckily, the waiter showed up as Cary took a deep breath and tried to collect herself.

"What will you lovely lady and gentleman be having for lunch this afternoon?" the waiter asked in that old-school Italian way.

"How's the veal today?" Vito asked, knowing full well that it was one of the house specialties.

"Delizioso," the waiter proclaimed.

"Then I'll have it," retorted Vito.

They were playing a game because Vito ate at Mike's nearly once a week, and the waiter, Giorgio, and he were thick as thieves. Cary thought it was endearing.

"And for you, young lady?"

"Um, how's the pappardelle with pesto?" Cary said, picking up on Vito's cue.

Giorgio gave her a wink and was off.

Although there were bigger things at stake, the veal order didn't sit well with Cary, who was on her way to becoming full-blown vegan, or at least vegetarian. But she knew she had to pick her battles, and this was one for another day. *The way people treat animals is appalling,* Cary thought. But she didn't know what she could actually do about it, except order the pappardelle.

While they were waiting for their lunch to arrive, Vito tried to get back to the subject at hand. He just didn't know what it was.

"So, Cary, how much longer are you going to keep me in suspense?"

As Cary was about to answer, Giorgio came back with their lunch and proudly set it down on the table in front of them, politely waiting for some oohs and aahs.

Cary thought she'd begin by feeling Vito out to see if he had heard about either the girls or the baby. She obviously couldn't bring up the deer.

"So much bad news lately," Cary began.

To her surprise, Vito chimed in, "You mean those girls...the ones in Wooster?"

"Why, yes," Cary answered. "And that baby in...um...I believe it was Eastshire," Cary continued, trying not to sound too invested in either incident.

"Yup," Vito added. "A little bad luck, and the game's up. Hit-and-runs really piss me off. If the guy, or woman, I guess—cops don't know who did it—had stopped and called for help, who knows if they'd still be alive. The girls, I mean. The baby, well, that's a different story, I guess. 'Lotta frenetic parents running around these days not paying attention to what they're doing, and the kids always pay the price," Vito concluded.

"Yeah, I guess," Cary added.

Vito promptly changed the topic of conversation, always interested in what Cary was up to when he hadn't seen her in a while.

* * *

On the way home, Cary recounted the lunch with Vito in her head. So, he knew about the Wooster girls but hadn't paid much attention to the details and clearly thought the police were assuming that it was a hit-and-run. The likelihood of catching whoever was behind the wheel was growing slimmer by the day. Cary had decided not to bring up the incident with the puppy, not yet. She'd save it for the next time she saw him. And as far as the baby went, well, he thought it was a tragic accident. Although Vito was probably only in his late sixties by now, his mind didn't seem as keen as it once was. Still, Cary believed he could be a useful ally.

* * *

The last thing Cary needed that night was a family emergency, but that's exactly what she got. No sooner had she closed the front door than the phone rang. It was her mother.

"Cary, it's your mother—I need you to come over *NOW*," she shrieked.

"On my way," Cary said, trying to hide her annoyance. She had reluctantly become a seasoned go-between for her mother and the local paramedics.

Her mother's blood pressure had spiked, and she wanted Cary to take her to the emergency room *again*. Her mother loved nothing more than self-medicating *against* her doctors' advice. So, Cary abandoned her plans of having a relaxing evening at home binging *Better Call Saul* and grabbed her keys to head over to her mother's condo. Felicia Mackin was a textbook narcissist. Cary wondered why it had taken her so long to realize it, but once she did, a lot of things began to make sense. Cary, Gayle, and their more or less estranged older sister, Rory, often competed for who was the most damaged. Sometimes Cary thought it was a three-way tie.

When Cary got to her mother's condo, she was surprised to see several emergency vehicles outside. She hadn't thought it was that bad. Her mother sounded okay over the phone. Cary ran in only to find her mother holding court with some very handsome EMS employees. The one she recognized, Stuart, gave her a knowing look, and they stepped outside.

"She's fine. She really is. Just needs to lie down and stop taking all that Xanax," he told her, and not for the first time.

"Believe me, I've tried, but I'm about the last person she listens to."

"Well, we're gonna wrap it up here. Just make sure she drinks some water and goes right to bed. But call us if you need us, okay?" he said reassuringly.

"Roger that," Cary answered.

Now that her mother had succeeded in ruining her night and corralling her onto her turf, Cary knew she was in for the Spanish Inquisition-light. Whether it was crime or medicine, Cary's mother had a way of treating her and her twin like they were ignorant regarding their own professions. Only Felicia knew *everything*. As Cary waited for the onslaught, she realized she couldn't remember her mother ever asking her a personal question. But somehow, everyone else in the world was a source of endless fascination for her. The main message her mother sent her growing up was that everything was her fault, and she did everything wrong. *Hmmm*, Cary reflected, *where did that low self-esteem come from?* A loving mother-daughter relationship seemed like sci-fi to her.

Deep in thought, Cary was brought back to reality by her mother's voice in the background.

"Eve looked so wonderful the other night. I love the new look of the show. Did you know they were going for a different look?"

"Yes, Ma. I *work* there," Cary answered, a bit sarcastically.

Well, not that much anymore, but her mother got the point.

"There's that attitude of yours again. You need to be up on things if you expect them to keep calling you back."

And there it was: the zinger of the evening. Cary just wasn't going to take the bait tonight. She was too tired and stressed and had way too much on her mind to get suckered into her mother's bullshit. So, Cary told her she wasn't feeling all that great either and made a hasty departure, risking incurring her mother's wrath.

As Cary was getting into her Jeep to drive home, a text popped up on her phone. It was Gene. Her mother must have conjured him up. They needed her tomorrow, and the "in" time would be 6:00 a.m. They would be taping at noon, as Eve had a family matter she needed to attend to in the afternoon. Sometimes Cary wondered if her life could get any worse.

FOUR

Cary hadn't been on Eve's show for more than a month, so she knew she would have to go through the standard freelance security routine when she arrived, which also meant she'd have to take an even *earlier* train. Whenever Cary knew she had to get up in the wee hours of the morning, especially to go to work, insomnia kicked in. Therefore, Cary got almost no sleep that night and was truly exhausted when she got to work. Upon entering the building, as she had often done in the past, Cary wished she could have traded places with any of the friendly, seemingly relaxed guards who functioned like maître d's. The stress level for everyone else was a killer.

Eve's show had become somewhat of a haven for refugees from CrimeTV, which meant Cary knew and had worked with several of the staff before she ever joined the show. But it had been a while, and it was good to see them again. She wished they would just make her permanent so that this back and forth could end, but there was no sign that was ever going to happen.

As soon as she arrived on the eighth floor, the usual "Hey, you're back, Cary" greetings began. The first two people Cary encountered were Ellyn Joseph, head of the department in which Cary usually worked, and Todd Zeff. Zeff was a twenty-something from Montreal who thought he was destined to be the next Peter Jennings and displayed little to no respect for staff who were clearly his seniors, at least age-wise. It didn't bother Cary. She actually found it pretty funny, but it irked the shit out of her other colleague and friend in editorial, Lee Snow. To Cary's disappointment, a fellow freelancer Caity Murphy was no longer working there. The two had bonded during Cary's initial stint on the show, as their mothers seemed to have read the same manual.

During her first few months freelancing, Cary discovered that Todd's real name was Jeffrey, as in Jeffrey Todd Zeff. That made for an easy nickname, behind his back, of course, to get their aggressions out: Jeff Zeff. When he really pissed them off, he was secretly referred to as "Jay-Z." Ellyn, Lee, and Cary weren't winning any awards in the maturity department, but it felt good all the same. Ellyn was a former CrimeTV producer, and Cary had enormous respect for both her and Lee. They were awesome, and she always looked forward to working with them.

"Well, if it isn't Cary Mackin back from the dead," Lee called out from her cubicle three doors down. "Are they *ever* gonna make you staff?"

Cary thought not.

Cary began her day by logging on to her computer and going through the backlog of emails that always awaited her when she came back from another forced hiatus. Before long, she was staring at a mugshot of a deranged clown who had just been arrested and charged with a string of murders in the Northwest. *Clowns and pig farmers*, Cary thought to herself. *They're batshit crazy.*

John Wayne Gacy put clowns on the map by raping, torturing, and murdering at least thirty-three young men and boys in the seventies. Known as "The Killer Clown," Gacy was executed in 1994, leaving behind two ex-wives and a son and daughter. Cary thought he took bisexuality to a whole new level.

Pig farmers were thrown into the spotlight when Canadian serial killer Robert Pickton was arrested for the murders of anywhere between six and forty-nine women. Pickton, a.k.a. "Pork Chop Rob," began killing in the early eighties and continued until his apprehension in 2002. Pickton confessed to forty-nine murders, telling an undercover agent that he had wanted to kill one more woman to make it an even fifty. But he got caught first; talk about being OCD.

In 2007, Pickton was convicted of the second-degree murders of six women and sentenced to life in prison with no parole for twenty-five years, the maximum penalty for murder under Canadian law at the time. Cary thought that was crazy; in December 2032, Pickton could be released back into society a free man. And some people thought the United States should emulate countries such as Canada and Sweden. *Why in the world would we do that?* Cary asked herself. In any event, clowns and pig farmers had always been on Cary's radar. It became somewhat of a dark joke at CrimeTV.

Cary didn't have a firm handle on what criteria dictated which cases made the cut and which didn't, how Eve and Gene made their decisions. CrimeTV was a whole other story, however. They went by the "stew standard." Among the plethora of grisly cases that came to the higher-ups' attention each week, certain ones were instantly deep-sixed and never aired on television. For lack of a better explanation, they included any case where the poor victim ended up being served as food at a soup kitchen. And then there was the ghastly case of Dawn Viens, whose husband, a chef, boiled her body for four days until little remained but the skull. Cary often wondered how she never lost weight from working there.

As Cary was attempting to get settled in for the day, Gene summoned her to his office. Cary had long since decided that it was nicer to be yelled at by someone with a Scottish accent. Brooke was there as well, the second-in-command. They wanted Cary to focus exclusively on the Connecticut girls today; apparently, there had been a development in the case. Cary wondered what that might be and if anyone had yet managed to connect the "baked baby" case to at least the "baked puppy," if not the dead girls. Cary decided that it was highly unlikely as the missing link was the incident with the deer, and as far as she knew, she was the only eyewitness to that atrocity. Intellectually, Cary knew the links between the cases were attenuated at best, but her instincts told her otherwise. JFK conspiracy theorists had nothing on her.

As Cary entered Gene's office, she was apprehensive about what she might learn about the girls.

"Grab a seat. Good to have you back, Cary," Gene said self-consciously. "We could really use the help."

Really? thought Cary. *Then why don't you hire me?*

As if he read her mind, Gene continued, "Wish we could bring you on board full time, but it always comes down to the money. You know if it were up to me..."

Gene used this line on her *every* time they brought her back, and so, Cary had decided that he must think it gave her some kind of incentive to take the job seriously.

Brooke, however, was a different story. Cary was never sure what to make of her. She considered Brooke a bit of an enigma. No one seemed to know much about her except that she had graduated number one in her journalism class at Columbia. But Cary always got the feeling she resented her long history with Eve and used it against her. And yet, Cary liked Brooke. She just didn't entirely trust her.

Since it didn't seem like Gene or Brooke was going to get to the point any time soon, Cary intervened.

"So what's up with the hit-and-run girls?" she asked.

Without hesitation, Gene responded, "They think they found the car."

All Cary could think was, *What the fuck*? It was time to have another meal with Vito.

As Cary headed home on the train that evening, it occurred to her that she didn't even know if the incidents with the deer and the two girls were related. It could be two completely different cars, two completely different drivers. If only she had gotten a better look. Cary wondered if she should ask Vito to meet her at the impound yard in Bridgeport tomorrow, but she thought better of it and decided to go alone. Cary had to have a better handle on things before she dragged him any further into this mess.

* * *

The traffic on I-95 was as bad as usual, but Cary didn't have to go back to the office after she checked out the car, so she wasn't really under any time pressure. As Cary would likely only be working half a day, Gene had cut her a break. As she was sitting in the traffic, barely moving, Cary had the following thought. More recently, her OCD had taken the form of thinking that she might have hit someone with her car and then having to retrace her steps to make sure they were all right. Cary often wondered how much gas she wasted as a result—probably enough to go back into therapy again, she figured. Apparently, as she learned more about it, that was considered a pretty typical form of OCD. Cary was sure, however, that it would sound certifiable to a *normal* person. And then it hit her: the irony. *I guess if you actually run somebody over with your car, you kinda know it.* Sometimes she made herself laugh.

When Cary pulled into the impound yard, she was greeted by a heavyset cop who had a permanently suspicious look on his rotund face. Just as Cary started scrambling in her bag for some form of identification, he motioned for her to put down the window.

"And what brings you here on this lovely day?" Officer Mahoney asked, rather out of character, Cary thought.

"I'm with LNN," Cary stated hesitantly, uncertain if that would help or hurt her cause.

"Is that so?" he responded.

Cary wasn't sure how to take it. Undeterred, she answered back, "Can I please take a look at the car you guys impounded, the one they think struck those two Wooster girls?"

"You sure can, ma'am, as soon as I see some form of identification."

If there was one thing Cary hated, it was being called "ma'am" by anyone, no less a thirty-something cop, but she kept it together and dug out both her work ID as well as her driver's license, just to be on the safe side. Cary didn't want this to take all day.

Appeased, Mahoney showed her where to leave her car and said he would personally escort her to the vehicle. Cary knew that was code for, *You're not going near that car alone.*

"Well, this is it," Mahoney declared as they neared the vehicle. "Right there is where the car made contact with the girls."

Cary just loved police jargon. *Made contact? You mean killed them?*

Cary couldn't help wondering if it was the same car that hit the fawns, but there was no way for her to be sure. The car in front of her was navy blue, pretty beat up, and had a big gash in the front where it had collided with the girls. Pending lab results, Mahoney said, the authorities were 90 percent sure it was the car that hit them.

"Where did you guys find it?" Cary inquired, going into producer mode.

"Seems like it was abandoned near Devil's Den. The son of a bitch had the gall to dump the car pretty much where he hit the girls.

Must've decided to lay low for a while then bring the car back there, arrogant prick. Yep, Devil's Den, you know it?"

Know it? Cary had spent more than her share of time hanging around "the den," as they had referred to it in high school, doing her share of whatever it is that kids that age do. Devil's Den was an enormous reserve known for its hiking trails and hangout spots. It was also around the corner from a legendary rock star who had lived in Wooster for as long as anyone could remember.

"Yes," Cary answered. "I've heard of it." She wasn't sure what vibe the officer was picking up from her, but she didn't really care.

"It's been wiped clean; stripped down, no plates or VIN. Whoever it belongs to, they did a pretty good job of getting rid of any evidence," Mahoney bemoaned. But he made it clear to Cary they expected a DNA match with the girls despite the Herculean efforts of the owner to sanitize the car.

Cary had the feeling the police still considered it a hit-and-run, not an intentional act of murder, but she decided it was best at this point not to tip her hand. As she made her way back to her car, she thanked the officer for his help. It was time for Cary to start putting the pieces of the puzzle together.

* * *

He liked this car better. And, anyway, whoever owned it would just go through insurance and end up with a big, fat check; auto theft was such a problem these days. No one would be the wiser; at least, that was his hope. Sure, he could have used one of his other vehicles—maybe even the Tesla—but why waste so much as a penny of his inheritance on *work-related* matters? Yes, money bought you freedom. But for what he had in mind, a more modest vehicle would do.

His old car had served its purpose, and it had been time to put it out of its misery. *People aren't very smart*, he decided. All he had to do was change the color and put his original plates on, and poof, it was his. They somehow accepted what was in front of them. Lucky him. He would just have to make sure to drive carefully so that he wouldn't be pulled over. Well, not *that* carefully. Sometimes he made himself laugh.

FIVE

This time, Cary decided to meet Vito for breakfast and get a jump on the day. Had she known she would get an unexpected friend request on Facebook late the night before, Cary might have made different plans, but it was too late to change them now. Mornings like this made Cary wish she had acquired a taste for coffee like every other adult she knew, but then again, the whole adult thing wasn't exactly her strong suit.

The friend request had come from Romy Baudin. Romy resided in Canada now with her husband. As far as Cary knew, they had never had children. Cary hadn't seen her in a very long time. Romy was her soul mate, as much as anyone had ever been, and the only person she had ever really been able to get close to. Their relationship had been intense yet unbalanced. Romy had crushed her emotionally, which is why the friend request led to a sleepless night. Cary hated to admit it, even to herself, but after all this time, she was still in love with her. Romy was *home*. Why did she think it was okay to reach out to Cary again and stir up all that pain? That's where Cary's head was at as she pulled up to her favorite diner to join Vito for breakfast and come clean. Cary had decided to tell him *everything*.

This morning, Vito looked better, more youthful if you can use that word about a sixty-something-year-old. Cary decided she would make the worst eyewitness ever. He was wearing a royal-blue jogging suit and had just come from a run. Apparently, the limp he exhibited at their last meeting had just been a cramp he had developed from exercising a bit too strenuously. Vito was actually in pretty good shape for his age. They were both ravenous and grabbed a booth in the back where they would have a bit more privacy. It would serve as a make-shift confessional.

Cary wasn't exactly sure where to begin, so she figured the menu would be the safest place to start.

"The lemon ricotta pancakes are fucking awesome here," she told him. How much trouble could that get her into?

Vito appeared to be in a particularly good mood this morning. Maybe it was the high from running, all those endorphins, but he decided to join her in the decadence and put his diet on hold, at least until lunchtime.

When the waiter came, they put their order in and then got down to business. It was Cary who got to the point, however circuitously.

"Remember when we had lunch, and I kept bringing up those dead girls and the baby?"

"Sure," Vito replied. "What of it?"

"Well, you may think I'm crazy, but I think there's some kind of connection."

"Connection?" he responded. "Could you please be a little vaguer, Cary?"

Vito could be a bit of a smartass, Cary decided. *But what private eye wasn't?*

"The girls in Wooster, I know they think it's just another hit-and-run...." Cary continued.

Vito wasn't following and appeared to be getting a little frustrated with her. So Cary decided she had to just blurt it out and deal with the fallout.

"I saw something, Vito, a few nights before. I haven't told anyone. Not even my sister…." Cary was getting panicky, and Vito sensed it.

"Calm down, Cary. One step at a time. Start from the beginning."

"The girls…the puppy…the baby…it's all connected," she began, rambling a bit incoherently.

"What puppy?" Vito said, a bit confused.

Of course, Cary thought to herself. He wouldn't have heard about the puppy, and she hadn't brought it up at lunch.

Cary described how she had run out late that night to get a sugar fix and told him what she had seen: someone in a car intentionally run over two helpless baby deer. She hadn't gotten a good enough look to identify the person who did it or the car. That's why she hadn't gone to the police. But Vito wasn't buying it. He knew her too well. *Fear* had kept her from contacting the police.

"I don't know, Cary," Vito began. "The girls…deer…around the same spot…days apart. It doesn't seem random. But I've seen crazier coincidences, believe me."

"I know, Vito. It's just…I mean, there's gotta be—" Cary answered. But Vito interrupted her.

"I know what you're thinking, Cary, but the rest…the baby…whatever happened to this puppy…I'm just not sure it's all connected. Not yet," Vito reasoned.

So at least Vito agreed that the deer and the girls in such close proximity both time- and location-wise was likely more than a mere coincidence. He just wasn't convinced yet that all four incidents were related. He did, however, tell Cary he was *in*.

* * *

As he finished his shake, the man took note of Cary's companion. He watched as Vito got into his car and thanked the DMV for vanity plates: EYE SPY. The man guessed that I SPY must have already been taken. *Life can be so unfair,* he pondered.

He had thought of getting vanity plates himself a while back but decided against it. It could come back to bite him in the ass. And anyway, BORNTOKILL was too long to fit, even if he changed it to BORN2KILL. The maximum number of characters allowed in any state was eight. He had done his homework.

It often amused him how average folks concluded that killers were somehow driven to malevolent behavior because they had bad parents or had been bullied in school. They just didn't get it. He was smarter than everyone else and had no trouble proving it. In a way, it was a game, a game that enabled him to use his intellect to run rings around whomever or *whatever* he set his sights on. All the judgmental do-gooders in the world with their moral superiority couldn't stop him. He always won. *So much evil, so little time.*

* * *

The next question Cary asked herself as she headed home was, *How can they prove the car hit the deer?* It occurred to Cary that the police weren't looking for animal DNA; they were looking for DNA from the girls. They didn't even know about the deer. *And whose fault was that?*

Whoever wiped down the car, i.e., the "Deer Killer," seemed more interested in distancing himself from the car than the *crime.* In other words, he didn't want the police to know *who* did it, but Cary didn't think he cared if they knew *what* he did, if that made any sense. Little did these days. In that regard, Cary believed the girls' DNA would come back from the lab and that the killer had only made certain to keep the cops from being able to identify the owner of the car.

In spite of the tragic circumstances, Cary couldn't help thinking that if all four incidents were indeed related, what an awesome case it would have been for them to cover—that is, if they hadn't all been fired. Knowing the unwritten code for what was acceptable for television, however, they might not have done it anyway. Cary had fought for every trial she believed in, although she lost as many battles as she won. This case was too graphic, and this case would be too long, and *blah blah blah*. Cary didn't want to think about how many amazing stories they had passed on because of arbitrary "TV" rules. But Cary had always trusted her instincts whether it be at work or in life; she only messed up when she went against them.

The next decision Cary had to make, however, was whether she should accept Romy's friend request. Now that one would be torture.

＊ ＊ ＊

Cary had decided a long time ago that animals were a lot more pleasant to deal with than people. And so, the only tangible benefit she saw in losing her beloved job was that it allowed her to spend more time with Obi. Obi, whose official name was Obelus—a long story—was her sister's family dog: a 192-pound Newfoundland with whom Cary had fallen in love. She credited her affection for him with giving up meat and awakening her to the cruelty people inflict on animals in general. Cary and Obi developed an instant bond when he was only a small puppy. She was his person, and he was her canine soul mate; her human one was a bit more elusive.

Cary was convinced Obi had helped her with her OCD, and she was devoted to him. So, as usual, she decided to head over to her sister's house and spend the afternoon with him. Recently, he had been diagnosed with laryngeal paralysis, a degenerative neurological disease, and Cary doted on him. He was the only thing in her life she hadn't messed up.

As Cary pulled into her sister's driveway and turned off the car, she took out her phone to check the ADT app that would allow her to see if the alarm was set. "Disarmed," it read in green. Her sister *never* set the alarm despite Cary begging her to do so. Cary was convinced that the average person refused to believe there were people like the "Golden State Killer" out there. But she knew better. More than forty years after his first known killing, Joseph DeAngelo had finally been arrested and charged.

Cary didn't understand how the case had gotten by her. She had never been aware of it, never even heard it mentioned in all the years she had worked at CrimeTV.

But as the facts came to light, it freaked her out, and she made her sister upgrade her alarm system. DeAngelo was a uniformed police officer when he started raping and killing total strangers. Ironically, he was thrown off the force for shoplifting supplies he planned to use in some of his crimes. The stats for DeAngelo were staggering. In total, it is believed he committed more than fifty rapes and one hundred-some-odd burglaries. He's also accused of brutally murdering at least thirteen people. When he was arrested in April 2018, his reaction was: "I have a roast in the oven."

The day the alarm system was installed, Cary met the ADT guys at her sister's house to make sure everything was done correctly. She had a comprehensive list of questions and Obi by her side. Cary laughed to herself when she recalled the men looking from her to Obi. She knew what they were thinking. *This girl needs an alarm?* With a nearly two-hundred-pound dog and a list of questions a mile long, they must've thought she had been gang-raped and beaten within an inch of her life at some point. Yes, Cary was damaged goods, and producing gruesome crimes for two decades hadn't helped.

As always, Obelus was happy to see her. Cary grabbed one of his balls, and they went outside in the back to get some exercise and have a little fun before she had to go home and face the daunting task of solving the latest Connecticut crime spree. Cary was convinced there was a serial killer on the loose; she just hadn't figured out a way to prove it yet.

Obi was slowing down a bit. He was shaky on his feet as his rear legs were bearing the brunt of the disease. But he was a trouper, and after a good game of fetch, they went back inside for his favorite treat: ice cubes. Every time Cary left him alone, she went through an exhausting routine of checking to make sure doors were closed, appliances unplugged, that he was safe. It was debilitating, but she couldn't help herself. So when she finished her checklist, Cary headed home. And yes, she set the alarm.

* * *

Having fallen asleep on the couch, Cary was awakened by an alert on her phone telling her that the alarm at her sister's house had been tripped. *Jesus fucking Christ*, she thought. Cary had forgotten to text her sister to tell her she had set the alarm and knew there would be hell to pay. The "it's not your house" speech would be coming momentarily. And then, right on cue, as if the phone had read her mind, it rang. Yes, it was her sister.

"Stop setting the alarm," her sister shouted through the phone. "It's not *your* house."

Gee, Cary thought, *I didn't see that one coming.*

SIX

As much as Cary hated getting up early, especially on a day she wasn't working, she knew that she was better off sitting in some traffic and getting to the Jeep dealer when it opened, rather than showing up later and having to wait all day. After thirteen years, her Honda Civic had finally died, and she had decided to treat herself to a Jeep Wrangler: a car she had always wanted. But her vehicle regularly popped out of gear. Thanks to the expertise of the mechanics Cary had grown so fond of, however, now her Jeep was as good as new. Cary had agonized over whether she should get an automatic or a manual, but she liked a challenge, so she had opted for a stick. Although Cary had driven a manual most of her adult life, she had given her Jeep more than its share of tough love. So in keeping with Cary's cautious nature, she considered it part of her normal routine to periodically stop by the dealership and have them check her transmission and clutch, just to be on the safe side.

Donny was her favorite Jeep employee. He managed the service department and seemed to be sympathetic to her situation. She always got the feeling he thought it was kind of cool that she had driven a stick for as long as she could remember. He seemed a little old to be called "Donny," but somehow it suited him. Cary was sure that he was due to retire in a year or so, and she would miss him. Cary *loved* driving stick. It made every seemingly routine ride into an adventure. And she liked to think she was good at it.

This morning's appointment had been quicker than most, and as Cary went to get into her Jeep, she thought she spotted a familiar face, just briefly; but he drove away too fast for her to get a good look. In any event, before she could collect her thoughts, a text came in on her phone. It was from Vito. The lab results had come back: *both* human and animal DNA had been found on the car. The human DNA belonged to the girls.

Vito had a close friend at the station who was more than happy to slip him the lab results. Cary had never met him, but she had heard all the stories of their days on the force together. According to Vito, Henry "Hank" Nowak would have trusted him with his life. They were like brothers, having trained as rookies together back in the day at the Connecticut State Police. And although they went their separate ways, Vito deciding to pack it in and open his own detective agency once his pension came due and Hank sticking it out on the force because that was all he knew, they never lost touch. And so much of their plan hinged on Hank's continued willingness to keep Cary and Vito up to date on the latest developments in the case. He just didn't know about Vito's silent partner—*yet*.

* * *

Cary had good days and bad. As she got into her Jeep to meet Vito, she wondered which this would be. As Cary drove along the winding roads of Wooster, she was anxious to get to Vito's and make a plan. So the bicyclist in the middle of the road was annoying the shit out of her, but she couldn't take a chance and pass him without risking an accident. *What in God's name is the point of the bicycle lane if none of the bicyclists use it?* she asked herself. The urge to run him down was overwhelming, but Cary opted to use her horn instead.

I guess he's deaf too, she told herself. *Fucking asshole.*

After several frustrating minutes, they came to a "T" intersection, and as she turned right and he turned left—*thank you, God*—his middle finger went up in the air.

Pissed, Cary thought to herself, *Don't they realize how ridiculous they look in those skin-tight little outfits?* But she couldn't afford to let stuff like this get to her today. Cary had far more important things to think about.

When Cary pulled up in front of Vito's house, she was surprised to find him outside watering his front lawn, bare-chested. She was taken aback by his build. He had the physique of a forty-something...a forty-something who worked out. Cary felt a twinge, a twinge of something she didn't understand. It confused her. She wanted things to be simpler, but Cary was often attracted, strictly sexually, to older men. Emotionally, she was detached, and they didn't really turn her head. Amy Adams did that. No, she decided, it was just a sexual impulse. *God*, Cary thought to herself, *if Vito knew what I was thinking right now...*

And then, as if awakened from a dream, she heard his annoyed voice.

"What the hell took you so long?" he blurted out.

"Sorry, I got stuck behind this asshole on a bike—" Cary started to explain, but Vito cut her off.

"Never mind, didn't mean to be so abrupt. We've got a lot of work to do is all."

And so, they began to go over what they knew so far and to strategize about what they didn't. Cary and Vito decided to turn his study into a war room. They needed to get organized. They decided to use an old whiteboard Vito had hanging on the wall that was blank. They proceeded to draw a chart of the four incidents that had occurred in the last month or so. Each incident would be listed as follows: eyewitness, if any; what happened; time; date; and location. They made a separate column for the latest developments.

#1: Cary saw "someone" deliberately run over two fawns with their car around 2:00 a.m. Friday, June 8, in Wooster;

#2: Two sixteen-year-old girls were hit by a car somewhere between midnight and 3:00 a.m. Wednesday, June 13, in Wooster;

#3: Cary and her sister witnessed a scene in the parking lot of Eat No Evil, a restaurant in North Canton, involving a woman and her dead puppy, who had apparently succumbed to heatstroke in the woman's car, around 1:00 p.m. Thursday, July 12;

#4: About two hours later, a man called 911 from his home in Eastshire, reporting that his infant daughter was trapped in his car;

Latest Developments:

#1: The car police believe hit the girls was discovered near Devil's Den in Wooster around 2:30 p.m. on Tuesday, July 24;

*Cary examined the vehicle at the police impound yard in Bridgeport the following day.

#2: A DNA match came back from the lab confirming both animal and human remains on the car; the human DNA belonged to the girls.

They decided to add a column that read, *What We Know and They (The Police) Don't*. The only thing on it was the deer. But Cary and Vito both agreed that since the authorities didn't know about the "Deer Killer" incident, they wouldn't think much of animal DNA being on the car. After all, people hit squirrels, raccoons, and even deer all the time. And so, as Cary headed home, she asked herself, *Where exactly did that leave them?*

* * *

Cary had trouble falling asleep that night. She thought what they really needed was a column that said, *What We Don't Know.* She'd mention that to Vito the next time she saw him.

When Cary awoke the next morning, she decided she could use an Obi "fix," so she texted her sister that she was going to head over to her house around lunchtime. When Cary got there, she checked her app as always to see if the alarm was on—*disarmed,* it read in green, as usual. Her sister could be infuriating. As she entered the house, Obi appeared to have been having a lazy day, but when he saw Cary, he went to find his ball. He struggled to get up off the floor every time. Seeing that always made Cary sad; he wasn't having the greatest life, she decided, but they were doing everything they could for him.

Although Obi had been showing signs that there was something wrong with him for a while, it wasn't until they finally went up to Western Mass Veterinary School outside Boston to have him officially diagnosed that they got the bad news. Dr. Luca Birchler was a world-renowned neurologist, born and trained in Switzerland. Cary had loved him on sight. He had a way with animals.

"And who have we here?" he bellowed the first time he laid eyes on Obelus.

After a couple of sniffs, Obi gave him his signature pawshake. A two-hundred-pound dog could be intimidating even to a veterinarian, but Birchler took Obi's size—and his drool—in stride. Cary thought Newfies were the best dogs in the world, but they came with some issues that a lot of people just couldn't seem to handle. They didn't know what they were missing.

And so, after taking one look at Obi, Dr. Birchler knew that he had a degenerative neurological disease for which there was no cure: long-nerve disease, in layman's terms. He just didn't know how quickly it would progress. Cary hoped it would take forever.

One day, it dawned on Cary that even Obi was connected to murder, if only by a few degrees. Cary was actually the one who recommended the breed to her sister when she had decided to get her older daughter another dog. Attorney Johnny O'Halloran, who had defended a notorious serial killer back in the nineties, was the one who had told Cary how awesome Newfies were. And that's how her sister came to get Obi. *Murder followed her everywhere*, Cary decided. *There was no getting away from it.*

SEVEN

Cary's father used to beat the shit out of her, mostly when he was having a bad day or had been drinking. It scarred her childhood straight through to adulthood. Then last year, she made the mistake of trying to talk to her mother about it. That went well. After pouring her heart out, Cary looked up at her mother's icy blue eyes, waiting for a response.

"Aren't you going to say anything?" Cary asked expectantly.

Without missing a beat, her mother replied, "Did you ever wonder why he picked *you*?"

Cary didn't have high expectations when it came to her mother, but this comment left her speechless.

He shouldn't have "picked" any of us, she thought to herself.

And that was the last time Cary attempted to have any kind of meaningful conversation with her mother.

* * *

Cary was supposed to meet a friend for dinner in the city, and she was running uncharacteristically late for no particular reason, regretting having made the plan. They were going to go to that Greek place right by Grand Central, so Cary told herself it wasn't really that big an effort. Still, just dealing with the train during rush hour was an ordeal, even if it was for a good cause: food.

Cary considered Anabeth Zielinski, who went by Anna Zee professionally, her best friend. They had worked together at CrimeTV for nearly fifteen years and shared a passion for the law and a likeminded sense of humor. Anna was one of the handful of employees WorldWideCommunications had retained when they demolished the network. Even the clueless execs, who failed to see the value in at least the brand, understood that they needed seasoned producers and reporters if they stood a chance of getting into the trials they wanted to cover. And so, Anna, along with a few others, had managed to get a stay of execution. But Anna's reprieve was short-lived, as she had been let go recently, along with the other reporters and field producers WorldWideCommunications initially kept as an insurance policy.

Cary spotted Anna at their favorite table in the back. Anna had texted her that she got there early, something Cary was notoriously known for—except today. Anna looked good. She had just come from a shoot and hadn't had time to change into more casual clothing. In addition to launching her own website, Anna had wasted no time lining up assignments for herself on magazine TV shows. It was difficult for Cary to listen to her go on and on about the latest case she was about to report on. That had been *her* world, but thanks to greed, Cary was no longer a part of it, except for the occasional stint on Eve's show. Cary knew that's what it had come down to: money.

As she joined Anna at the table, Cary tried to put all these negative thoughts out of her head and just enjoy dinner.

"You look great, Anna," Cary began.

"So do you, peanut," Anna replied in kind.

Anna called everyone peanut. Cary was actually somewhat hurt when she first realized that. She had always thought it was a special nickname just for her. But it didn't bother Cary anymore. Not really. She knew Anna cared about her, and she would always consider her one of her closest friends.

Halfway through the meal, it occurred to Cary that Anna might be able to help her connect the dots, or at least prove that they were connected. Anna had been an ADA in the Manhattan District Attorney's office well before she joined CrimeTV. She had even worked alongside JFK Jr. and had the stories to prove it. Anna had the sharpest legal mind Cary had ever encountered, and she also knew Vito. He had been a chronic talking head on the network for years. In fact, that's how Cary met him and, hence, how he came to work on her sister's divorce. What a team the three of them would make. But Cary wasn't sure if she should go there and thought it best to run the idea by Vito first. And so, they wrapped up dinner with their favorite dessert: the chocolate molten cake with fig ice cream. It was orgasmic.

Cary tried to relax on the train ride home, but an annoying couple with their crying baby made that nearly impossible. Each time the conductor passed by, he made such a fuss over the infant that you would think he'd never seen a baby before. After ten minutes, Cary had enough. So she started texting Anna to vent. All of a sudden, the thought crossed her mind that likely every serial killer has had the same experience as a toddler. Overblown antics from some dumb-ass stranger they'd never see again, gushing over a budding psychopath. It made Cary laugh, the whole idea of it. Anna texted back several *LOLs*. They were always on the same page.

As the family of three detrained at Stamford, Cary texted Vito that she had an idea and needed to talk to him. Yes, Anna might just be the ticket. Cary was pleasantly surprised at Vito's receptiveness to having Anna join the team—that is, *if* she was willing. But first, he thought they needed to do a little more digging. So they agreed that the next step, which had actually been on Cary's mind for a while, was to make contact with the woman who lost her puppy. Although the reception was spotty as always, Cary was able to make out what Vito was saying over the phone, more or less.

"I'll just...Hank pu...the po...ice report."

"An...will...do that?" Cary wasn't sure how far this guy would go for them. Well, for Vito. But he seemed certain that Hank would get them all the details they needed: name, address, and so on. They would just have to come up with a plan to approach the woman, and Vito thought it best if Cary did the dirty work.

* * *

As Cary headed to the woman's house, she couldn't help thinking, *Dogs are the only thing that makes this planet bearable*, and this woman had just lost hers. But thanks to Hank, they knew the woman's name, where she lived, and what she did for a living. Now Cary would have to do the rest. Apparently, according to Hank, it hadn't even dawned on the police to check out the woman's car. They just went on the assumption that she misremembered leaving the windows open, and the dog died as a result. She was so distraught that they hadn't even considered charging her with some kind of animal cruelty offense, so the investigation ended before it began. Case closed.

As soon as the woman came to the door, Cary understood why eyewitness testimony is often unreliable. The woman looked nothing like what she remembered. In retrospect, Cary realized that she hadn't taken notice of the woman at all. She had just gotten wrapped up in the chaos and, quite honestly, wished they had picked a different restaurant so she and her sister wouldn't have had to deal with the situation.

The woman standing in front of her now was striking, exactly Cary's type. Clad in worn-out jeans, donning an "I Kissed a Dog and

I Liked It" tee shirt, Cary hoped she liked kissing girls too. She felt an instant attraction she hoped didn't show. Maybe if she tried picturing Vito with his shirt off again...*nah.*

Oh boy, Cary said to herself. *Here we go.*

She wished she had taken more time to get ready this morning. Cary believed, however, that someone was either attracted to you or they weren't, and whether or not you made an effort didn't usually change that reality. Cary would have been all over the woman before her, for example, if she had just rolled out of bed.

Cary hadn't been in a relationship for a while. It was all too draining emotionally, and anyway, she was very picky. She often pondered the fact that people tend to couple off, and the more she thought about it, the odder it struck her. Just getting picked for teams in school or finding a partner for a field trip was enough of an ordeal. And then she was supposed to find a permanent one. *No thanks.* But Cary imagined the woman standing in front of her now could change her mind.

At first, the woman reminded her a bit of Robin Wright, with a little Lena Headey thrown in—mid-to-late forties, reddish-blonde hair, and a charming smile she used to mask her pain. Cary was drawn to broken people: she was one of them.

"Hi, I'm Cary," she began self-consciously. "Thanks for meeting with me."

"Come on in," the woman replied. "Please excuse the mess. It's not usually like this.... It's just with all the..."

Cary responded in her head, *Please excuse my mess. I'm not usually like this....* But Cary knew what the woman was going to say next, so she tried to take the conversation in another direction.

"You have a lovely home," Cary continued, looking around for family photos that might provide some clues; as to what, Cary wasn't sure. She just didn't want to see a picture of her with a man, or a *woman* for that matter. Cary laughed inside.

Focus, Cary reminded herself. There was a great deal at stake, and how she handled the woman could prove critical. A lot was riding on this meeting. If she fucked it up, Cary might not get another shot. She had to gain the woman's trust. She had to like Cary. Cary *definitely* liked her.

Cary already knew the woman's name from the police report Hank had so cooperatively provided them with, and they had spoken over the phone to arrange the meeting. So the fact that she forgot to introduce herself in person to Cary wasn't really a problem. It just would have been nice. The woman's name was Kimberly Hunter, she lived in Fairview on a sprawling plot of land, and she was a photographer. Her home resembled a barn, and it appealed to Cary right away. She also had a studio, but Cary hadn't gotten that far yet. As she looked around, Cary decided she could be very happy there.

Stop it, Cary, she told herself. *Enough.*

Cary had arranged the meeting on the pretense that she worked in television, which was actually true, well sort of, and was a huge animal lover, also true, and volunteered at local shelters, *not* true, and had heard about what happened to her dog and wanted to reach out. But Cary's goal was to get a look at the car or, if she got really lucky, learn something directly from Kimberly during the visit. In that vein, Cary decided it was time to show a little sympathy.

"I'm so sorry about your dog...your puppy," she began, somewhat awkwardly.

"Thanks.... Andrew was the sweetest.... I don't know what I'm going to do without him," Kimberly continued in a shaky voice.

Cary felt a little guilty that she wasn't being totally honest with Kimberly, but she had to keep her eye on the ball. If Kimberly was positive that she had left the windows cracked, it could go a long way to connecting her dog's death to the baby's. And so, just as Cary was trying to figure out where to begin, Kimberly broke down in tears and, before she could stop herself, blurted out between sobs, "I saw a *man...* by the car, running away." One word came to Cary's mind: *Bingo!* Cary wondered why Kimberly hadn't told the police, but in reality, she already knew: fear. She guessed they had more in common than she thought.

Cary couldn't let Vito know she was attracted to the puppy's owner, but he was a detective after all, so if he figured it out on his own, so be it. He would tease her mercilessly, but she didn't see any reason why it should affect their investigation. Or could it? Either way, Cary figured she had some explaining to do. She never got to take a look at the car. Yet Kimberly had held back key information from the police that she shared with Cary, for whatever reason. Cary guessed she must have gained her trust after all. She figured the next step was to add *Kimberly, puppy owner, saw a man*, under the column *What We Know and They (The Police) Don't.*

* * *

Cary often wondered what makes a killer. She used to think anyone who murdered someone had to be crazy, and then she realized that some people are just pure evil. *Intimate* murders, killings between couples, people who may have been provoked, however, were a bit more relatable. *God knows women could drive you to anything*, she thought. They used to joke at work that marriage kept them in business. Also, if someone really screwed you, hot-headed people who lost control and regretted it afterward, that was relatable as well. But why would anyone kill a stranger? In any event, she believed this guy was completely certifiable and, yes, *evil*.

Cary tried to make up a profile of the suspected killer in her head. Was he a loner? The type of guy who's invisible? Or could he be a family man with a wife and kids like Dennis Rader, known as

"BTK"; Joseph DeAngelo, the "Golden State Killer"; or Gary Ridgway, a.k.a. the "Green River Killer"? The kind of person no one would ever suspect could do such a thing. Rader was married to the same woman for more than thirty years. DeAngelo married his one and only wife, Sacramento attorney Sharon Marie Huddle, in 1973. And Ridgway was married three times, his most recent marriage lasting more than ten years. As Woody Allen said, "It bothers me that I've never had a relationship that lasted as long as Hitler and Eva Braun's." Cary had to laugh.

Ridgway's son, Matthew, remembers him as a "regular soccer dad." And yet, his father pleaded guilty to murdering nearly fifty women and confessed to killing as many as twenty more. Ridgway avoided the death penalty and instead got life without parole by agreeing to disclose the location of some of the missing women's remains. Body bargaining had never sat well with Cary. The double lives some notorious murderers led blew her away. She couldn't even imagine what their children and spouses went through once they knew.

Dennis Rader was also a father and husband whose wife of thirty-four years, Paula Dietz, was granted an emergency divorce after he was identified as the notorious "BTK," Rader's self-proclaimed moniker that stood for bind, torture, kill. Rader terrorized the Wichita area on and off from the mid-seventies until the early nineties, murdering ten people. He said sexual fantasies drove him to kill.

Like Ridgway, Rader managed to weave his murderous impulses into his regular life, holding down a job with ADT, a security company, ironically, for nearly fifteen years, before becoming a compliance officer for Park City, Kansas, a Wichita suburb. *ADT, the same alarm company my sister uses*, Cary bemoaned upon discovering the coincidence. Word has it that as a Cub Scout leader, Rader once left an overnight to kill, returning to the campsite afterward. Taunting the police, however, eventually led to his arrest in 2005.

* * *

Anna and Cary's sister had become close friends. They often commiserated about their challenging social lives with men, having both gone through difficult divorces. And Anna had become an honorary second aunt to Cary's two nieces and nephew. She was family. So, in a somewhat veiled attempt to bring Anna into the investigation, Cary invited her out to Connecticut to have dinner with her and her twin and then spend the night. Anna always stayed at Gayle's place when she came out from the city, as she had more room and a private guesthouse that Anna found cozy. Cary, however, intended to get her alone the next day and explain what had been going on and ask for her help before she had to face Vito again. Cary needed a bit more ammunition and a plan.

Cary and her sister picked Anna up at the Fairview train station. It was the closest one to Wooster. She had taken the 5:52 that was due in at 7:00 p.m. sharp. Gayle spotted Anna as she got off the train and flagged her down. They were planning to go to their favorite Thai restaurant, but they all decided they were pretty Thai'd out, so they opted for Italian instead. As always, Anna brought a fresh batch of her signature brownies she considered the best in the western world. Cary had to admit they were pretty damn good.

As they sat down to dinner, Anna, as usual, kicked off the conversation with a listing of her next television appearances.

"...and I think I'll be on *Nightline* next Tuesday discussing that case in Michigan, and then *20/20* wants to use me for..."

Luckily the waiter came and spared Cary the rest. It wasn't that she was jealous of Anna for doing a better job of landing on her feet, but Cary was hardly working anymore and just couldn't listen to what she was missing out on. Her sister, however, hung on every word. Anna was somewhat of a celebrity to her family, but not to Cary.

Cary decided dinner had gone well. The three of them always had a good time, and she always made Anna laugh. But it had gone later than she planned, so after Anna got settled into her sister's guesthouse, Cary decided to call it a night and head home. But before she took off, she gave Obi a good belly rub, and he, in turn, gave her his paw, draping his leg over her arm. It warmed Cary's heart. How she loved that dog!

They hadn't ordered dessert, and Anna had really brought the brownies for her sister, so as Cary got into her car, her sugar craving felt unsatisfied. She decided to head toward the diner in search of some relief. It was probably the closest place open at this hour, and she was thirsty too, so a thick chocolate shake would do just fine right about now. Cary pulled into the parking lot, turned off the engine, and sat for a moment, thinking about everything that had taken place in the past several months.

Cary hoped she wasn't making a mistake bringing Anna into the picture, but she felt they needed another criminal mind and set of eyes to take a fresh look at the situation. And then, just as Cary was about to get out of her car, she spotted three clearly drunk teenage boys totally out of control. At first, Cary thought nothing of it. Then she reminded herself of one simple rule: when you come upon a potentially dangerous situation, you never let your guard down because that's when something will go terribly wrong. But she needed that shake. So Cary waited another twenty minutes to no avail. They weren't going anywhere any time soon, and so Cary reluctantly drove away.

Sugar is going to get me killed one day, she contemplated, *one way or another.*

* * *

Cary was stirred up as she tried to fall asleep, so she turned to the one thing that always helped her unwind. Even in today's world, she believed that people considered masturbation a taboo subject when it came to women while accepting it as quite normal for men. *Why weren't feminists all over that one?* she wondered. Now that's a cause she could get behind. Sometimes Cary thought she was so good at it that she should have a cigarette afterward. But she didn't smoke.

EIGHT

Cary often thought people who suffered from obsessive-compulsive disorder were just trying to make order out of a hopelessly chaotic world. And just as no two snowflakes are the same so, too, do OCD behaviors vary dramatically from person to person. Cary's were partly sexual in nature, and partly excessive neurosis regarding the well-being of her nieces and nephew and, of course, Obelus. And then there was her recurring fear that she had hit someone with her car that fortunately, to date, had turned out to be false. And so, she thought it wouldn't be easy for anyone to be in a relationship with her.

Cary and her twin sister were total opposites. The only thing Cary thought they had in common was their love of dogs. While her sister was generous to a fault, Cary was, shall we say, very careful with money; while her sister was a bit on the slovenly side, Cary was meticulous; and while Cary was predominantly gay, her sister was classically *boy crazy,* if that term can be used about a professional woman. Her younger niece, Sharon, always said that if you put the two of them in a blender, you'd have one normal person.

* * *

Cary had a lot of things on her mind this morning, such as how she would get Anna to agree to help Vito and her solve whatever the fuck was going on in Connecticut. Food would definitely help. As she was driving to pick up Anna, Cary decided the best place to take her was the Olde Country Inn just around the corner from her sister's house. Cary had a weakness for pancakes, and she was convinced this place served the best in the state. It was the ultimate indulgence that Cary usually denied herself. She often reflected that her epithet would read: *She should have had the pancakes.* But this morning, Cary would ply Anna with them.

When Cary got to her sister's house, Anna was outside on her phone. If Wooster was known for anything, it was bad cell phone reception. As Anna made her way to Cary's Jeep, she continued the conversation, motioning to her that she would only be another minute, and then abruptly ended the call.

"I thought we'd just go over to the Inn. It's right around the corner," Cary said as Anna got into the car and started putting on her seatbelt.

"Sounds good to me, peanut," Anna replied.

When they got to the restaurant, Cary's usual waitress, Candi, short for Candace, showed them to a corner table for two. As she handed them the menus, Cary got the feeling that she recognized Anna. As Candi asked if they wanted anything special to drink, she gave Anna a knowing look.

"Excuse me, I don't mean to be rude, but aren't you Anna Zee?" she inquired.

If there was anything Anna loved, it was being recognized, even if it was just in a small, out-of-the-way eatery like the Inn.

"Why, yes," Anna said, feigning surprise. "What's your name, peanut?"

Anna hadn't known Candi for more than thirty seconds, and already she was a *peanut.* Cary gave up.

When it came time to order, Candi recommended the pancakes, so they both decided to indulge. Now it was time to get down to business. Cary decided there was no beating around the bush, so she got straight to the point. She filled Anna in on what she had seen the night the man ran down the deer then moved on to the girls, the puppy, and the baby. At first, Anna seemed somewhat skeptical, but when she learned of Vito's involvement, it seemed to bolster Cary's credibility.

The single point that seemed to resonate most with Anna, however, was Kimberly's confession. Cary had been looking for an excuse to see Kimberly again, and Anna just gave her one. So Anna decided she could stay over another night if Kimberly would agree to meet them the next day. *Just leave it to me*, Cary thought to herself. But to Anna, she replied, "I'll see what I can do."

Cary was afraid Anna might pick up on her attraction to Kimberly, so she did her best to play it straight, as it were. When they pulled up to Kimberly's house, Cary instinctively fixed her hair and took an uncharacteristic glance at herself in the mirror. *Stupid me*, she said to herself, but Anna didn't seem to notice. So, when Kimberly came to the door and invited them inside, Cary figured she was in the clear. The only thing she wondered was whether Anna was going to make Kimberly a peanut too.

As they went inside, the woman turned to Anna and, with the cutest grin Cary had ever seen on a human face, said, "Hi, I'm Kim. So nice to meet you, Anna."

"*Hi, I'm Kim?*" Cary thought to herself. *What the fuck?*

And so, to Cary's surprise, *Kim* and Anna hit it off right away. Apparently, Kim was a big fan and had followed Anna's career for some time, having watched many of the high-profile trials she had covered for CrimeTV. Kim went on and on about how much she missed Anna's astute reporting and wondered where else she could see her these days. Anna was more than happy to provide her with a road map. Cary was beginning to see no end in sight to this mutual admiration society forming before her, so she tried to think of a way to discreetly change the subject as to why they were there in the first place.

Just as Cary was figuring out the best way to bring up the demise of Kim's puppy, she spotted a picture of the two of them on a bookcase in the corner. Cary had to admit Kim and her dog looked very happy together. There's nothing cuter than a golden retriever puppy, Cary thought, but for the life of her, she couldn't remember his name. *Shit*, Cary said to herself. *What a reporter I'd make.* But before Cary could save herself, or would need to, Anna unwittingly came to the rescue.

"What a precious picture," Anna said, directing her comment to Kim.

Anna had spotted the same photo, and while Cary was driving herself crazy trying to figure out a way to bring up the dog without remembering his name, Anna, in her usual blunt manner, just did it, with no fallout.

Anna seemed to have gained Kim's trust rather easily, and so she responded in kind, "Why, thank you," as her eyes welled up with tears. "Andrew meant a lot to me. It hasn't been easy."

Andrew. Damn it. That's right. How could I have forgotten that? Cary asked herself. God only knew where she'd be in another twenty years or so. She could barely remember her own name anymore.

Just as Cary was beginning to feel like the third wheel, Kim turned to her and said, "Excuse me, I'm afraid I'm not being a very good hostess. Can I offer you something to drink? Either of you?"

Well, I'm in, Cary thought, but she wasn't sure what to ask for.

And then, as Anna said she'd love a cup of coffee, Kim replied, somewhat embarrassed, "I'm so sorry, afraid I only have hot chocolate."

And Cary thought to herself, *Yes, things were definitely looking up.*

The three of them sat down at Kim's heavy wooden kitchen table, hot chocolate in hand. It was a uniquely beautiful piece. When Anna complimented it, Kim replied that she had designed it herself. Cary thought Kim seemed pretty artsy, potentially a good sign that she might be at least partially on Cary's team. At least she hoped.

Cary began to relax, knowing full well that Anna would take over from here and get the ball rolling in terms of their investigation into recent events. Anna laid out the other incidents, only one of which Kim had even heard of: the girls. Still, Cary could see an understanding in her eyes that something was terribly wrong. Kim, however, was unable to give them much of a description of the man she got a fleeting look at as she returned to her car on that fateful day.

So, Anna blurted out, "Can we take a look at the car?"

If there was one thing Kim was certain of, it was that she had left the windows cracked. There was simply no doubt in her mind about it. And Anna seemed to believe her. Cary did too.

As the three of them approached the garage, there seemed to be another sign from God that Kim was the perfect woman for Cary: in front of them was a vintage MG convertible, most likely from the sixties. It had always been Cary's dream car; she would have given anything to own one. As Cary tried to take a closer look, Kim walked past it, bringing them to the actual car in question: a silver Subaru. Cary thought it best to let Anna do the talking.

The windows were all the way open, so as Anna bent down to take a peek inside, she reached into the front driver's seat and held up a set of keys.

"What's this?" she turned to Kim.

"Oh, I always keep an extra set of keys in the car. God knows why. It's just a bad habit."

"Were these in the car when you left Andrew to pick up lunch?" Anna inquired.

"Um...yeah, they must've been.... I wasn't thinking..." she continued.

"Do the police know about this?" Anna said, her tone taking a more serious turn.

"No, I...forgot about it...then the man...I wasn't sure what to do...." Kim continued disjointedly.

And so, the three of them instantly understood that the man Kim thought she had spotted running away from her car could easily have raised all the windows and left poor Andrew to die. It wouldn't have taken long.... It had to have been nearly ninety degrees in the shade that day. And he was only a little puppy. Kim began to break down, sobbing at the reality of it all. Cary and Anna both thought she had enough for one day.

NINE

People rarely took Cary for a lesbian, whether they were straight or gay. She didn't give off the right vibe and didn't have the look. She guessed that, to the average person, she appeared heterosexual. How ironic. In reality, she had never fit in with the gay community, and she was never exactly sure why. And yes, she could be attracted to men too, so Cary believed she hadn't made a very good lesbian and tended to get involved with straight women. Now that she thought of it, Cary realized she had never really been with a gay girl. They just didn't click.

Cary hadn't made a very good adult either. The only home Cary had ever really made for herself was the carriage house she was living in now. Located in Wooster, the same town as her sister, she found herself currently residing on the estate of an actor, albeit D-list, who, fortunately for him, came from enough money to be able to chase his dream. But she rarely saw Brandon, as he traveled all the time. So Cary had her space, and the only thing he asked of her was to water his plants when he was away and bring in his mail; *deal*.

As Cary headed over to her sister's house the following day to take Obi for his rehabilitative swimming appointment, she decided that living so close to her had its advantages. She could see Obi any time she wanted, as he had become the single most important thing in her life.

As soon as Cary pulled up, she could hear him barking. After checking the alarm—*disarmed*—she entered her sister's house. When Obi saw his harness in her hands, he knew he was in for a treat: a car ride. And so, after getting him into her sister's Sequoia, the only vehicle they owned between them that Obi could comfortably fit in, she headed to the rehab center. When Cary got there, she had to wait, as always, for the dog before them to finish; they were always running late, but Cary didn't mind. It gave her more time with Obelus.

Leslie, the woman who owned the place, was a pleasant, crazy animal lover who had taken a liking to Obi. She handled his two-hundred-pound frame with ease—*sometimes*. Today she wanted him to do seven laps. Obi agreed. After putting on his life vest, a daunting task in itself, she gently got him into the pool with the help of her assistant, Drea. After completing the laps, the two women got Obi out of the pool and began to dry him off, another challenging undertaking.

As Cary made her way to the check-out desk, she asked Leslie and Drea, as usual, for help getting Obi back into the car. They gladly obliged. Cary always felt good after these appointments. Swimming seemed to help Obi's condition, and Cary and her sister both thought he was moving better in general. At least she prayed he was.

* * *

The man watched as Cary got back into her car. *That's quite a dog*, he said to himself. More like a small pony. He checked out the license plate again, just random numbers and letters. *Hmmm*, he thought to himself. She was a lot smarter than that man she hung around with, *stupid fuck*. Vanity plates were God's gift to criminals.

As the man sat there for a moment, reflecting on recent events, he couldn't help thinking he had never been a very good student. And yet, he had always been an avid reader. The percent of useful information they taught you in school could fit into a small thimble as far as he was concerned—all just a colossal waste of time. He had always had better things to do, and now, thanks to his financial independence, he had the time to do them. Ridding the world of the weak, the trusting, the unsuspecting, the *interfering*; yes, that was his calling.

* * *

Cary believed gratuitous violence permeated American culture, particularly in film and television. It was hard to find almost any movie or series without an excessive amount of bloodshed. Yet if she looked back on her childhood, most of Cary's earliest memories were of horrendous *actual* murders she heard about growing up. Maybe that's where her phobia came from. It was impossible to know.

One of the first was Kitty Genovese, the young woman who was stabbed to death in New York City reportedly in front of thirty-eight witnesses, none of whom called the police for help even though most of them were supposedly out of harm's way, looking down from their windows as they heard her screams. Or so the *New York Times* said. It was difficult for Cary to admit to herself that she might have been one of them. She hadn't even gone to the police over the deer. And although that version of events has since been mostly debunked, Kitty's murder nevertheless affected Cary profoundly from a very early age.

Cary only recently discovered that Kitty had been a lesbian and lived with her girlfriend. That was back in 1964. Cary couldn't help thinking that Kitty must've been somewhat of a trailblazer. Kitty's brother Bill devoted his life to uncovering exactly how his sister died.

And although that question has never been answered entirely, his sister's murder impacted at least one key decision in Bill's life: to enlist in the Marines and go to Vietnam. Bill equated dodging the draft with the people who, he believed at the time, let his sister down. Eventually, Bill lost his legs in Vietnam. As he lay in a paddy waiting for someone, anyone to save him, he finally understood how his sister must've felt as she was dying.

Kitty Genovese's murder spotlighted the "bystander effect": that one person alone is more likely to take action than twenty, as it took decades for contradictory accounts to poke holes in the original story. Her murder also is largely credited with developing the 911 system. It also encouraged people to embrace the mentality of getting involved and, if they see something, to say something. That is Kitty's legacy.

And so, Cary's entire career had been based on helping murder victims and their families. Whenever they began a new trial, if a victim's relative reached out and asked the network to use a particular picture of their loved one, Cary was more than happy to oblige. It was a small enough request. Anything Cary could do to make the families feel the slightest bit better made her feel that she was accomplishing what she had set out to do.

When Cary learned that the mother of a nine-year-old girl who had been savagely murdered didn't have the funds to attend the execution of her daughter's killer, Cary sent money. And when they covered the sentencing hearing of two particularly cold-blooded killers, Cary made sure the victims' photos were aired constantly during the proceedings. In the end, honoring the victims and helping to remember them was all she could really do. Cary couldn't necessarily get people to help. Not even herself.

But Cary wanted to help Kim and to catch whoever was terrorizing the neighborhood, even if people didn't realize it was happening.

She and Vito and now possibly Anna were the only three who really got what was going on. But now, maybe Kim would join them.

Cary couldn't read women very well. She didn't have a handle on whether Kim could be bisexual or gay, and if so, whether she might have any interest in her. Cary guessed it was a long shot, but she hadn't felt this way about anyone in a while and couldn't let it go. She had to find out, but how? The last thing Cary wanted to do was fuck up the case. And nothing terrified her as much as the thought of approaching a woman romantically, so she put her plans for Kim on hold for the time being and tried to focus on the investigation. *Men are so much easier*, Cary contemplated. Maybe she should have given them more of a chance.

After bringing Obi back home, Cary decided to chill for the rest of the day. It was already four o'clock, and she was emotionally drained. Anna had gone back to the city but agreed the three of them—or possibly four—would have to meet, and soon. So as Cary struggled to open the mayonnaise she bought earlier in the week, she bemoaned the nutjob in Chicago who decades ago tampered with Tylenol. Ever since, people all over America were one step away from throwing jars of pickles and condiments against their kitchen walls. *Yes*, Cary decided, *people were inherently evil*. All one needed to do was observe the security at an airport for proof.

* * *

Cary was woken up by a text alert. She had fallen asleep on the couch watching a movie on HBO GO—*Nocturnal Animals*—more irony, more Amy Adams. As she picked up her phone, a bit disoriented, she saw that it was nearly five o'clock in the morning. However, in spite of the disruption, that brought her great relief. Five o'clock was the hour where she knew she would be safe. Lunatics didn't go around breaking into houses and murdering people in their sleep at 5:00 a.m. No, that's when Cary knew she had bought herself another day. It was all so exhausting.

The text was from Anna. She was heading to the gym in an hour and just wanted to make sure Cary was all right. *I was all right*, Cary thought to herself, *until you called and woke me up at five in the morning.*

Cary tried going back to sleep, but she never could after being woken up, so she decided to make herself some breakfast. Scrambled eggs and toast would do just fine right about now. But food alone always triggered Cary's sugar craving, so she would have to take care of that too. This morning, she thought she'd treat herself to a chocolate croissant at the French bakery up the road in Fairview: true decadence. After running some other errands, Cary returned home to regroup for the day. She realized she hadn't heard from Gene and Eve in a while and was fast losing hope that they would call her back again any time soon. But Cary had a serial killer to catch, so that would keep her more than busy for the time being.

＊ ＊ ＊

Cary, Vito, and Anna had decided to gather in the city this time. The meeting was set for tomorrow afternoon. So Cary had a day to kill and needed to find a way to de-stress. She couldn't help wondering what Kim was up to. She had to make a move, or nothing was ever going to happen. It was time to get a little personal. Cary realized that, with all her fantasizing, she didn't know much about the woman except that she loved dogs. She didn't even know if Kim had ever been married, or if she was married.

So Cary decided to just go for it, to be spontaneous, and to casually drop by Kim's house; on what pretense, she wasn't sure. She'd figure that out when she got there. But Cary never got the chance. As she pulled up to the house, she saw Kim outside, leaning into the front driver's seat of the MG Cary loved so much. At first, Cary couldn't make out what she was doing as the house was set somewhat back from the road. And then, as Kim straightened up and backed away from the car, Cary spotted a man in the front seat. He put the top back up, and Kim got into the car. And it rocked back and forth for what seemed like an eternity. Cary was crushed.

* * *

Vito and Cary took the train into the city together, and Anna met them at Grand Central. Cary had been uncharacteristically quiet on the trip in, but Vito didn't seem to notice. He had other things on his mind. But when Anna saw her, she knew instinctively that something was wrong. Cary was done with women—for good this time. She couldn't deal with the pain anymore. How had she let herself get so wrapped up in a stranger she knew almost nothing about? *Fucking idiot,* she reprimanded herself. She couldn't believe how much it hurt. And she didn't even know her. It was just the whole picture, how many times this had happened to her. *Will I ever learn?* Cary asked herself. She felt that panicky, sick feeling that love caused people to feel. She knew it would pass but not soon enough. Well, maybe at least she'd lose a couple of pounds. Lovesickness trumped Weight Watchers any day of the week. But Cary decided there was also comfort to be taken in food.

When she thought of her plan to surprise Kim, she cringed at what a fool she almost made of herself. At least Kim was none the wiser, and Cary could just suffer in silence—a small consolation. She decided she'd best stick with dogs. They were the only living creatures that always made you feel better no matter the circumstance, and Obelus was the best of them. They had bonded from the get-go. He brought her nothing but joy and peace. How she loved him. She just hoped he could hang in there because she didn't see how she could go on without him.

Cary reluctantly decided Kim hadn't really done anything wrong. She most likely had absolutely no idea that Cary even had a crush on her. But it hurt all the same. So, as they sat down to lunch, Cary was deep in thought when Anna's voice snapped her out of it.

"So what are you going to order, peanut?"

It was then Cary realized she had no memory of even walking to the restaurant. *God*, she thought to herself, *I wonder if I sleepwalk too*.

They had decided to go to Trattoria Dell' Arborio, right around the corner from Lincoln Center. It was one of Cary and Anna's favorite restaurants and, at this hour, wouldn't be too busy. They grabbed a table in the back where they would be able to talk and get down to the business at hand. They had to stop a killer, but first, food. Cary was a creature of habit and always got the same thing wherever she ate, and at Dell' Arborio, that meant the lobster spaghetti carbonara *without* bacon. She felt kind of guilty about it as she was no longer comfortable eating lobster or anything else that had once been alive.

Well, at least the pig would be spared, Cary rationalized.

But picturing Kim having sex like a banshee in that little MG had rattled her, and thus, Cary decided that *just* for today, she would take comfort in any food she chose. That also meant putting in her usual request for the banana cream pie they served at their other restaurant. It was legendary, and today, Cary might just need two pieces. She got a kick out of the waiters running next door to get it for her. Anna got the same thing as Cary, only with the bacon, and Vito ordered the meat lasagna. They weren't winning any vegan awards anytime soon.

While they were waiting for their lunch to arrive, Anna went into reporter mode and asked to be brought up to speed on their investigation, if you could call it that. And so, Vito began.

"This is how we see it, Anna. The girls were run down by the same guy who ran over the deer. Gotta be the same guy," he continued. "We just can't prove it...*yet*."

"And the lab came back with human and animal DNA from the car...." Cary added. "The girls' DNA. So that's gotta mean something. I mean, right?" she continued.

"And it was 100 percent confirmed to be the girls' DNA, the Wooster girls, correct?" Anna said in her best DA voice, attempting to confirm one measly fact in this whole mess.

"Thing is," Vito interrupted, "we haven't been able to tie the puppy's and baby's deaths to the other two incidents.... Hell, we haven't even been able to tie them to each other...not yet. But the animal/human MO...it's weird.... I mean, what are the odds?"

Anna took out the little brown notebook she carried around with her everywhere and started writing. Cary thought it would serve as a *Catch A Killer* to-do list.

Anna took matters into her own hands, drawing up a detailed plan to jump-start their investigation. So far, they were looking at four incidents that had occurred in the Wooster area in the past few months, none of which the police considered intentional acts. At least, that's what Vito believed. No one except the three of them even knew about the deer. Had they mentioned it to Kim? Anna couldn't remember. But there was no sign it was on the authorities' radar.

As far as the girls were concerned, the trail had gone cold except for the discovery of the car. And while it was still an open investigation, Anna was certain the police had it on the back burner for the time being, pending an unexpected break in the case. It appeared the incident with the puppy was simply ruled accidental, as the police didn't know about the man Kim spotted fleeing the scene and had apparently never bothered to examine the car. But Anna would get to that later. The baby's death, however, well, they had to find out what the police made of that one. *So where did that leave them?* Anna wondered.

She believed the next step was to maximize their resources. So Anna decided to assign each of them a task, and then they would meet up again and brainstorm. The way she saw it, one of them would have to talk to the girls' parents, friends, whoever knew them best, and try to get a handle on why they were out so late at night. Who did they hang out with? Were they in relationships? And so on. Anna's instincts told her this needed a woman's touch, so she felt Cary should handle it: done.

Anna decided she would be the best one to interview the baby's father. She knew how to mask tough questions. She would be sympathetic and gain his trust and hopefully elicit some piece of information that could move the investigation forward.

That left Vito. He was the one who had an inside man on the force, Hank, so Anna believed Vito should try to gather any hard evidence he could somehow manage to dig up. Maybe get another look at the police reports, put two and two together. Vito could be pretty resourceful, and he knew his way *around* the law. Most importantly, however, Anna trusted her gut, and right now, it was telling her that there was a crazed serial killer on the loose with an ax to grind. They had to stop him before he struck again, because all indications were that he would.

* * *

The man decided it was the best banana cream pie he had ever eaten. He thought he'd get an extra piece to go. He loved the city. He could get lost in it. He thought he would treat himself today and take an Uber back to Connecticut. The new woman with them was pretty hot. He thought he might treat himself to her too. But he had a busy week ahead of him, so he thought he'd put a pin in that one—for now.

* * *

As Cary headed over to the first girl's house to see if she could speak with her mother, she realized she hadn't seen her own in weeks. *Could it be that long?* Cary asked herself. Well, there was no time now, but maybe she could try to at least call her on the way back. In spite of the issues that she had with her mother, Cary felt guilty when she let too much time go by without seeing her. Sometimes she felt like Jessica Lange in *Frances*. One theme in her mother's life that she repeated constantly was, *It's always the unexpected*. Somehow that resonated with Cary. Murder was *unexpected*. At least if you were normal. But Cary thought about it all the time.

And yet she knew that just because someone had a deep-seated fear of being murdered didn't mean they would be, and vice versa. How many murder victims ever thought in a million years that this was how they were going to die? *Probably none*, Cary guessed. But then there was Ritchie Valens, the singer. He had had a pathological fear of dying in a plane crash and actually did. It was all so random.

With those thoughts going through her head, Cary pulled up to the first girl's house: a small yet charming-looking home that could have used a little work on the outside but was somehow appealing all the same. As Cary made her way to the front porch, a rather large, drooly Saint Bernard appeared to come out of nowhere and ran straight over to her. It was a friendly dog who Cary guessed picked up on Obi's scent. He took an instant liking to her. As Cary summoned up the courage to knock on the screen door, she thought the dog might help break the ice.

The woman who answered appeared to be in her late thirties, with brown hair, brown eyes, and the most distraught look on her face Cary had ever seen. Losing a child. Cary couldn't even imagine losing one of her nieces or nephew, or Obi for that matter. *What this poor woman must be going through*, she thought.

"Can I help you?" the woman asked her.

Cary knew she should have tried to get in touch with the woman beforehand and not surprise her like this, but she was afraid she might refuse to see her. Cary thought she'd have a better shot in person.

"You have an awesome dog here," Cary began. "What's his name?"

"It's a *she*," the woman responded, not unkindly. "Mischa."

Damn. Did it again, Cary thought. *Do I notice anything?*

Cary loved it when people gave their dogs human names: Mischa.

"Who are you, and why are you here?" the woman continued, appearing to get a little frustrated with Cary.

"Oh, so sorry," Cary continued. "I work at LNN, the Legal News Network. We cover crime, and I wanted to ask you a few questions about your daughter."

Cary feared the woman would slam the door in her face, but her reaction was quite the opposite. She seemed to be grateful that anybody still gave a shit.

"Why don't you come inside?"

Cary started to relax.

"I just made a fresh batch of iced tea. Would you like some? Then maybe we can go sit on the porch and talk."

"That would be nice," Cary said.

She liked this woman instantly; there was something about her. Cary was more intent than ever on finding the evil piece of shit who had taken her daughter away from her *forever*.

"I'll just be a minute in the kitchen," the woman continued. "Have a seat if you want."

But Cary used the time to snoop around and see if anything struck her as unusual. Her daughter was beautiful. There were pictures of her everywhere. It made Cary angry, what had happened to her.

And then the woman came back with a tray holding two tall glasses of tea, some freshly baked chocolate chip cookies, and a large pitcher in case they got really thirsty. It was a brutally hot day. Cary knew she would need it as the woman escorted her to a picnic table.

As they sat outside in the shade, it was the woman who began.

"Em was my only child, my only family. I'm afraid it still hasn't registered that I'll never see her again. It's impossible to grasp the reality of it all," the woman went on. The pain etched on her face was truly unbearable to look at.

If I ran the world, Cary said to herself, *cruel and unusual punishment would be the norm*. Every murder victim gets the death penalty for sleeping, jogging alone, walking to their car in a darkly lit parking lot; so why shouldn't their killers? Cary never understood the logic: why a murderer should be guaranteed a better deal than their victim, by law no less. It angered her. But all she could think of to say was, "I'm so very sorry."

The woman's name was Siobhan Browne. Cary detected a hint of an accent she couldn't exactly place, but she assumed she must be Irish. She loved Irish names and accents and people for that matter. Cary had always considered herself honorary Irish and, with a name like Mackin, figured she must have some Irish blood. Siobhan had gotten pregnant at a relatively early age and had raised Em, given name Emily, on her own. Losing her was devastating. As they continued to talk, Cary discovered that she was indeed from Ireland, and most of her family was still back there. She had come to the United States to get away.

Although Cary was actually enjoying the conversation, it was already getting toward mid-afternoon, and she still had the other girl's family to get to. So it was time to start asking questions.

"Did Em have a boyfriend, if you don't mind my asking?" Cary started.

She sensed a hesitant look in the mother's eyes, but then she replied quite simply,

"No, a girlfriend."

Cary was completely taken aback. She didn't know what to say. *When did everyone in the world become gay?* she pondered. But Cary saw no reason to drag herself into this.

"She was seeing somebody?" Cary tried to sound nonchalant.

"Em was...um...she spent a lot of time with Amanda, Mandy, the girl she was with that night," Siobhan explained.

As Cary was trying to decide where to take the conversation next, Siobhan continued.

"Em was confused.... She was only sixteen years old.... She had dated boys.... She saw some guy for a while, but it didn't work out."

"Can I have his name?" Cary asked bluntly.

"I never knew it. I think he was older. I never met him. Em was secretive about the whole thing. But then it just sort of ended abruptly, so I never gave it another thought. I always got the feeling she was forcing herself to go out with him to prove something."

Cary thought she understood. The discovery of the car seemed to provide Browne with some hope that her daughter's killer might be apprehended. But Cary got the feeling it hadn't crossed her mind that the driver might have run over her daughter and Mandy *intentionally*. Cary saw no reason to bring it up, not yet. It had been enough for one afternoon—for both of them. Amanda's parents would have to wait.

TEN

Cary was emotionally drained when she got home, so she indulged in something she rarely ever did: a long relaxing bath. *Why don't I ever do this?* she asked herself. After drying off, Cary decided she was hungrier than she had realized, so she went into the kitchen to scrounge up some dinner. Her fridge was nearly empty, as usual, but she remembered that she had bought a box of high protein pasta and a jar of tomato sauce, marked "V," the other day. Yes, Cary decided, she was doing her part to stop the slaughter—well, at least more than most people.

As she waited for the water to boil, Cary thought it might not be a bad idea for her to make some notes about the meeting with Siobhan. So she grabbed her laptop and opened up Word. But as she started to create a document labeled, *What Cary Found Out,* she remembered she had forgotten to accept Romy's friend request. After the Kim debacle, Cary decided why not torture herself a little more and see what Romy was up to. So she hit the confirm button. Did she really want to start looking at pictures of Romy and her family, her husband? No, but curiosity got the best of her. Facebook was like quicksand; there was just no getting out.

Cary went to Romy's wall and began to look through her photo albums. Romy looked great. *Damn*, Cary thought. *Am I going to be self-destructive enough to start going through her posts?* The answer, of course, was yes. As Cary took a look at the first one, it triggered that familiar panicky feeling. It was Romy's wedding anniversary, and Cary was currently staring at a rather large, old, black and white photo of her and her husband locked in an embrace, kissing and looking madly in love. How Cary hated her.

But Cary knew what had gone on between them, and even though it had been a lifetime ago, there was no doubt in her mind that Romy had loved her. It had taken Cary a long time to accept the fact, however, that Romy was just a straight girl who had put her own curiosity first and Cary's feelings a distant second. When they broke up, Romy started to walk it all back: She had never been *attracted* to Cary; she had just been *drawn* to her. She never *missed* her; she had just *thought* about her, and so on. Yes, Romy was the queen of semantics. Cary thought Romy wasn't being honest with herself and couldn't handle the fact that she had somehow gotten involved with a woman romantically. It was a long time ago, but to Cary, it seemed like yesterday.

Cary decided this wasn't a productive way to spend the evening, so she circled back to what she had learned from Emily's mother. Now that she thought about it, Cary still didn't know why the girls were out so late. But she hadn't spoken yet with Amanda Caldwell's parents. Maybe they would shed some light on the situation. Cary couldn't help wondering if they were even aware there might be something sexual going on between their daughter and her best friend. But was that even relevant? Cary wasn't sure. She realized she hadn't gotten much useful information out of Siobhan. The *girlfriend* thing had thrown her. The most interesting thing was the ex-boyfriend, but she didn't even know who he was. Well, Cary thought to herself, hopefully Anna and Vito would fare better.

* * *

As she drove up to the Caldwells' house the next day, it was quite a different scene from Emily's. *Did anyone really need four garages?* Cary asked herself. As she was being ushered to an outdoor terrace by a servant of some kind, Cary couldn't help thinking, *Do people really have butlers anymore?*

Amanda's parents seemed completely clueless. They put on a brave front, but Cary guessed behind the stoicism lay intense grief. There was no sign whatsoever that they remembered their daughter as anything but a straight-A student who aspired to great things. Cary thought they'd be shocked at the thought something sexual may have been going on between Mandy and Emily. So Cary decided to steer clear of the subject and see what else she could find out.

"I'm so sorry about your daughter," she began.

Like Siobhan Browne, the Caldwells welcomed Cary with open arms, although they appeared to be somewhat more guarded. Still, they loved their daughter very much and wanted to see justice served. They seemed comfortable with the fact that Cary worked, well *had* worked, at a network such as CrimeTV. Cary got the feeling they really wanted to help. That was half the battle.

"Is there anything you can tell me about Mandy that might help us?" Cary continued.

Rebecca Caldwell was the first to answer. Cary guessed she was in her early forties and had gone to a school like Wellesley. She gave off a proper, preppy vibe but seemed like a nice enough woman.

"*Amanda* was a lovely girl. We were—*are*—very proud of her," she replied.

Then breaking down in tears, she continued, "We miss her."

They called her *Amanda*. Cary had to remember that.

"Do you have any idea what Amanda was doing out so late at night?" Cary asked.

This time it was the father, James Caldwell, who responded.

"When they catch that son-of-a-bitch who did this to our daughter, there will be hell to pay." His tone startled Cary, but she guessed they were on the same page when it came to the death penalty. And then Amanda's mother interrupted, adding: "The only thing I can think of is that Amanda might have been going to meet her *boyfriend*."

"Her boyfriend," Cary replied, trying to sound nonchalant.

"Yes, Tim...Tim Shaw."

Cary guessed sexual *fluidity* was rampant these days.

* * *

As Cary was driving home, she decided it would be a good time to touch base with Anna and tell her what she had found out. Except for the mysterious boyfriends and the possibility that the girls were more than just friends, Cary had pretty much come up empty-handed. And so, she decided she would try to reach Anna and see what she made of it all. "Siri, call Anabeth Zielinski—home," Cary directed her phone. To Cary's frustration, she got Anna's voicemail. "Call me," Cary said. "I think I may have something."

It only took a few minutes for Cary's phone to ring. When she picked up, it was Anna.

"Sorry, I was in the shower. What's up?" she inquired.

"Not sure," Cary began.

She filled Anna in on what the girls' mothers had told her, that Emily and Amanda may have been involved romantically but that they had either once had or did have boyfriends. Cary wasn't sure where this might take them.

"You've got to talk to the boys," Anna told her.

"The mother doesn't seem to know who Emily was seeing," Cary continued. But, she told Anna, Amanda's mother had been more than happy to provide her with the name of her daughter's boyfriend. They agreed that that was the next step.

On her end, the only thing Anna had found out so far was that the baby's father was out of town for another week and would call her back when he returned. So the two women decided that the only way to move things forward was for Anna to put her life on hold for the time being and come out to Connecticut for a while until they could figure things out. Her sister's guesthouse would serve as Anna's second home.

* * *

With a quick phone call to Vito, Cary was able to get Shaw's address. As she drove up to the boy's house, she wasn't sure what to expect. Cary tried to picture what kind of guy Amanda would be attracted to, but there was no way to know. She had never even met her. The only thing Cary was able to ascertain so far was that Amanda wasn't slumming it; whoever this guy was, he came from money. So that was one thing Amanda and Tim had in common.

Cary parked her Jeep where the guard at the front gate pointed and took a deep breath. She wasn't really comfortable around people in general, which made running around to strangers and asking them invasive questions a daunting task for her. But she had to find out what was going on. And while it was entirely possible that the girls' deaths were completely random—*wrong place, wrong time*—she was positive they weren't accidental. Whoever did it had acted deliberately, whether he knew them or not. Of that, Cary was certain. She also had a strong hunch that it was the "Deer Killer." She just didn't know who he was.

As Cary made her way to the main house, she spotted a young man walking alongside a chestnut-colored mare. Cary thought horses were the most beautiful animals in the world. This one was particularly stunning. The boy was wearing a white V-neck tee shirt, torn jeans, and worn-out cowboy boots. He looked drained.

"Hi, I'm Cary Mackin. I'm here to see Tim Shaw. Do you know where I can find him?" she inquired.

"Yeah, I'm Tim," he answered, a bit suspiciously. "What do you want with me?"

Cary explained that she worked for a television show that covered crime and that they were investigating a couple of unusual incidents that had taken place in the area over the past couple of months. She didn't think saying "sort of worked for" would bolster her credibility.

"So what does that have to do with me?" he asked.

Cary told him they were trying to help the police catch the person who ran over the Wooster girls and that Amanda's mother had given her his name.

He seemed a bit taken aback while trying to appear cooperative.

"So what do you want to know?" he replied.

Cary wasn't exactly sure how to bring up his alleged relationship with Amanda. But before she knew what she was saying, she blurted out, "You were seeing one of the girls, Amanda, right?"

And then, to Cary's astonishment, he said rather coldly: "I was *doing* both of them." It took a lot to shock Cary these days, but Tim Shaw had somehow managed to do so.

* * *

Cary went to pick Anna up at the train station. It had been a couple of days since she had met with Tim Shaw, and she hadn't been able to talk to Anna about it yet. Anna had a lot to do before she could hole up in Connecticut for a while, and Cary didn't want to distract her. When she spotted Anna on the platform, she wondered if she would have enough room in her Jeep for herself, Anna, and all of her belongings.

Anna had enough luggage with her to last a normal person a minimum of three months without doing laundry. It reminded Cary of the time they had been sent out to a trial together in Michigan. The case hadn't lasted more than three weeks, but when it ended and they checked in at the airport for their departing flight back to New York, the ticket agent asked Anna where she was moving to. It made Cary laugh just thinking about it.

In any event, none of that mattered right now. Cary couldn't wait to get Anna settled into her sister's guesthouse and then spill the beans about what Tim Shaw had told her. Cary had already stocked the fridge with all of Anna's favorite things, so there was nothing much left to do but let her unpack. Cary figured she'd drop Anna off at the cottage and visit with Obi while Anna was settling in. Then the two of them could grab a bite and catch up.

Anna was more tired from the trip than Cary had expected. When she went back to pick her up, Anna suggested she make them lunch and they sit outside on the patio and talk. That suited Cary just fine. They needed privacy, and this way, she could spend more time with Obi. Anna was a big dog lover, and Obi's issues—that is, drool—didn't bother her. She was good-natured about it. So as Anna began to fix them something to eat, Cary went back to her sister's main house and rounded up Obelus, his harness, and his favorite ball. It served as a pacifier. Cary could've used one too.

When Cary returned, Anna had already set the table outside and was loading a tray with sandwiches and her famous red rooibos iced tea. Cary hoped it was the peach-flavored one.

"Sorry, Anna. I meant to be back in time to help," she said apologetically.

"No worries, peanut. Everything's almost ready."

Cary recognized a familiar smell coming from the oven: Anna's brownies. She had already whipped up a batch. They would go great with the tea. *Hmmm*, Cary thought to herself, *what's the rush to solve this thing again?*

Food was one of Cary's major obsessions, and her former colleagues were like-minded. Whenever they had to work late, usually when CrimeTV was airing a trial on the West Coast, Cary's corporate card sprang into action. A platter of deli sandwiches from the late great Carnegie Deli or pans of Carmine's legendary manicotti and lasagna were a welcome distraction from autopsy photos. Cary and her coworkers often joked that since all they talked about was food, maybe everyone at the Food Network was obsessed with crime. They never found out.

So, as Cary took a bite out of the "veggie option" sandwich Anna had prepared especially for her, Cary's mind wandered back to Tim Shaw. She took a long sip of the iced tea, peach-flavored, fetched Obi a large bowl of cold water laced with ice cubes, and began.

"I found Amanda's boyfriend," Cary said bluntly.

"What's his name again?" Anna inquired.

"Tim Shaw."

"Tim Shaw," Anna repeated. "So what did he tell you?" she asked Cary, going straight into reporter mode.

"He said," Cary continued somewhat hesitantly, "that he was *doing* both of them."

Cary was somewhat taken aback by Anna's reaction: there was none. She just proceeded to process everything they knew so far about the girls. After some thought, Anna shared her current theory of the case with Cary. She believed that Emily was attracted to Amanda, but she wasn't sure how Amanda felt about her. Anna, therefore, deduced that Amanda knew Emily liked her but might just be toying with her, while really being in love with Shaw. And that Emily might have been willing to have a three-way in order to hold onto Amanda. That all sounded reasonable to Cary. They both also agreed that none of this might have anything to do with how and why the girls died. It was getting a bit too complicated for Cary's liking.

And then Anna got to the point. Did Tim Shaw see anything that night? Did he see the man, the same man Kim saw? But somehow, that question never came up. Shaw had manipulated Cary. She hadn't even managed to ask him if he was with the girls the night they had been killed. But she knew Anna was right: if the girls were on their way to meet up with him, he could have seen *everything*.

* * *

As Cary headed home later that afternoon, she reflected on the meeting with Anna. The instant Kim's name was mentioned, Cary realized she hadn't thought about her in days. It was like something out of the past. *That must be a good sign*, Cary told herself. Maybe she was over her. Cary wondered how she would feel the next time she saw Kim. But she couldn't think about that right now. The next step was to cozy up to Shaw and see if she could get him to tell her anything. Anyway, it was Anna's turn to see what she could get out of the baby's father.

Meanwhile, Cary thought, when she got home, she'd take another one of those soothing baths she had recently grown so fond of. But as she pulled into her driveway, two texts came in simultaneously: one from Vito and the other from Anna. *This can't be good*, Cary mused. She was right. They told her to check her phone. A woman, her four-year-old daughter, and their dog had been sideswiped by a car. The thirty-three-year-old woman survived but was in critical condition; her young daughter and dog did not. Before Cary even had a chance to get out of her car, she sent Anna a text: *I'm on my* way *back.* She headed to her sister's house.

When Cary got there, she was surprised to see Vito's car. She didn't realize Anna had even told him where she was staying yet. But in the end, Cary didn't think too much of it. She just knew it was going to be a long night.

ELEVEN

Although Cary had always done her best to avoid looking at the autopsy photos at work, she couldn't sidestep all the grisly details. It was an impossible task. So the death of this little four-year-old girl inevitably conjured up that awful picture of Caylee Anthony: just bones. When Cary first saw the photo, she wasn't even sure it was real. The little bones laid out for the jury to see. Is that all that's left in the end, bones? Cary couldn't bear to think about it. What right did anyone have to steal someone's life away and turn them into that? They needed to pay.

As Cary, Anna, and Vito settled in, they realized that none of them had eaten dinner yet. To Cary's relief, they opted for Thai this time. Much as she loved Italian, Cary didn't think she could eat any more pasta. Thai was a nice vegan alternative if you ordered the right dishes. So Cary got the steamed veggie dumplings and tofu Khao Soi, her favorite soup she discovered on a trip to Northern Thailand. Anna opted for kale fried rice, and Vito, as usual, ordered a meat dish: the beef Massaman Curry. Cary would have to have a talk with him about his eating habits one of these days.

As Cary headed to the bathroom before dinner arrived, she had a thought. Some killers stalked their victims *after* they murdered them:

crashing their funerals, calling their homes. Sick stuff like that. Maybe they could lay a trap for this guy, lure him in. The little girl's memorial service would likely be a mob scene. She thought she'd run the idea by Anna and Vito after they ate. When the doorbell rang, Vito answered and brought the food into the kitchen.

"Would anyone like some of my rooibos iced tea?" Anna inquired. "I made a fresh batch."

Cary thought it would go great with Thai food. Anna's culinary skills were pretty much limited to iced tea and brownies, but Cary couldn't even do that, so who was she to judge?

As Vito passed out the containers, Cary noticed two wine glasses and some cheese near the fridge. She guessed Anna thought they might not have ordered enough food, and Cary didn't drink.

The guest cottage wasn't particularly big. It consisted mainly of an open kitchen area that led straight into the living room, which boasted a beautiful stone fireplace. The bedroom was down a narrow hallway just past the powder room. They opted to eat dinner on a couple of chairs and a couch that surrounded an antique wooden coffee table near the fireplace.

Vito had already been briefed by Hank on the details of the case. From all appearances, it seemed like the police had another hit-and-run on their hands. Someone driving too fast around a curve struck a woman, her four-year-old daughter, and their Bernese mountain dog. Only the woman survived, albeit with life-threatening injuries. Cary couldn't help thinking that if it was the same guy, the "Deer Killer," he must've been sending a message—but to whom?

"The woman's name is Blair Riordan: thirty-three years old, stay-at-home mom, stopped working temporarily to raise her daughter, husband's name is Richard, same last name. She's in the ICU." Vito continued, bringing them up to speed on what Hank told him.

"The mother doesn't know about her daughter," Vito went on. "She's not responsive, and even if she were, they wouldn't tell her anyway, not yet. The news could jeopardize her recovery."

"So what do we do?" Cary asked, despite having a pretty good idea.

"One of us has to keep tabs on Riordan and, if she comes out of it, talk to her," Vito answered.

Cary realized Anna had been uncharacteristically quiet during the exchange. As if Anna read her mind, she chimed in, "Cary should do it."

Cary wasn't exactly sure why Anna wanted to assign her the task. And then it dawned on her that it was all over the news that the mother was still alive, which meant whoever had been driving the car knew that too.

"The killer...I mean everyone knows she's still alive.... What if..." Cary continued.

"Relax, Cary," Vito began, interrupting her. "People can't just wander into the ICU.... I'm sure if the cops think she needs security, they'll do the right thing."

So Cary agreed she would stake out the hospital and monitor the woman's progress. But she also brought up the theory that killers sometimes stalk their victims posthumously and threw out the idea that one of them should attend the little girl's funeral to see if they spotted anyone who seemed suspicious. Both Vito and Anna agreed. They also acknowledged that this was most likely no ordinary hit-and-run; it was the "Deer Killer" taunting the police. They had no way of knowing he was also goading them.

* * *

As Cary headed home, she couldn't help thinking about lone survivors of horrific crimes she had seen over the years. They were rare, but it happened. She had become particularly obsessed with the victims of a brutal crime spree in Wichita, Kansas. After being terrorized for the better part of the night, five friends had been taken by two killer brothers to a soccer field and shot execution-style. Then, for good measure, they ran them over with one of the victims' truck. After the murders, the killers returned to the home looking for more valuables, beating a victim's dog named Nikki to death with a golf club in the process.

The dog's owner, the sole surviving victim, known as HG, had managed to cheat death on that cold, snowy night. A barrette she had in her hair deflected the bullet just enough to prevent a fatal injury. And the snow somehow padded her from the weight of the car. Her friends didn't fare as well. Reginald and Jonathan Carr were arrested, tried, and sentenced to death for the murders of Jason Befort, Brad Heyka, Aaron Sander, Heather Muller, and Ann Walenta. Walenta, the Carrs' fifth homicide victim from an attack three days earlier, was able to identify Reginald Carr before sadly succumbing to her injuries.

Cary thought HG's impact statement in court was truly the most poignant account of a crime and its effect on the victims she had ever heard. During the invasion, while the Carrs were ransacking the home, the engagement ring HG's boyfriend, Jason, had bought for her was discovered hidden in a popcorn box. That's how she found out he was about to propose. If there was one person in the world Cary wanted to meet, it was HG: the woman who owed her life to a hair clip that stayed stubbornly in place throughout murder, rape, and torture, the woman who faced Cary's greatest fear and came out alive.

* * *

In spite of all that was on her mind that night, Cary slept like a dead person. When she got to the hospital the following day, she parked her Jeep in the visitor's lot and proceeded to the information counter. Cary wasn't sure the best way to approach the woman behind it. She looked anything but friendly.

But just as Cary was collecting her thoughts, a text came in from none other than Gene. They were planning to lead with the Riordan story tonight and wondered, since it was geographically expedient, if Cary would be willing to go to the hospital and follow up on the mother's condition. She didn't dare tell him she was already there, as Cary decided the truth only gets you so far in life; but lies, there was no limit to where lies could take you. *Sure Gene*, she texted back. *I'd be more than happy to.*

Her day rate was up to four hundred fifty dollars, so Cary figured it was easy money, as she was in the process of doing the same thing for free.

Bolstered by Gene's request, Cary found the courage to be direct with the woman behind the bullet-proof glass.

"Excuse me," she began. "Can you tell me where I might find Blair Riordan?"

"Are you a relative?" the woman asked, somewhat timidly to Cary's surprise.

"No, afraid not," Cary responded. Then, deciding to go with the *truth,* told her, "I'm a journalist with—"

But the woman cut her off. "I'm so terribly sorry. I'm afraid I can't help you. She didn't make it. We're trying to reach the family. Afraid your timing couldn't have been worse. She just passed. I'm so sorry."

Cary was completely taken aback. She sat down to get her bearings and texted Gene what she had just found out. A wave of sadness came over her. She was tired of dealing with victims; she wanted them to win, but it seemed like the victory always went to the killer. Gene texted her back almost immediately. *Never mind. We already scrapped the story; some guy in Colorado just killed his whole family.*

Cary rarely got a *but thanks anyway*. Still, she knew she'd get paid for the day. That wasn't what was bothering her. What disturbed her was the callousness. In the end, as much as Cary tried to convince herself that she was doing good, it was just a ratings game. And she was complicit. Gene thought the "Killer Dad" would rate better than some woman who got sideswiped along with her daughter and dog. It was that simple. Cary thought she should start a Murder Victims' Lives Mattered movement, but she feared it wouldn't catch on.

As she headed to her car, Cary realized she had forgotten to tell Anna and Vito that the woman had died. So she picked up her phone and told Siri: "Call Anabeth Zielinski, mobile." After two rings, Anna picked up.

"What's up?" Anna inquired.

"Blair Riordan, the mother. She didn't make it." Cary sounded despondent.

"Gotcha," was all Anna said back. And then she added, "We're on our way to a funeral."

Cary decided to go straight home and try to unwind. As she drove away from the hospital, for a brief moment, she thought she was being followed. So Cary did what she always did in that situation: pulled over to see if the car would pass her by. It did. *I'm really losing it*, Cary said to herself.

* * *

I never fall for that one, the man said to himself. The mother had succumbed to her injuries—another bullet dodged. He decided if someone was going to have a good day, it might as well be him. Humility was not his strong suit. He failed to see where it got anyone. We live in a world where you have to know what you want and go out and take it. He could check both of those boxes.

* * *

The first thing Anna noticed as they took their seats in the back of the church was a picture, blown up to poster size, of four-year-old Dakota Riordan and her dog, Nelson. Anna found it difficult to look at. With the mother's passing just minutes before her daughter's funeral was to begin, Anna figured the Riordans would have another service to plan. *Why did people like the "Deer Killer" have to exist?* Anna pondered. There, of course, was no answer. The fate of the Riordan family was just another senseless act in a world spiraling out of control. She took comfort in being there with Vito. He was the sharpest private eye she knew, and the most charming. She had never gotten over him, and apparently, he felt the same.

It was a shame all hell broke loose the night they intended to rekindle their romance. Anna wondered if Cary had picked up on anything. The wine glasses and cheese were a dead giveaway, but Anna saw no sign that Cary noticed. *She wasn't very astute sometimes*, Anna thought. There really was no reason they couldn't be honest with Cary, but right now, Anna didn't want to complicate the situation. As Anna was deep in thought, she heard Vito's voice in the background.

"Just keep an eye out. Anything, anyone looks suspicious, just nudge me," he directed her.

"Yes, of course," Anna answered him. "I'm all over it."

Anna was straight as an arrow, but it bugged her that Cary had zero interest in her. It was just an ego thing. Cary just wasn't the least bit attracted to Anna, and Anna knew it. But Vito was a different story. *They* had chemistry. He loved her blonde curls and contagious laugh. Anna was only five feet, three inches tall, but she always told people good things come in small packages. Vito seemed to agree. They made a handsome couple.

The sound of an organ snapped Anna out of her irrelevant thoughts, and she heard sobbing coming from the front pews. Frank Riordan Sr., his son Frank Jr., and Richard Riordan—now a widower with no children—clutched hands. Just looking at them broke Anna's heart. Killers destroy whole families, not just the individuals they kill. And closure was bullshit. Anna couldn't even stand the word. The three men stared down at the tiny coffin little Dakota would spend eternity in; an urn, presumably with Nelson's ashes in it, stood next to the casket on a small stand. It just didn't get any more depressing.

After heartbreaking eulogies delivered by Dakota's father, grandfather, and uncle, the church cleared out as people made their way to the cemetery. Vito and Anna followed suit. That's where the killer might position himself. It was a long shot, but they had to try, as there had been no sign of anything out of the ordinary at the actual service. As the tiny casket and urn were lowered into the ground together, emotions ran high. Anna had to look away. They had seen no indication that whoever did this had decided to insult the victims with his presence at their final resting place. Truth be told, Anna was relieved.

* * *

He sensed they were looking for him at the funeral. Why else would they have been there? But he could be invisible when he wanted to, and they had no idea what he even looked like. They were clueless. The man thought the woman and Vito looked awfully cozy together. Yes, he knew Vito's name. The DMV had made that possible. Today he was also able to get a better look at the woman. Well, if it wasn't Anna Zee in the flesh. He was actually a big fan. *Who doesn't like crime, after all?* he asked himself.

* * *

As the pair headed back to Vito's car, Anna noticed a rather tall, lanky man staring at them as he said his goodbyes to poor Dakota's family—or rather, what was left of it. He was following them with his eyes, as if he didn't want to lose sight of them. And then, before she could open the car door, he was somehow standing right in front of them. Mainly addressing Anna, he began, "I hear you've been looking for me. Tom Cooper."

It only took a moment for Anna to place him. It was the baby's father, the baby who had suffocated in the hot car the same day Kim's puppy died. Anna recognized him from a photo Vito had managed to obtain. She thought the picture must've been from his driver's license. Anna decided that in spite of the torture it shelled out to the average Joe on a daily basis, the DMV did have its benefits.

Before Anna could process what he was doing at little Dakota's funeral, Cooper gave her the answer. "Just thought I'd come by and pay my respects," he explained. "We have a rather *unfortunate* bond."

Anna hadn't had a chance yet to express her sympathy, but Tom Cooper just gave her the opening.

"I'm so sorry," she began somewhat awkwardly. "That's what we wanted to talk to you about," she continued.

Cooper didn't answer right away, so Vito used the pregnant pause to introduce himself. He wasn't sure Anna would ever get around to it.

"Mr. Cooper, I'm Vito Loggia. Anna and I used to work together. I'm a private detective." And then Vito added rather clumsily, "I believe we know each other."

This time, without missing a beat, Cooper responded, "Yes, I know who you are. You handled my divorce. My *wife* hired you."

Anna sensed the kind of tension you could cut with a knife. She was used to the city, where people could pretty much stay anonymous if they wanted to. Things were different in Connecticut. *Everyone* seemed to know each other.

Anna always believed the best plans were spontaneous, so in the spirit of *no time like the present,* she suggested that the three of them grab some coffee and talk for a bit. Cooper was on board. So he followed them to the diner just off I-95. They grabbed a booth in the back and settled in. Anna and Vito sat on one side while Cooper took the seat directly across from Anna. She wasted no time getting down to business.

"What can you tell us about the day your daughter died?" she began.

"Daughter?" he responded, confused. "Elsie was my *niece.*"

Anna couldn't help but wonder how they got their wires crossed on that one. Then as if answering a question that she hadn't asked, at least not out loud, Cooper continued, "Actually, there's been some confusion on that score. Let me explain."

So it turned out Tom Cooper's younger brother Jimmy had substance abuse problems, as did his girlfriend. When she got pregnant, Tom agreed to help them out financially and take care of the baby on one condition: that she stop doing drugs until she gave birth and that both of them check into rehab—*again.* Cooper caught Lynda, the baby's mother, smoking weed late in the pregnancy but hoped no harm had come to little Elsie. He made good on his promise and took the baby in. End of story.

The couple was currently in rehab in Arizona, and Cooper wasn't sure if they had really been planning on coming back for Elsie once they got clean. A drug addict is a drug addict, and their stints in various facilities in the past had only gone so far. But then, well, "We all know what happened next," he lamented.

Sad story, thought Anna. But they needed to know the details of Elsie's death, so she tried steering the conversation back in that direction.

And so, Tom Cooper relived that awful day, the moment he would never forgive himself for. He had taken little Elsie to protect her from the people he deemed to be irresponsible parents, including his own brother, but he was the reason she was dead. At least that's how he saw it.

Apparently, Cooper was already living the hectic life of a single "parent," as he had never remarried following the divorce. So, after backing his car out of the garage and strapping Elsie into her car seat, he ran back into the house to look for his cell phone.

"I cracked the windows. I even turned the AC on," Cooper recounted with a pained expression on his face.

"So you left the car running?" Anna asked, trying to nail down the facts.

"Yeah, I thought it was only going to be a minute or two. But I took the call," Cooper elaborated. "I took the goddamn call. Sorry, I just…"

"The *call*," Anna and Vito said simultaneously.

"I…uh…found the phone right away because it was ringing when I went back inside," Cooper continued. "It was my wife—my *ex*-wife—I should have let it go to voicemail. It's always the same fucking thing with her. Wasn't even important, and that call's probably the reason Elsie is dead," Cooper went on, beating himself up for what was probably the millionth time.

"It's okay," Anna tried to say in a reassuring way. "None of this is your fault."

"Sure doesn't feel that way," Cooper answered.

"How long were you on the phone?" Anna inquired.

"About five minutes, maybe more. She was getting me all riled up. Stupid of me to let her get to me like that. The police must have the exact time in their report," Cooper suggested.

"And what happened next?" Vito interjected.

"I…uh…I…ended the call and went back to the car. I couldn't open the doors. They were locked. The windows were closed…. Elsie was…

she was gasping for breath," Cooper continued, his voice cracking with emotion.

"The engine was still running.... I called 911.... Then I went into the garage to try to find something, anything to break the glass," Cooper continued to explain. "By the time I grabbed a hammer, the police had arrived. But by then, well, it was too late. Elsie wasn't breathing.... They tried CPR...oxygen...everything, but she was gone," and with those words, Tom Cooper broke down.

Cooper collected himself and got to the point. After examining the car, the police simply concluded that when he shut the door to run back into the house, the vehicle automatically locked with the keys inside: a tragic accident.

"And what did the autopsy show?" Anna inquired.

"Autopsy?" Cooper repeated, looking morose. "There was no autopsy.... I couldn't bear it. The cops believe I *thought* I cracked the windows...same with the AC."

"What are you getting at?" Anna asked him.

"Elsie was fourteen months old. It should have taken longer for her to die, but the heater was on, not the AC," he continued.

"The heater?" Anna and Vito seemed surprised.

"The police said when they opened the car the heater was on.... They think I was rushing and made a mistake," Cooper continued. "I don't know what to think.... I was sure..."

Anna hadn't realized Elsie was more of a toddler—fourteen months. She thought she remembered everyone calling the little girl a *baby*, but then again, having worked in the news, that shouldn't have come as any surprise. In the ratings war, babies trumped toddlers any day of the week.

The cops had ruled the whole incident accidental. But Anna thought she knew better. The killer made it *look* like an accident. He must have been trolling for a victim: a human victim that complemented the dead puppy just hours before. What luck that Tom Cooper left his phone in the house. All the killer had to do was seize the moment, close the windows, and then lock the car from inside and shut the door. It was as easy as that.

Once they were alone, Anna turned to Vito to see what he made of it all.

"Sick fuck," Vito began.

"What if he smothered her?" Anna suggested.

"Without an autopsy, who knows?" Vito began to answer. "But the motherfucker must've switched the AC to heat, so I'm sure he thought that would do the trick. He thinks on his feet. I'll give him that. I'm gonna ask Hank for the police report just to check on Cooper's story. Can't hurt," Vito concluded.

"Vito," Anna began. "It's all connected. It's got to be. I thought Cary was being paranoid at first, but it's the same guy, right?"

There was no doubt about it, they agreed; the incidents were indeed related. A psychopath of sorts was terrorizing Fairview County. But then Anna had another thought.

"Vito, how do we know he wasn't there? I mean, at the funeral... the grave...I mean just because—" Anna continued, but Vito cut her off.

"We don't," is all he said in return.

TWELVE

Cary hadn't heard from Anna or Vito since she told them about Blair Riordan's death earlier in the day. It was nearly dinnertime now, and she was dying to hear their report about the funeral. Cary was exhausted but hungry. Her mother had texted Cary about an hour ago to see if she wanted to come over and have a bite. Cary knew she had been neglecting Felicia lately, but she simply had no desire to subject herself to an evening that would inevitably lead to self-loathing. So she ignored the message. If and when her mother called her out on it, she'd simply say she never received the text. Yes, lying had its advantages, especially when it came to mothers—at least mothers like hers.

Cary had also been lax about collecting Brandon's mail for him while he was away, which was almost all the time now since he had landed a recurring role in some Hulu limited series that would probably end up being not so limited. But Cary didn't think it would debut until next year; how cool. Cary also hadn't seen much of her sister recently despite hanging out at her guesthouse with Vito and Anna.

So Cary thought she'd jump in the shower to freshen up, check on the main house, and then head over to her sister's. She thought she'd surprise Vito, Anna, and Gayle with dinner. Cary decided to swing by Antonio's and pick up a couple of pizzas: eggplant with fresh burrata was her favorite, and her sister and Anna liked that one too. She thought she'd get the meat lover's for Vito. Cary could handle being an enabler for the time being, at least until whoever the fuck was wreaking havoc all over Fairview County was caught.

When Cary pulled up to her sister's house, she could tell she wasn't home yet, but Cary went inside anyway to feed Obelus. *Disarmed,* the app read. Obi was, of course, happy, as always, to see her. She texted Gayle to meet them at the guesthouse and headed over. When Cary got there, it was dark inside, but Vito's car was outside. Cary wasn't sure what to make of it. So she gently knocked on the door, a nearly two-hundred-pound Newfie and two burning-hot pizzas in tow. A light went on, and as the door opened, she saw Vito clad only in a robe, looking straight at her, somewhat embarrassed. *What the fuck?* Cary said to herself. She should have gone to her mother's after all.

Cary never knew about Vito and Anna, that they had a history. She couldn't believe Anna never told her about it and that they had managed to keep it secret. It turned out they had begun an affair when they were all back at CrimeTV—Anna as a reporter, Vito as a talking head, and Cary overseeing the live trial coverage. Cary had never pried into Vito's personal life; she didn't think it was any of her business.

The reason Anna and Vito never made their relationship known at work was simple: they just didn't want to deal with the drama. They thought it could hurt both of their careers. And then WorldWide-Communications took care of that anyway. But the affair ended before the network was dismantled, and they hadn't had any contact since, until now. Cary guessed they had her to thank for that. Unwittingly, she had played Cupid. *I wonder what broke them up*, Cary contemplated, but she wasn't about to bring up the subject. She couldn't help thinking this was going to take some getting used to.

After the unexpected revelation, the three of them devoured the pizzas, leaving one lonely piece Cary had put aside for her sister. Gayle arrived as they were cleaning up and immediately sensed some tension. When they told her, she let out a laugh and simply said, "I was wondering when the two of you were going to get together." And that seemed to settle the matter.

Gayle only stayed for a little while. She had to get up early for work the next day and still had charts to go through and was expecting a phone call from her son. With the three-hour time difference, the call alone would cut into her sleep, but Gayle was devoted to her children and, night or day, was always there for them. Gayle had had her kids when she was young and tended to dote on them all the more. So Cary waited for her sister and Obi to leave before getting around to the subject: Dakota Riordan's funeral. Gayle was under the impression that Anna had come out from the city to work on a book she had been thinking of writing. And for the time being, Cary thought it best to keep it that way.

So Anna and Vito briefed Cary on what Tom Cooper had told them about the day his *niece* died. They agreed that the killings, although connected, were most likely random acts by an evil piece of shit who got off on destroying living creatures, human and otherwise. The specific motive was unclear. In fact, there may not have been one. *Just thrill kills*, Cary decided. But she couldn't help thinking that the last act, running down the Riordans and their dog, was some kind of a warning. The Riordan incident somehow tied everything up in a neat package.

Nights were hard for Cary. That was when she felt the most vulnerable. One evening, years ago, when she was having a particularly difficult time of it, Cary ended up sleeping in her car. No one could surprise her there. And yet, she had never acted on her fear. Although she had thought about getting a gun for years, something had stopped her. Maybe it was her nieces and nephew. When they were younger, having a firearm around seemed risky. But now they were all grown up, and there was a serial killer on the prowl. *Yes, now might just be the time.*

Like most millennials, Cary's nephew and nieces were anti-gun, so she wasn't about to tell them that she was thinking of getting one. And since they rarely came home these days, as the three of them were starting their adult lives, Cary didn't think they needed to know. Her nephew, Martin, was a writer living in Los Angeles trying to break into the entertainment industry, while her older niece, Jane, was in school out West in Colorado. Cary's younger niece, Sharon, was still figuring things out, and what better way to do that than to take a year off from college and travel? So Cary didn't think they factored into her decision at the moment.

As Cary attempted to get some sleep, not knowing what lay ahead for tomorrow, she couldn't help thinking about what had happened to Kelly McGillis, the actress. Before she was famous, McGillis had been repeatedly raped by two men who broke into her New York City apartment and threatened to beat her to death. Rumor has it that at some point after the attack, she had a secure bedroom door installed in her home, not unlike the post-9/11 ones used for cockpits. Cary often thought of following McGillis's lead.

Cary was convinced the three things anyone needed to stop a killer in their own home were: a) a wireless alarm system that couldn't be tampered with, b) an impenetrable door, and c) a gun. Cary had none of the above. She had been too busy worrying about everybody else. *Do as I say, not as I do*, she thought to herself. *What an ass I am.* She could imagine the thoughts that ran through a murder victim's mind upon the realization they were about to be killed. *If only I had....* Cary never wanted to be in that position. She'd have to work on that one starting tomorrow.

Cary woke up thinking about the first notorious deadly home invasion: the Clutter family case, which inspired the book and subsequent movie, *In Cold Blood*. Back in the fifties, in Holcomb, Kansas, people didn't even lock their doors. And there weren't any cell phones. So the Clutters never stood a chance when they were targeted by two ex-cons who were told by a former farmhand that Mr. Clutter kept a safe full of money in his home. That tip turned out to be false, but it tragically led to the brutal murders of four members of the Clutter family: Herb and Bonnie along with two of their four children, their daughter Nancy, sixteen, and son Kenyon, fifteen. Their two older daughters, Beverly and Eveanna, were not at the house at the time.

Today things are very different, and yet, deadly home invasions happen all the time. In 2007, nearly fifty years after the Clutter family tragedy, the Petit family of Cheshire, Connecticut, met a similar fate. Two men broke into the home and held the family hostage for hours, eventually killing both daughters and the wife. Dr. William Petit managed to survive, beaten and tied to a pole in the basement. Like the Petits that horrific night, statistically, most people with alarm systems rarely set them. *They lived with the illusion of safety*, Cary thought, *not the reality*. But she didn't want to start the day like this, so Cary tried to put murder out of her head and begin on a more positive note: researching the requirements and procedures for gun ownership in the state of Connecticut.

Cary wasn't sure how hard it would be to get a gun, legally, in her home state. She knew the laws had changed since the massacre at Sandy Hook Elementary School in Newtown in December 2012. The shooting claimed the lives of twenty children and six adult staff members at the school, as well as the shooter's own mother. So Cary thought she'd run the idea by Vito, as the results she found online were confusing. The only gun Cary had ever fired was her father's shotgun back when she was just a child. She remembered hitting those clay ducks one after the next.

Truth be told, Cary was a natural. The look on the faces of the guys who worked at the range amused her to this day. They couldn't believe a ten-year-old girl could shoot like that. Cary remembered the shotgun being heavy for her at the time, but she determinedly fired away, hitting nearly every duck. To this day, Cary could recall the rush she felt just holding it. The first time she picked up a gun, Cary understood the power it gave someone. It was hard to imagine how it made a true psychopath feel.

Vito actually thought it wasn't such a bad idea for Cary to get a gun. After all, he had an arsenal of sorts in his basement and knew she only wanted it for protection. And there *was* a serial killer on the loose; Cary, Anna, and he were certain of that. A quick Google search hadn't been all that helpful, but Vito was. Although he strongly recommended that she obtain the firearm *legally*, he was happy to bend the rules a bit, lending her one of his own handguns until she had fulfilled all the requirements necessary to get a permit. As far as Cary could tell, the penalty for possessing a firearm without a license in her home state was up to two years in prison, a fine of up to five hundred dollars, or both.

But Cary decided to do a little more research and found an article in Wikipedia titled "Gun Laws in Connecticut." The state has some of the toughest firearm statutes in the country, but it also appeared that the overall licensing system for open and concealed carry was less restrictive. Cary was surprised to discover that Connecticut was an open or concealed carry state as long as you had a license.

That didn't sound so intimidating to Cary. She wanted a concealed carry permit, and the process didn't seem as difficult as she had imagined. Still, she was anxious to get started, so Vito and she decided to spend the following afternoon at his favorite shooting range in New Canaan. *New Canaan:* the town where Kitty Genovese was buried. Everything seemed to come full circle in Cary's life when it came to murder.

* * *

As Cary drove up to the entrance of the shooting range, she spotted a guard in a small booth and sensed he would give her a hard time before admitting her. He was a friend of Vito's, however, so Cary thought most of the theatrics would be for show. She was right. Mike turned out to be a really nice guy who admired a woman who had the guts and where-withal to do what it took to protect herself. Vito had given him a heads up that Cary would be coming, so after a quick introduction, he let her pass, pointing out the best place for her to leave her car.

Meanwhile, Vito texted her that he was running a bit late and asked Cary to get them a table inside. He'd be there as soon as he could. The range and its amenities were much more upscale than Cary had been expecting. *Leave it to Vito*, she reminded herself. He was a *private* detective, after all, and this was clearly a private shooting range. She had just assumed they would be going to the same place where cops go for target practice. In retrospect, she should have known better. She remembered how much it had cost her sister to hire him to spy on her husband—more money down the drain.

As Cary was deep in thought, the maître d' showed her to a window table with a lovely view of the grounds, and she waited patiently for Vito to join her. *I wonder what's holding him up*, Cary asked herself. Hopefully, Anna hadn't distracted him. Cary put the thought right out of her head.

As the waitress came to take her iced tea order, she spotted Vito at the entrance. He looked great. *Guess all that sex with Anna agrees with him*, Cary said to herself.

"Sorry I'm late," Vito began apologetically. "I got held up—"

But Cary didn't give him the chance to say anything more. Interrupting, she said matter-of-factly, "So, how's the food here?"

"Not bad, actually," Vito replied. "I usually have the bleu cheese burger."

Cary wondered if they had pappardelle. When the waitress came back with the menu, Cary looked it over dismissively and decided on the avocado toast with black sea salt and sweet potato fries. *That would save an animal or two,* she assured herself.

"So, where are the guns?" she asked Vito rather unabashedly.

"Slow down, Bonnie Parker," he laughed. "What's the rush?"

Cary wasn't sure if Vito had to smuggle them in. She didn't know what the protocol was in a place like this. She was a fish out of water.

"They're in my car," he reassured her. "We'll go get them after lunch."

So she tried to relax and enjoy the meal. Cary was surprised by how nervous she felt. She hadn't fired a weapon in a long time and didn't want to embarrass herself in front of Vito. When the check came, Cary reached into her bag to grab her wallet, but Vito, always the gentleman, wouldn't hear of it. *Old fashioned isn't so bad*, Cary considered. *Especially if you're a cheapskate like me.*

As they walked to Vito's car, he started instructing her on gun etiquette. Never point a firearm at anyone; keep the ammo and gun separated at home; if small children are in the house, keep the gun locked in a safe location; and so on and so on. Cary couldn't help wondering if all these safety precautions were taken, where would that leave her if someone broke into her home in the middle of the night? It didn't matter; she knew *her* gun would be locked and loaded, right by her bed.

Vito had two handguns with him. Cary assumed hers would be a smaller, lighter version of whatever he brought for himself. But she was wrong. He took out two identical guns so that he could properly teach her how to use it. That made sense to Cary. She was starting to realize how little she really knew about firearms. What the differences were. How to know which one was the best for her. But, she gathered, that's what Vito was there for.

When Vito took out the weapons, Cary was struck by their beauty. They had a way of drawing you in. The two Dan Wesson Specialists were titanium in color with a faux wood panel running up the sides. They were striking. Cary felt guilty just looking at them, considering the escalating gun problem in the United States. And yet, she firmly believed that good guys with guns were the only way to stop bad guys with guns. The Texas Church Massacre and Maryland school shooting were evidence of that.

It is just a shame that firearms were ever invented, she thought, *but this is the world we live in*. The only way to level the playing field was to fight back. People couldn't just sit at home waiting for armed killers to steal their lives away from them. Cary would never let herself be in that position.

Suddenly, Cary tripped over a small branch and realized she had probably missed most of what Vito had said so far. What a bad student she was.

"Cary, are you with me?" he inquired.

"Yeah, sorry. Can you repeat what you were saying?"

Vito frowned. "This is serious stuff, Cary. You gotta pay attention."

So noted, thought Cary.

And so, Vito continued, describing the Wesson in detail. This particular handgun was designed for use by law enforcement. It was a .45 ACP 1911 with tritium night sights, 1913 accessory rail, an ambidextrous thumb safety, and had just about every feature you could want for personal defense. Cary didn't really understand what any of that meant, but she thought once she knew how to fire it, she'd feel a lot safer than she did now. *What took me so long?* she wondered.

Once Vito completed his dissertation, he took Cary over to get the necessary eye and ear protection: goggles and earmuffs. Vito followed suit. They were then assigned a shooting position on the firing line. Vito waited until they were on the *ready* line before taking out the ammunition. He carefully showed Cary how to load her gun, and *now* she was paying attention.

Vito fired first, aiming at one of those generic-looking paper targets with a shadowy figure in the middle. He, of course, hit the equivalent of a bullseye. After he emptied his weapon, it was Cary's turn. Holding the gun with both hands, she began firing. The first shot jolted her as the gun had a relatively strong kickback. Vito had *forgotten* to mention that little detail. He gave her a knowing smile. It was his way of initiating her into the club. She didn't mind. She loved Vito.

Then Vito startled her by coming from behind and pressing himself against her, placing his rather large, strong hands over hers and guiding her next shot. Cary knew he didn't mean anything by it, but she couldn't help it; it felt *good*. Cary knew she wasn't interested in Vito romantically. Her response was just animalistic. She was a sexual creature and could respond to a stimulus, even if it came from a man. That's all. She was technically bisexual but emotionally gay. The repetitive analysis was getting old. And anyway, he was Anna's now. She refocused her attention on the Specialist.

Vito backed away in anticipation of Cary's next attempt. Without hesitation, she emptied the gun; the shadowy man was in tatters. She blew him away, and Vito too.

"Nice shooting," he told her. "I'm impressed, Cary. Really."

Cary was relieved. She knew deep down she could shoot, but if she fucked it up, it would have completely shattered her confidence. Apparently, it was just like riding a bicycle.

As they made their way back to their respective cars, Vito gave her a big kiss on the cheek. *It's a good thing he didn't stick his tongue down my throat*, Cary joked to herself. And then he laid what Cary considered a bombshell on her.

"I'm gonna go talk to Hank," he began. "I think it's time we tell the police what we know."

Cary wasn't exactly sure where that left her.

THIRTEEN

Apparently, bringing the police into the loop, officially, even if it was only Hank for the moment, was Anna's idea. *No surprise there*, Cary told herself. Anna was notorious for stirring the pot. Cary wasn't sure if she should be there when Vito briefed Hank on what they theorized was going on all over Fairview County: that a serial killer was committing car-related murders of both people and animals. Cary had never put it in those terms, and yet, that was exactly what was happening. And while she knew killing animals wasn't *legally* considered homicide, Cary failed to see the difference. *People murder animals all the time*, Cary bemoaned. *No matter what they call it.*

So far, the killer had either used his car as a weapon or messed with other people's cars to carry out his murderous spree. She tried to anticipate Hank's response when Vito presented him with their theory. She had to get it all straight in her head. To date, there had been five separate incidents: the fawns, the Wooster girls, Kim's puppy, Tom Cooper's niece, and Blair and Dakota Riordan, along with their dog, Nelson.

What worried Cary the most, however, was what might happen if Vito told Hank about the deer. Cary wondered how he would react to the fact that she had witnessed someone intentionally run over two baby deer but never called the police to report the incident. She didn't know if Hank would even bother looking into it, for that matter, unless they could convince him that it wasn't an isolated event, that it was connected to the others.

Still, as far as Cary knew, the police were treating the Wooster girls and even the Riordans as hit-and-runs, as criminal but likely *unintentional* acts, not necessarily committed by the same person. They didn't even know about the deer—*yet*. And as far as Kim's dog and Tom Cooper's niece went, Cary didn't even think they were being categorized as crimes, just tragic accidents. Kim, like Cary herself, had never even told the police what she had seen, or rather *who* she had seen, the day her dog died: a man she probably couldn't identify running away from her car. So where did that leave things? Cary thought Vito might just be the one to make sense of it all. And then it occurred to Cary that she still hadn't met Hank. No time like the present.

* * *

Anna had to go back into the city for a few days to take care of her mail as well as a project she was working on for one of the cable stations. So when Vito asked Cary to accompany him to meet Hank, she was more than happy to oblige. They decided to have Hank meet them at Vito's house, but first, the war room had to be updated. There wasn't that much more information they could add to their chart, but they wanted to be as detailed as possible. They might only get one shot at convincing Hank something sinister was going on.

When Cary pulled up to Vito's, she grabbed her bag and went inside, trying to keep it all straight.

"Hey, babe," Vito called out to her as he heard the door swing open. "I'm in the back."

Babe? Cary didn't recall ever hearing that word come out of Vito's mouth before. She blamed Anna. She must like it when he calls her that, and now it's probably become second nature for Vito to address any woman he's around that way. Anna could be a bit of a narcissist herself.

In any event, Cary headed to the rear of the house where the war room had been set up, conflicted about the predicament she now found herself in. When she saw Vito, she gave him a quick kiss on the cheek. He seemed to sense her apprehension about what they were about to do: expose themselves and everything they had worked on for the past several months to the police.

As if Vito read her mind, he tried to reassure her, saying, "Don't worry, Cary. Hank won't take it any further without our say-so unless it's absolutely necessary."

Unless it's absolutely necessary? What the fuck was that supposed to mean? But all Cary answered back was, "I'm trusting you, Vito. The last thing I need right now…"

"Relax, Cary. Hank is like family. We're doing the right thing."

Cary was never sure what the stats were on doing the right thing, how frequently it blew up in your face. She guessed fairly often.

So Cary and Vito got down to business. They began by filling in the names of the people involved in each incident. Under the Wooster girls' column, they added Amanda "Mandy" Caldwell and Emily "Em" Browne, labeling them victims and noting Siobhan Browne along with Rebecca and James Caldwell as the parents. Under the puppy incident, they added Kimberly "Kim" Hunter as the owner and noted the dog's name was Andrew, a four-month-old golden retriever. Tom Cooper was listed as the uncle, not father, of fourteen-month-old Elsie, the toddler who had suffocated in a car only a few hours after Andrew had done the same. Cooper's brother, Jimmy, and his girlfriend, Lynda, were named as Elsie's biological parents, currently living at a rehab facility somewhere in Arizona. And lastly, they added a new column for thirty-three-year-old Blair Riordan, her four-year-old daughter, Dakota, and their Bernese mountain dog, Nelson.

Efficient as always, Vito had already printed out pictures of all the parties involved and asked Cary to help him place them on the chart accordingly. Then all that was left to do was, under *What We Know and They (The Police) Don't*, to change "Kimberly, puppy owner, saw a man" to "Kim saw a man running away from her car and left an extra set of keys inside." And then it hit Cary: staring right at her under two columns was the word "deer." Hank couldn't know. And then, just as Cary was trying to figure out the best way to ask Vito not to share that incident with Hank, he had the same thought. Sensing Cary's uneasiness, Vito turned to her and said, "Don't worry," and proceeded to erase the "Deer Killer" notations from both columns.

"Hank doesn't have to know…. Not *yet*," he reassured her.

They decided to break for a bit before they tackled the *What We (Still) Don't Know* column. Maybe Hank could help them with that one. Vito had made lunch for the three of them. Now all they had to do was wait for Hank to arrive.

Cary helped Vito set the table out back. He had prepared a bunch of hearty sandwiches. Then, just as they were almost done, the doorbell rang.

"Mind getting that, Cary?" Vito asked. "I'm just gonna finish straightening up in the kitchen."

"Sure, Vito, no worries," Cary answered.

She had heard so much about Hank over the years, Cary was curious to finally meet him. As she opened the door, a striking woman, about early forties, with blondish colored hair and the most beautiful green eyes Cary had ever seen, stood before her.

"Can I help you?" Cary asked, a bit perplexed.

"I'm Hank," the woman replied, putting out her hand.

If this wasn't a *what the fuck* moment, Cary didn't know what was. Taken aback, she responded, "Hi, I'm Cary. Vito's friend. So nice to meet you. He's in the back. Come on in."

Then Cary thought to herself, *I'd run a red light for her.*

Vito gave Hank a warm greeting and motioned to Cary to pour some iced tea for the three of them. *Yes, massah,* she said to herself. Cary didn't see any sign that Vito noticed her confusion, so she decided to just play along and talk to him about it later.

"How's your father?" Vito asked Hank. "Last time we spoke, I was worried about him."

"Oh, he's fine. It was just the flu. You know what a baby he can be," Hank responded.

"I do indeed. Must be hot as hell in New Mexico right now," Vito added. "Never understood why Hank didn't retire to Florida like everybody else. Then again, he's always been a rebel, that's for sure."

Hank? Just how many Hanks were there? Cary wondered.

Then Cary put it all together. The Hank she would be eating lunch with momentarily had to be the *other* Hank's daughter. Cary wondered what her real name was. Hank had to be a nickname, just like it was for her dad. Well, she could always ask Vito about it later if the subject didn't come up naturally in conversation. Cary feared *this* Hank could put an end to her moratorium on women, however. She was making her forget all about Kim, and Romy, for that matter.

Cary found women with a badge and gun irresistible, especially if they looked like Hank did. She reminded Cary of Jennifer Carpenter in *Dexter*—not the face, just the look. *Nothing wrong with that,* Cary mused. But Cary was intimidated by beautiful women, and she hoped she wouldn't make an ass out of herself before the day was over.

Her hot chocolate bond with Kim seemed irrelevant now. Looking back on her crush, Cary couldn't help thinking, *What's the difference if they both liked hot chocolate?* She was sure there were people all over the world who felt the same way to whom Cary would never be able to relate. The idiotic things people cling to in order to convince themselves they've found their soul mate. But Cary thought she could spend the rest of her life with Hank, even if she lived on coffee and took it black.

So the next question, naturally: was she gay or at least sexually fluid? That seemed to be the way one approached dating these days. And then Vito threw Cary with one simple question, "How's your girlfriend?"

Now we're getting somewhere, Cary thought.

Apparently, Hank had been seeing a woman for the past year, and thankfully, it ended recently for a variety of reasons she didn't exactly want to get into. Cary was getting all flustered just thinking about what she should do next. It was probably too soon to approach Hank if she had just gotten out of a bad relationship. And Cary was too much of a coward to make the first move anyway. So she decided not to do anything for the time being and just let Vito direct the conversation. He brought it around to food.

As Vito set down a rather large platter of sandwiches for just three people, he said in a voracious tone, "Well, I don't know about you people, but I'm starving."

Cary hadn't realized how hungry she was until now. They each grabbed a plate and began the selection.

"I made some veggie ones for our friend Cary here, always trying to save the animals. But for Hank and myself, well, that's a different story," he continued. "We are proud carnivores. Right, Hank? So try not to moan orgasmically when you taste my latest creation: sliced skirt steak, rare, with my special homemade horseradish and pickled red onion. It's beyond." Cary couldn't help thinking Vito was starting to sound like a Valley girl. *Damn, Anna.*

Oh, God, Cary moaned to herself, and not in the way Vito warned Hank. Eating meat could be a dealbreaker. But then Hank gave her the most endearing smile, not unlike Kim Basinger in *LA Confidential*, and Cary's heart melted. *Guess we can work on that little issue*, she told herself, *if I ever get that far.*

Cary helped clear the plates after they had finished eating and overheard Vito and Hank talking from her vantage point in the kitchen. She had offered to clean up as the thought of being left alone with Hank was too much to bear. As Cary came back to the table, she wished more than anything for something sweet to settle her nerves. Vito, always the gracious host and hyperaware of Cary's addiction, never let her down.

"Sorry, guys, there's something I have to get from the kitchen," he explained as he got up from his chair. And then before Cary knew it, he placed a box of Double Coat Tim Tams in front of them, alongside a couple of quarts of their favorite ice cream from The Creamery in Newtown: Lost in Paradise and Mocha Madness. Vito may have needed some guidance in the protein department, but he shared Cary's sugar habit down to the chocolate sprinkles. But to Cary's dismay, Hank chimed in, "None for me, thanks. I'm not much of a dessert person." *I'm not much of a dessert person*, Cary repeated to herself. *Women*, she pondered. There was just no winning with them.

It was time to get to why they were all there in the first place: convincing Hank that there was a serial killer on the loose and then enlisting her help in catching him. Although Hank had provided them with information about the incidents in question, she was more or less in the dark about their true intentions. Vito never told her that he thought the cases were related. He also hadn't explained his, Anna, and Cary's theory that a serial killer was operating in the area.

Vito suggested they move to his study, their makeshift war room. As they entered, Hank immediately took note of the chart. Vito walked her through each incident, pointing out everything that seemed relevant to connecting the crimes to each other, as well as to the same perp. Hank seemed to get it right away. And while Cary may have been a stranger, Hank had known Vito since she was a little girl and trusted him and his instincts implicitly. It all seemed to make sense to her. After all, she was a detective and obviously smart and had no trouble putting the pieces together.

"Let me see what I can find out," she finally said. "I'm gonna have to do a little digging before we even consider bringing the force in on this in any official capacity. There'll be no turning back then."

Cary couldn't help worrying about what this could all mean for her. She had hidden information from the police, information that might have helped stop a killer. It made her feel awful and guilty, but she didn't think there would be legal consequences. Cary knew some states had Failure to Report laws, but she didn't think Connecticut was one of them. She would have to do some research, but Cary was pretty sure there weren't any statutes on the books that would apply to what she witnessed.

As Cary cleaned up with Vito, she wasn't sure how to bring up the "Hank" mix-up. Cary had pretty much figured it out already anyway, but Vito knew Hank very well and might be able to help her romantically. Cary was surprised how cool Vito seemed to be about the gay thing. She just always assumed he was old-fashioned that way and had never even told him about herself. But now that seemed foolish. Cary had no way of knowing whether Vito suspected she was gay, bisexual, whatever, but she had never felt comfortable bringing the subject up. On her end, Cary had always assumed that Vito was more or less a confirmed bachelor, and they both tended to stay out of each other's personal lives—that is, until Anna showed up.

"So what'd you think of Hank, Cary? Isn't she great?" Vito began.

Cary didn't want to tip her hand yet, so she tried to answer nonchalantly.

"Yeah, she seems really smart," she responded.

"That's all?" Vito prodded her. "I thought I sensed a little chemistry."

"I don't know what you mean," Cary tried to sound clueless.

And then Vito cut to the chase. "I think you two might be good together."

Cary's face turned red, and she couldn't formulate the appropriate response, so Vito helped her out.

"Come on, Cary. I'm a goddamn detective, for Christ's sake. A girl like you would have had a million boyfriends by now if you were interested."

Damn, Cary thought to herself. Vito, of all people, knew she wasn't really straight, but almost every gay girl she had ever known assumed she was. Go figure. They misread her at every turn. Truth was Cary just didn't fit into the whole lesbian scene even though she knew she was meant to be with a woman. Cary considered herself the black sheep of the gay community. Now that she thought of it, she didn't really fit in anywhere. Cary just needed to find the right person, and, at the moment, she hoped that person would turn out to be Hank.

It was time to fess up, but she couldn't get bogged down in all the minutia—gay, bi, whatever. She just needed Vito's help to get to Hank. So Cary told him he had pegged her right and that she would kill to go out with her.

"That's more like it," Vito said.

"So, what can you tell me about her?" Cary asked, kicking off her next investigation.

"Well," Vito began, "she comes from a family of cops. At least fourth generation, I believe. At least, that's what Hank has always led me to believe."

Cary intuitively understood Vito was referring to the *other* Hank, her dad. *Guess that's a start*, Cary told herself.

And then Vito promised he would do everything he could to help her, that he would feel Hank out. As Cary headed home, she wondered if having a homicide detective for a girlfriend might help her sleep at night, might allay her fears. But that wasn't what this was about; it would just be a bonus. Cary really liked Hank—more than she had liked anyone in a very long time. Hank made her Kim obsession seem adolescent and silly. And then it dawned on Cary: she still didn't know Hank's real name. Maybe that would be a good conversation starter on their first date—if Vito did his job right.

FOURTEEN

Cary tossed and turned most of the night. She had too much on her mind. The thought of dating scared her, yet she couldn't help herself. Love and attraction were powerful forces. But that wasn't the only thing keeping her from sleeping. Cary wasn't sure what was going to happen if Hank started stirring things up, even if it was at their request. Cary stayed up half the night going over everything in her head. She should have followed the "Deer Killer's" lead and turned off her own headlights as soon as she saw what he did. It was stupid of her to leave them on when the car was off, just a bad habit. She should have waited for him to leave before starting her car too. Cary had no way of knowing if he had spotted her. Cary wondered where he lived, where he worked, if at all, if he was still in the area. There were so many questions left unanswered.

Cary woke to the annoying sound of the phone alarm she forgot she had set. She could have used more sleep. But now that she was up, Cary decided today would be a good day to take Obi to the dog park for an hour or so. He needed the exercise; it helped slow the disease. So she put on her sweatpants and running shoes and her Antarctica tee shirt that served as a constant reminder of bucket list things she had yet to do and texted her sister that she was going to borrow him for a while.

There were always some regulars at the park, but Cary wasn't in the mood to deal with them today. She just needed some time to herself. So she took out Obi's ball and began to throw it, not too far, conscious of his limitations. It was now early September but still pretty hot. She knew he couldn't stay out too long. As he was bringing the ball back to her for another round, an unruly Old English sheepdog came running right toward them. Cary was afraid the dog would bang into Obi and injure him, so she tried to intervene. Just as she went for the dog's leash, she heard a voice cry out.

"Barry, come here *now*." As the woman turned around, Cary saw it was none other than Hank. "Oh my God. Cary? I'm so sorry. He got away. I hope your dog is all right," she said apologetically.

What were the odds? Cary asked herself. Well, 100 percent because it happened; that's what a friend of hers used to say. And she looked like such a mess this morning, donning her favorite slobber outfit. *Jesus, can I get a fucking break when it comes to women? I mean, really*, she told herself.

But to Hank, she simply replied in a discombobulated way, "Oh, no worries, we're both fine. What a beautiful dog you have. Do you come here often? I don't think I've ever seen—"

But Hank interrupted, saying, "We don't have a dog park in Fairview, so I always bring Barry here when I get the chance. We must be on different schedules."

Yes, different schedules, Cary thought, and hers was the on and off unemployment kind.

Cary explained to Hank that Obi was her sister's dog but that, for all intents and purposes, he was hers. They had bonded from the first time they laid eyes on each other, and she simply adored him. She decided not to get into his condition at the moment. Cary didn't see the point. Then Hank asked her, rather bluntly, if she'd like to come back to her place and have some *coffee*. She'd just have to make a quick stop on the way home. *Oh, well*, Cary thought to herself. *At least she likes dogs*. Cary was pleasantly surprised by the invitation but didn't want to read too much into it, at least not yet. She couldn't imagine Vito had worked his magic that quickly.

So Cary got Obi back into her sister's Sequoia and followed Hank. Fairview was just a couple of towns over from Wooster. The section Hank lived in was almost farm-like and relatively close to Kim's house. *When worlds collide...* thought Cary. Hank lived on three acres with a main house and a barn-like structure she used for guests and family. Cary couldn't help wondering how she afforded all of that on a detective's salary. Her question was soon answered.

"I inherited this place from my uncle," Hank explained. "It's my little haven from the world."

Lucky Hank, thought Cary. She was afraid to tell her where *she* was living at the moment: the guesthouse of a local actor in the process of trying to make it big. That sounded so transient and unstable. Cary wasn't sure what Hank would make of her current living and work situations, so she decided that there was no need to go there unless she brought it up.

"Can I offer you something to drink?" Hank continued. "I make the best cappuccino this side of Rome."

"That sounds lovely," Cary responded. Unbeknownst to Hank, she was about to try it for the first time.

"Why don't you have a seat? I'll only be a minute," Hank replied.

Cary pulled up a kitchen stool while simultaneously attempting to keep an eye on Obi and Barry romping around in the back. Hank's property didn't have a fence, but she had assured Cary they were far enough back from the road that the dogs weren't in any danger. If it had been anyone else, Cary would have insisted on bringing Obi inside, but she didn't want to do anything to push Hank away. Why was it when you *liked* someone, you automatically started doing things you would never normally do? Cary wished she had the answer.

"Here we are," Hank said as she carried a tray with two cappuccinos and some yummy looking chocolate croissants to the counter area where Cary was sitting. They were Cary's latest addiction. *How did she know?* Cary asked herself rhetorically.

Cary had watched Hank as she prepared the mugs. She even did that decorative thing with milk that Cary often saw on other people's cappuccinos or espressos or whatever the fuck they were. She was adorable, Cary concluded, just too cute.

As Hank pulled up a stool right beside her, Cary felt Hank's knee touch the upper portion of her left leg. It sent a chill up her spine that Cary hadn't felt in a while. *Jesus*, she said to herself. *Settle down.* And then Cary reminded herself again that she wasn't even sure if Vito had spoken to Hank yet or if she had any idea what Cary's story was—that is, that she was basically gay and interested. *Oh, God*, Cary thought, *what have I gotten myself into now?* She felt vulnerable and worried that she was about to be preemptively rejected. And then Hank did the one thing that in Cary's experience always indicated at least some level of interest: she brushed the back of Cary's neck with her index finger as she placed her mug down in front of her. Cary's face was flushed. She hoped Hank hadn't noticed.

"You like chocolate, right?" Hank continued. "I don't usually indulge, but these croissants..."

Those words snapped Cary out of her erotic state, and she nodded an affirmative yes. Then Hank became a bit more businesslike and started asking her normal get-to-know-you questions: personal ones that had nothing to do with the "Deer Killer" case. So far, all Hank had succeeded in getting out of her was what she did for a living, or rather used to do, as her freelance gig had all but dried up. Cary spun it in as positive a light as possible, given the circumstances. Hank actually seemed sympathetic to her plight: booted out the door of the best-kept secret in television along with the rest of her work family. But Cary was a long way from sharing any of her secrets with Hank yet. She barely knew her, after all. She just knew that she wanted to.

"I've been dying to ask you," Cary blurted out rather suddenly. "What's your given name? It can't be Hank, right?"

From Hank's reaction, it appeared this wasn't the first time she had been asked this question. "I was wondering when you were going to bring that up," she responded good-naturedly. "Harriett."

Harriett? Cary wasn't sure what she expected her to say, but Harriet wasn't it. Still, it was a nice enough name. "Does anyone actually call you that?" Cary continued.

"Only my grandmother and my older brother. He can't deal with having a father and sister who share the same name. It freaks him out," she laughed.

Cary thought Hank was funny. She wondered if she was upset with Vito for outing her at lunch the other day, but she couldn't exactly ask her. It just meant that unless Vito had told her more than Cary was aware of at this point, Cary knew more about Hank than Hank knew about her. That could work to her advantage. And then Hank really threw her with the following words: "Sorry about Vito the other day. I think he was trying to play matchmaker." Cary had absolutely no idea how to respond, so a nervous stutter would have to do.

"I...I'm not sure what you mean." Cary tried to sound nonplussed, but Hank saw right through her.

"It's okay, Cary, I told him I thought you were straight," she continued, "and then he sort of spilled the beans...."

Why does every gay girl think I'm straight? Cary asked herself. It was exasperating. But all she said to Hank was, "It's a little complicated...." Before Cary got to finish her thought, however, just as she was trying to get up the nerve to take things further, Barry and Obelus came running through the back door covered in mud.

"Oh, shit," said Hank. "They must've gotten into the shed."

"Oh, God," seconded Cary. "My sister's going to kill me. I better get him home."

And that concluded their first date.

* * *

Anna texted Cary that she was coming back to Connecticut the day after tomorrow and would try to make the 3:35 p.m. train out of Grand Central. They had a lot of catching up to do. So Cary figured it fell to her to get the guesthouse ready for Anna's return. Obi's fur was still wet from the hosing Cary had given him the previous afternoon. But at least the mud was all gone, or most of it. Her sister hadn't noticed. She was always too distracted to focus on the details.

In any event, Cary decided to head over to the cottage and change the bedding and straighten up a bit so Anna wouldn't have to deal with it. She checked the fridge in the small kitchen area—empty except for some condiments and an old carton of almond milk that smelled just as rancid as regular milk when it turns sour. Cary tossed the milk and headed to Dan's Market in the center of Wooster. Word was that Christopher Walken shopped there regularly, but Cary had never seen him. *He must be a hundred by now*, she guessed.

Getting Obi into any car, no less a Jeep, was an ordeal, but her sister had taken the Sequoia to work, so Cary had to make do. It was difficult to maneuver him, but Obi spent so much of his time cooped up these days that Cary took any opportunity she could to get him out. When she pulled up in front of Dan's, she tried to get the closest parking space she could find and cracked the rear window just a bit so the cool breeze would keep Obelus comfortable while she shopped. As she went through the aisles selecting some of Anna's favorite foods, it occurred to her that she should probably pick up a couple of things for Vito too. After all, once Anna was back, he would likely be staying there as well, at least some of the time. And he was trying to help her get something started with Hank, so she owed him.

Cary couldn't help thinking about the other day. Hank must've had no idea how attracted she was to her. Barry and Obelus had seen to that. So, as she was checking out, Cary decided she had nothing to lose by being a bit spontaneous and asking Hank out to dinner. After she loaded the groceries into the back of her Jeep and checked on Obi, she sent her a text: *I think the dogs interrupted us. Wanna grab dinner?* Cary sent it before she could stop herself and then regretted it almost immediately. Hank's reply, *Sounds good*, came right back. Well, she certainly wasn't playing games. Cary didn't know where they should go, or when for that matter, but at least she had made her move.

Sometimes Cary wasn't sure which was more stressful: chasing a woman or a serial killer.

* * *

It was good to see Anna. Cary found her mere presence reassuring in a way she couldn't put into words. Somehow Anna always made her feel like everything was going to be all right. When she got into the car, Anna gave Cary her usual greeting: "Hi, peanut." Today it felt familiar. Cary was dying to tell her about Hank, but the investigation took priority, so she would have to fill her in on that first.

"So, what did I miss?" Anna inquired.

Cary told her that Vito and she had met with Hank and laid out their suspicion that there was a serial killer in the area committing car-related murders.

"Did she buy it?"

She? Cary thought. Guess Vito was more explicit with Anna than with herself.

"Yeah, I think she got it. I'm pretty sure she agrees with us that all these deaths are or could be related. That it's the same guy."

"So what's next?" Anna asked.

Cary explained that Hank was going to poke around and see who she could get on board. She wasn't entirely sure what that might entail, whether Hank would want to question some of the relatives or friends of the victims. But at the moment, she knew more than any of her colleagues on the force. They told her that Kim claimed she saw a man fleeing the scene and that she had also left a spare set of keys in her car that inadvertently enabled whoever did it to trap Andrew. What they hadn't shared with Hank yet was that Cary had witnessed the killer run down the fawns. Even Vito agreed to hold back on that one until they knew what they were getting into. Now that Cary thought about it, they hadn't mentioned the deer at all. Cary told herself it could wait. She guessed it might be the first lie, or, rather, *omission,* in their yet-to-be-determined relationship.

Now that it was out in the open, Anna kept Cary fully informed about her comings and goings with Vito. After she dropped Anna off at the cottage, instead of inviting Cary inside for a bit, Anna told her Vito would be there shortly, and she had to unpack and get ready. He was going to cook a welcome back dinner for her, but she needed to shower first and most likely squeeze in a nap. It was already nearly five o'clock, so that didn't give her much time. Cary got the hint.

"I'll call you in the morning," Anna told her. "Peanut."

So Cary decided she would pick up one of Pepe's goat cheese pizzas on the way home; she wondered if they used cheese made from animal rennet, but she thought she'd give herself a pass tonight. Her dietary options were shrinking. Figuring out what to eat was becoming quite an ordeal. But before Cary got as far as the driveway, her sister texted her: *Mom is coming over for dinner. Wanna join us?*

Oh, God, thought Cary. But she decided that, in spite of her mother's antics, a family night might be good for her, so she headed down the little dirt path that connected the guesthouse to her sister's. When she got there, her mother's car was out front.

It usually took no more than five to ten minutes for her mother to get her in a bad mood. Tonight was a personal best. She kicked off the night with a dig at Obi—an obvious cheap shot, but it worked. Whenever her mother came over, Obelus was relegated to the mudroom right off the kitchen. So that's where Cary headed first. When her mother saw her snuggling with him, she proclaimed, "Getting emotionally attached to a dog is a sign of mental illness." Cary wondered if they had added that one yet to the latest edition of the *Diagnostic and Statistical Manual of Mental Disorders*.

When she got back to Brandon's estate, Cary checked the mail on the way in and dropped it off in his kitchen. Only one plant looked like it was on life support. *Not bad*. Then she headed to her nook of the property. Cary vowed to avoid her mother for the time being. She couldn't deal with this kind of bullshit while she was in the midst of a murder investigation. It still mystified Cary that, at her mother's age, she still worried about what everyone else thought instead of what *she* herself thought. Maybe her mother was lucky, focusing on inane shenanigans of her own making instead of seeing the bigger picture— that in the end, none of it really mattered.

Cary knew she would have trouble sleeping tonight, but she changed into her favorite scrubs anyway, the ones that her sister had given her; they served as her summer pajamas. It was well into fall by now but, occasionally, still brutally hot. Cary longed for winter. She decided to take out her laptop and start googling. She selected the images option at the top and typed in Amanda Caldwell's name.

Immediately pictures of the two girls and their parents popped up. It gave Cary a wave of panic. Tim Shaw's picture popped up too. Cary thought that was a little weird, but strange things often presented themselves when one googled.

Sometimes when Cary had a bout of insomnia, she would pass the time by looking up pictures of some of the murder victims whose trials they had covered—the ones who had really gotten to her. Often, before she had a chance to look away, a grotesque photo would catch her eye, and it would take days for her to get it out of her head. One of the most haunting photos she had ever seen was of a different kind: Tracy Paules, serial killer Danny Rolling's last victim, staring straight into the camera. A picture taken before she had the slightest idea of what was going to happen to her.

And yet, after her horrendous murder, Tracy's sister, Laurie Lahey, gave an interview where she said she had had a feeling that she would never see Tracy again once she left for college in Gainesville, Florida. Lahey told the reporter Tracy's response was, "Stop, you're scaring me." But Tracy went anyway. Who would change their college plans, after all, on that kind of information? Cary often wondered if that thought went through Tracy's mind as Danny Rolling was terrorizing, raping, and murdering her.

Cary couldn't help thinking what went through anyone's mind once they understood they were about to be murdered. The realization that they were going to die; it must be the most horrific moment. Tracy's picture wasn't the only one Cary had focused on. There was just something eerie about it. Photos of people like Charlene and Lyman Smith, two of the "Golden State Killer's" victims, posing for a snapshot not knowing what the future held, haunted Cary as well. It could happen to anyone. Cary thought how few people really understood that.

As Cary finally began to nod off, a text alert interrupted her slumber. It was from Hank: a bitmoji indicating she couldn't sleep either. Cary was beginning to think they were as compatible as she had hoped. But she decided not to answer it. She'd deal with Hank in the morning.

* * *

When Cary awoke, she texted Hank that she had been asleep when Hank tried to reach her last night. She guessed that was her second lie, but a minor one. Hank wrote back, *Wanna grab breakfast?*

Why not? thought Cary. But this time, she would put her best foot forward. So Cary jumped in the shower, blew her hair out, and put on her jeans and favorite tee shirt a friend had brought her back from South Africa; it accentuated her best feature. *Relationships*, Cary thought. When she got to Hank's, she honked her horn and waited a minute for her to come out. *Sunglasses on or off?* Best leave them on. Everyone looked better in sunglasses. Sometimes Cary thought romantic relationships were truly the most superficial of human interactions.

Hank looked great this morning. She was in tight jeans, one of those short blouses that accentuated the belt, and worn-out, royal-blue PF Flyers. Cary guessed she was five feet, six inches tall. Her long hair literally glowed in the sunlight, its reddish-blonde hue coming out. She accessorized her outfit with a detective's shield. There was no sign of a gun unless she was carrying it concealed. Cary couldn't help thinking if all cops were this hot, the crime rate would skyrocket.

"Hey, Cary," Hank greeted her with an unexpected hug and kiss on the cheek. Cary would have been more than happy to skip breakfast.

"I thought we could go to the diner," Cary began, "if that's okay with you."

"Sure, I go there all the time. Best blintzes around," Hank replied. So they headed into town.

"Have you always driven stick?" Hank asked her. "It's a dying art."

"Yeah, it's my only vice," Cary joked. She sensed Hank appreciated the witty response.

When they got inside, they were greeted by Xanthe, the regular hostess.

"Well, if it isn't two of my favorite customers," she proclaimed. "Sit anywhere you'd like."

Cary sensed the gossiping was about to commence, but she didn't care. She decided that when you got down to it, there were generally two types of lesbian couples: ones that appeared to mimic a man and a woman and ones where they looked like sisters. Cary didn't want to be either, but at five feet, five inches tall, she was just a hair shorter than Hank, had warm brown eyes, and auburn hair. That put them in a third category: the hip, cool, you'd-never-think-they-were-gay group. Cary was more than fine with that. Of course, they weren't exactly a couple yet, but that was beside the point.

They settled into their booth and grabbed two menus that were reliably kept between the salt and pepper shakers and the wall. So far, a romantic relationship with Hank only existed in Cary's head. Women were so hard to read, especially straight women; it was so easy to misinterpret every move. Just because Hank had recently been with a woman didn't mean she was flat-out gay. Not these days, anyway. Cary would have to lower her expectations; yes, low expectations were the key to happiness. If you expected anything more, you were setting yourself up for disappointment.

Cary wasn't even sure if this was a date or not. Breakfast at the local diner hardly screamed, "I love you, Cary." She'd just have to see how things went. After ordering—Hank stuck with the blintzes, and Cary decided to go for scrambled eggs, well done, on a lightly toasted pita with butter—the conversation got going. But not the way Cary was hoping. Hank got right down to business.

"I've figured out my strategy for looking into your case," she told Cary. "I'm going to try to talk to some of the players off the record and see what 1 can get out of them. Then, if you and Vito are ready, are okay with it, I'm going to go to my boss, because 1 believe you guys may be onto something." Cary knew she had to come clean about the deer, but she wasn't sure she had to do it just yet.

"Sounds like a plan," Cary responded.

And then Hank said cryptically, "Cary, I'd like you to come with me."

After they had finished eating, Cary drove Hank back home, pretty much in silence. They didn't know each other well enough for it to be that comfortable type of silence, and yet, it didn't feel particularly awkward either. Cary took that as a good sign. When they pulled up to the house, Hank surprised Cary by asking her inside. It was nearly noon now, and Cary didn't have any specific plans for the afternoon, so she acquiesced. Hank explained that she had taken the day off so that she could organize her thoughts about how best to proceed with the investigation. She'd have to figure out a way to work it into her regular schedule.

When Barry spotted Cary, he gave her an enthusiastic greeting. He had been lying near the fireplace, and Cary hadn't noticed him until he ran over to her. He was a sweetie, just like her Obelus. Hank decided to let him outside for a while to get a little exercise. She thought he had been putting on weight lately, which was bad for his joints. Once Barry was in the backyard, Hank suggested they sit on the couch. Cary was getting a little apprehensive. It felt like something was about to happen, something she wasn't sure she was ready for.

Hank picked up on her tension. "You seem stressed, Cary. Here, let me help you."

And with that, Hank got to work on Cary's neck muscles and continued down her spine. She had strong hands—not surprising for a cop. And then, without warning, Hank deftly moved her fingers from Cary's lower back to under her shirt, rubbing her breasts with a motion that almost caused Cary to come. *When is she gonna break out the handcuffs?* Cary wondered. They made their way into the bedroom, where Cary would proceed to spend the best two hours of her life. Yes, her mother told her. It's always the *unexpected*.

* * *

What man didn't like watching two women together? he asked himself. Certainly not him: only his therapist. *He* clearly had issues. The afternoon had provided an unanticipated bonus. As he finished pleasuring himself, he reflected on what he had just witnessed: *This could get interesting.*

Therapy had been just another huge mistake. He should never have let his family talk him into it. When Adam Lanza shot up Sandy Hook Elementary School, the person the public turned on was his mother, who was, ironically, Lanza's first victim. The same outcry followed nearly every school shooting. Why didn't the family do something before it was too late? Well, his own blood relatives had tried to steer him in what they believed was the right direction but clearly failed. *Clueless fucks.*

Dr. Sheldon Ackerman, a.k.a. "Please call me Shelly," spent more time on his own issues than he ever did on those of his patients. Sometimes the man thought Ackerman should have been paying *him*. In one bizarre session, Dr. A. hijacked the conversation into a one-sided dissertation on how he must be the only man on earth who didn't get aroused by the thought of two women having sex with each other.

Doc Shelly almost seemed proud of it, as if it put him on a higher plane somehow.

That was the final straw as far as the man was concerned. How could he continue seeing a shrink who didn't even appreciate the most basic pleasures in life? How could he pay someone he couldn't relate to in the least to solve what other people believed were his problems? And that was the end of that.

FIFTEEN

Cary went to sleep that night wishing they hadn't taken it that far that fast. It could mess everything up, from the investigation to their relationship. Everything was out of order now; they hadn't even had an official first date yet. She wondered what it would be like the next time she saw Hank, and who was supposed to contact who first. Cary decided to wait until she heard from her. She wasn't sure if the next text would be about business or pleasure. This was going to get messy.

Cary spent the better part of the following day checking her phone to see if she had missed any texts. She hated what relationships did to people, to her. Not a word from Hank. Well, she could be busy. She *had* to be busy now that she had doubled her workload. But still, how long did it take to send someone a text? *Five seconds*, Cary thought. She was close to recruiting Vito for advice, but she didn't want him to know what had happened. If it didn't work out, it would be embarrassing, to say the least. She'd rather suffer in silence than have to deal with his pity.

It had now been more than twenty-four hours, and no word from Hank. Tonight would be Cary's second evening in limbo. *Screw her*, she thought. For all Cary knew, it had just been revenge sex for Hank.

She might not be over her girlfriend. Cary should have asked more questions, found out more before she literally jumped into bed with her. It was a stupid move on her part, and she was getting agitated as a result. *Never take someone on the rebound seriously*. How many times had she told herself that? And then she fell right into her trap. Hank might sleep with a different woman a day for all Cary knew. Or a different *man*, for that matter. And Cary was already falling for her.

Cary tried to put Hank out of her mind and get some much-needed rest. And then her phone's text alert sounded. It was Hank. Cary was afraid to read the message. When she finally got up the nerve, it simply said: *Can you meet me tomorrow?* Cary wasn't sure what to make of it. It could mean anything. But she answered: *Sure*. A few moments later, Hank answered back: *Great. I want to talk to that woman who lost her dog.*

Damn, Cary thought, *messy indeed.*

* * *

The thought of being in the same room with Hank and Kim was unnerving. Add to that thought that she hadn't seen Hank since they slept together and that Hank's recent texts hadn't even acknowledged that something had happened between them, and it was almost unbearable. This was going to be a migraine-inducing afternoon. Cary offered to pick Hank up so that she wouldn't see where she was living. It was infantile, but Hank had a beautiful home, inherited or not, and Cary was crashing in a guesthouse. It gave Hank the advantage in the relationship. She didn't deserve that yet.

When Cary pulled up to Hank's place the next day, she texted her: *Out front*. She felt funny going inside after the decadent afternoon they had shared the other day. Cary had no idea how Hank was going to act. *Never mix business with pleasure*. If it didn't work out, she'd still have to see Hank all the time because Vito had dragged her into this mess. Hank was on her phone when she opened the car door, but Cary could only hear her end of the conversation. Hank seemed distracted. There was no hug and kiss for Cary, and she showed no sign of ending the call. So Cary drove on in awkward silence. If it had been Cary, she would have been using the phone as a shield, but Hank seemed oblivious.

When they arrived at Kim's house, Cary put her Jeep in gear and waited for Hank to take charge of the situation. She finally wrapped up the exchange with the words: "I'll call you later." There was no way for Cary to know if the call was personal or work-related, and she wasn't about to ask. Then, with no further explanation, Hank simply said, "Let's go."

Let's go? Cary thought. *What the fuck? Do you even remember who I am?*

As soon as Kim opened the door, Cary felt an irrational, jealous pang, of whom she wasn't even entirely sure. It was just misery being in the same room with the two of them—*women*. Kim was straight as far as Cary knew, and there was no reason to think the meeting would be anything but professional. Still, Cary was feeling desperately insecure, and Hank had done nothing so far to reassure her.

"Hi, I'm Kim," she began.

"Hank. Thanks for meeting with me."

With *me*? What about *us*? Cary deduced there was no *us*—not yet anyway, personally or otherwise.

"I'd like to ask you a few questions if you don't mind," Hank continued.

So the three of them went over what happened on the tragic day Kim lost her beloved Andrew. Hank tried to get her to remember even the tiniest detail that might help them connect the cases. After coming up empty-handed, Hank got an idea.

"Can I take a look at your car?" she asked.

So they walked over to the garage, passing the defiled MG Cary could barely stand to look at. When they got to the car in question, Hank opened the doors and searched inside. And then, she reached in between the seats and pulled out a card, the type that people leave on windshields to get business.

"What's this?" Hank asked.

Kim didn't recall seeing it. Her only thought was that someone might have left it under her wipers, and she took it off and threw it in her car.

"Think, Kim. This is really important," Hank continued. "Did you find this card stuck to your windshield the day Andrew died?"

Hard as Kim tried, she couldn't be sure. But it was definitely possible. She couldn't describe the man either.

When they got back to Cary's Jeep, Hank took a closer look at the card. On the front, it simply said: "ODD JOBS?" The back was blank, not even a phone number. To Hank, that could only mean one thing: whoever left the card wasn't soliciting business. There was something more nefarious going on. Hank thought she had what she needed. If they found another one of the cards at any of the other crime scenes, it might mean the killer was taunting the police and could connect the cases. As they drove away, Hank touched Cary's leg, then leaned over and kissed her on the cheek. Cary wondered if a Jeep could give a little MG some competition in the rocking back and forth department.

* * *

First, they had to see if they could lift prints off the card. Hank could take care of that discreetly. She had access to fingerprinting kits at the station. Then they would have to check each crime scene to see if any more cards were lying around or if any of the players remembered seeing one. By Hank's calculations, if she was on the right track, there could be three other cards where the Wooster girls, Elsie, and the Riordans were killed. Hank still didn't know about the deer. They decided to start with Tim Shaw as he may have been with the girls the night they were killed. Talking to Amanda's and Emily's parents didn't seem to make sense as they were never at the scene where their daughters had died.

Cary thought of one more thing: what they might find inside the car at the impound yard if they tore it apart *French Connection*-style. But that might entail telling Hank about the deer incident. Cary wasn't sure she was ready to do that yet. Much as she hated lying to Hank or, at a minimum, keeping things from her, she feared the disclosure could jeopardize their relationship. It would be a last resort. She would see what else they could find out first.

Cary hadn't gotten any useful information out of Tim Shaw the first time she met with him. She was so taken aback by his "*I was doing both of them*" comment that she never got around to asking him whether or not he was with the girls the night they were killed and, if so, if he saw anything suspicious. She hoped Hank would be able to get him to talk.

This time, Hank picked her up, but at her sister's, and they made their way to Tim Shaw's place. He greeted them at the entrance to the property and took them to a patio with a lovely view of the pool and grassy green area where the horses were kept. *How did I miss the pool the first time around?* Cary asked herself. What a detective she'd make. A young, Thai-looking girl brought them some iced tea and a plate of what appeared to be homemade chocolate chip cookies. Cary felt at ease. Then Hank began her interrogation.

"Were you with Amanda and Emily the night they were killed?"

Cary thought Hank should have worked her way up to that all-important question, but she guessed the detective in her thought otherwise.

"I was supposed to meet up with them, but they never showed. It got late, so I took off."

"So you never saw them that night?"

"No, ma'am," Tim continued.

Cary thought he was lying, but she left it to Hank to dig deeper. She knew Hank wouldn't tell him about the card; he was still a person of interest, whether he realized it or not, and if he was involved in any way, it was better if he didn't know what they knew. Hank would have to be careful.

"Anything else you can tell us? Something that may have caught your attention?" Hank continued prodding.

"Not a thing. Have you guys been up there? There's stuff all over the place. I didn't even get out of my car that night. It was raining. Just split when I decided they were blowing me off."

So Hank did what she always did in these situations: handed him a card, but not the one they found in Kim's car.

"If you *suddenly* remember anything give me a call," Hank said. And she wrote her cell number on the back. Cary figured this was all *off the record*, well, sort of. She guessed it depended on where the investigation took them.

Since they had struck out with Shaw, they decided to head up to Devil's Den and check out the general area where the girls were killed. Maybe they would find something there. Hank wasn't that familiar with Devil's Den, but Cary knew it well. It made her feel important, if only briefly. The expanse of the den would have overwhelmed anybody else who was looking for something. But Hank was a cop, so she knew precisely where the girls had been struck. When they got to the exact spot, there was still police tape lying around and the remnants of chalk where the girls' bodies had been outlined.

"Where do we even begin?" Hank bemoaned.

The comment surprised Cary. Hank was the detective after all, so if she didn't know how to approach the search, how should Cary?

"Why don't we start at the center and move out from there?" Cary proposed.

So the two of them did their best to sift through the leaves and occasional trash they came upon in the hopes of finding one of the man's calling cards. But after a three-hour, exhaustive search, they came up empty-handed.

"What a waste of time," Hank said. "The sooner we bring the force in on this, the better."

Cary got an uneasy feeling.

It had been a long day, and since Cary had to be dropped off at her sister's anyway, she and Hank said goodbye with a quick kiss and an "I'll call you tomorrow." But as Cary drove home, she thought about the one place that needed checking—the area where the fawns had been run down. She'd have to do that on her own. There was still enough daylight left, and as Cary didn't foresee much sleep in her future, she turned around and headed up the Post Road toward where she thought the deer had been hit. She wasn't sure of the exact location; panic had engulfed her that night, and she had driven off without taking note of any particular landmarks. Cary cursed herself now for not being more in command and realizing at the time how critical it was that she be able to pinpoint the spot.

When Cary got close enough to the general area, she pulled over and turned off her car. Then, using her phone as a flashlight, she began to pick through the tall grass that covered the ground. After about ten minutes, all she had uncovered were some cigarette butts, beer bottles, and a couple of clearly used condoms. *Another reason to slide toward the women end of the scale*, she lamented. Cary wished she had had the foresight to bring gloves with her, but that was the price of spontaneity. Cary determined that she might be a little off the mark, so she drove her car about a quarter-mile down the road and repeated the same routine. The search turned up nothing.

Cary decided to leave her car by the side of the road and continue walking further into the woods. This area seemed more familiar somehow. After a few minutes, she found herself at the end of a narrow dirt road about fifty feet from the main street. As Cary was about to give up for the night, something caught her eye. As she shone the light from her phone onto the ground, she spotted what appeared to be crumpled paper of some sort. She reached down and picked up the debris. It was getting dark now. Her impromptu investigation had lasted longer than she had anticipated. When she held the light directly on her palm, she could just make out the letters: O_D _OB_? *Holy shit*, thought Cary.

The first thing Cary did when she got home was put the card in a safe spot until she could figure out what to do with it. She couldn't give it to Hank unless she was prepared to tell her *everything*. She needed to talk to Anna and *now*. So Cary got back into her Jeep, texted Anna she was heading over, and drove back to her sister's house. When she got there, Vito's car was out front. *No surprise there*, Cary thought. She decided she best tell both of them anyway. Everything had happened so fast that she and Hank hadn't even had time to fill Vito and Anna in on the card they found in Kim's car.

Anna and Vito were happy to see her. When she first saw Vito's car, she was afraid she might be interrupting something. But from the looks of things, it appeared they were just watching a movie. The movie could wait.

"What's going on, peanut?" Anna asked. She had a concerned look on her face.

"There's something I have to tell you, both of you. It can't wait," Cary began.

"Slow down, Cary. Have a seat. Can we get you anything?" Vito asked.

Before Cary had the chance to answer, he went to the fridge and brought out a tray of Anna's brownies and some Pellegrino. *That works*, Cary thought.

"Does this have anything to do with the investigation?" Vito continued.

And he's a private eye, Cary thought. *Of course it has to do with the investigation.* But all she said was, "Yes."

"Then let's have it."

So Cary filled them in on what Hank had discovered in between the seat cushions of Kim's car: the "ODD JOBS?" card with nothing on the back. They agreed it was odd, to say the least, no pun intended, and that finding another one at any of the scenes would be enough to go to the police *officially*. Cary told them that she and Hank had spoken with Tim Shaw but came up empty-handed, so they had searched as much as they could of Devil's Den where the girls were killed but found nothing. Then Cary got around to the reason she was there.

"I found one of them, one of the cards near where the deer were killed," she announced. *That* caught their attention. Cary explained that she had hidden it in a safe place and that the one they found at Kim's was now in Hank's possession, pending fingerprint analysis. But before Cary could get to her predicament, Vito and Anna gave each other a knowing look and asked almost simultaneously, "So, are you going to tell Hank? Tell her about the deer?"

That's what Cary had to decide. She guessed it was no longer a choice. She had to come clean and face the consequences.

* * *

It occurred to Cary as she awoke the following morning that neither Vito nor Anna knew that she and Hank were involved. Vito may have had his suspicions, but he had no way of knowing. Much as it would devastate Cary if the confession cost her her evolving relationship with Hank, she no longer had a choice. Cary would have to decide how to spin the whole thing.

Cary thought the revelation would be delivered best over dinner, so she texted Hank to see if she would be free to meet up around seven o'clock at The Seefood Shack in Roton. It had the best lobster rolls in Connecticut. And although Cary was on the fence about consuming the red-colored crustaceans these days, she thought tonight she just might need one. One thing in particular that tormented her about *that* night was what would have happened if she had gone to the police. Would Amanda Caldwell and Emily Browne be alive? Kim's dog? Little Elsie Cooper? The Riordans? The tragic consequences of that decision plagued Cary with guilt. The enormity of it all overwhelmed her.

Cary spent the better part of the afternoon deciding what to wear to dinner. And then it dawned on her: tonight would be their first real date—if you could call confessing to withholding evidence from the police a date. All they had done so far was have sex and join forces to move the investigation along. It sounded a little strange when Cary put it that way. She should never have slept with Hank, at least not so soon. It was another one of her bad decisions. But attire-wise, she decided on her worn jeans with her favorite black V-neck sweater and shit-kicker boots she stole from her niece. She didn't want to look like she was trying too hard, but she wanted to look hot. It was a delicate balance.

Cary got to the restaurant first and self-parked, passing on the valet parking as she didn't trust anyone to drive her Jeep. Hank was running a bit late, as usual, but had texted her that she would be there soon. Cary couldn't help wondering if it was a power play. Yet Hank couldn't have had the slightest idea of why Cary wanted to see her tonight. She must've assumed it was purely social. At least that's what Cary presumed. She had no idea how Hank would react to the news or what she would do with the information. Tonight could be a shit-show, Cary concluded, and she'd be standing right in front of the fan.

As Cary waited for Hank to arrive, she took out her phone to give the appearance of looking busy. She started checking Romy's page on Facebook. It was adolescent, but she couldn't help herself. Cary wasn't even sure how she really felt about Hank. When you did everything out of order, the feelings got jumbled. While the sex had been mind-blowing, Cary was starting to realize she barely knew Hank, and after tonight, God only knew where their relationship would go. *Probably nowhere*, Cary thought. She had fucked up morally, if not legally. *There oughta be a law*, Cary told herself.

Lost in thought, Cary was startled by a finger moving sensuously across her back. It was Hank. *God, she had the touch*, Cary sighed. They had never been in public together before, not in what could be perceived as a romantic context, unless you counted the diner. She wasn't sure how Hank would act, how demonstrative she would be. And then Hank greeted her with, "Hey beautiful," and Cary's heart raced.

They were seated at a corner table with a breathtaking view of the water: the perfect setting for a first date, not so much for what Cary had in mind for the evening. Cary didn't drink—not even tonight—but Hank was off duty and almost immediately ordered a vodka on the rocks.

"The menu looks awesome," she began. "What do you usually get here?" Hank seemed clueless as to Cary's true motives behind the dinner. Cary usually ordered the lobster with spinach fettuccine whenever she ate at the Shack. But tonight, she took pity on the little red critters and decided to spare them, opting instead for broiled sea scallops. *Scallops didn't fight for their lives like tuna*, Cary reasoned. She wasn't sure where that left the poor lobsters, however. It may have been a silly distinction, but rationalizing had gotten Cary through a lot in life.

The server who came to take their order gave off a gay vibe, but he wasn't obvious. Hank seemed to pick up on it, and they hit it off right away. Cary hadn't noticed how social she was. They hadn't been in this kind of setting before. Hank was charismatic and charming, and their waiter definitely noticed. *She would always have the upper hand*, Cary decided. He introduced himself as Jon and recommended the filet mignon as a fish alternative, which Hank seemed all too eager to order. *Put a pin in that one*, Cary told herself. Cary stuck with her decision to get the scallops, and Hank selected a bottle of wine from the comprehensive alcohol menu.

It was time to get down to business, come what may. But as Cary tried to begin the uneasy conversation, Hank revealed her agenda for the evening.

"So I guess, technically, this is our first date," Hank began. "Although I must say, you look awesome without clothes."

Only Hank could somehow manage to pull off a line like that, Cary decided. This wasn't going to be easy. And then Hank had a confession of her own to make.

"Cary, we never talked about my ex. I think it's only fair you should know what's going on," she continued.

Before Cary knew it, the deer were a distant memory. She started to get that panicky feeling that this conversation was going to hurt.

"It's over. It was a mistake. Rose wasn't who I thought she was," Hank continued to explain.

"How long were you two together?" Cary asked, uncertain if she wanted to know any more.

But Hank forged ahead as she attempted to clarify where she stood at the moment, relationship-wise.

"About a year romantically, but we knew each other casually for a while through mutual friends," Hank said matter-of-factly.

Cary got the sense this was as much as Hank cared to reveal at the moment as her next words were, "I'm starving. Where did Jon go with our food?"

No sooner had the words left her lips than Jon returned with their dinner. It looked mouthwatering. As they ate, Hank began to drink the rather large glass of wine Jon had poured for her and was clearly enjoying the filet mignon, noting that few seafood restaurants knew how to cook meat properly. Cary bit her lip.

As the night progressed, Cary knew she'd never get around to bringing up the real reason she had asked Hank out this particular evening. The dinner had turned romantic, and they started trading stories about their pasts. God knows how it came up, but before she knew it, Cary was telling Hank about the time when, as a kid, she decided to run away from home.

"So I packed a pillowcase full of my favorite stuffed animals and some candy and got into the little blue car my parents had bought me for Christmas and drove away right down the middle of the road."

"Was it a stick?" Hank asked.

"No. But my sisters woke my parents up and ratted me out, and my father dragged me back home, none too pleased," Cary continued. "What a little rebel I was."

"I like it," Hank said approvingly.

Cary began to blush. Hank was breathtaking and sensuous and funny and smart. *God, I better not fuck this up*, Cary admonished herself.

Hank passed on dessert, so Cary followed suit. When the check came, Hank insisted on paying over Cary's objections. She had assumed they would split it, but Hank's generosity boded well for the rest of the evening.

"Why don't you follow me home?" she suggested to Cary. *Done.*

By the time they got back to Hank's place, it was almost eleven o'clock. The dinner had lasted longer than Cary had realized. *Not bad for a first date*, she mused. The fact that she had chickened out on her confession didn't seem to factor into the rest of the night. Cary knew what was coming. The sex just kept getting better and better. Tonight, it was particularly passionate. Maybe it was the wine, but Hank's inhibitions, if indeed she had any, were nowhere to be found. Every touch, every move, every kiss was pure ecstasy. Cary couldn't get enough.

When it was over, Hank draped her arm over Cary's midsection and kissed her on the back of the neck. Cary wanted to stay there forever. But she was taken aback by what came out of Hank's mouth next. In an offhand kind of way, she simply asked, "Do you date men?" Almost immediately, Cary got a bad feeling regarding what more she would learn about Hank tonight.

Cary didn't know exactly how to respond, so she went with, "Well, it's sort of complicated."

"What do you mean?" Hank asked inquisitively.

The last thing Cary felt like talking about after having out-of-this-world sex with the woman of her dreams was the nuances of her attraction to men. So she decided to turn the tables and then wished she hadn't.

"Well, what about you?" Cary began. "Since you're the one who brought the subject up."

"Yeah, sure. I guess it just depends on the person," Hank responded, appearing oblivious to the effect these words would have on Cary.

And so, to Cary's dismay, Hank was a *depends on the person* kind of woman. The ramifications of that statement were mind-boggling. Although Cary was never sure of Hank's true orientation, she had hoped that Hank was just gay, simple, end of story. This was a whole other mess to deal with. Cary knew the stats on bisexual women didn't bode well for her. Most who were married had spouses of the opposite sex, and those in serious relationships were overwhelmingly involved with men. And Cary was worried about her ex?

"Think we could just table this for the time being? I'm exhausted," Cary said, as she reached for Hank's hand.

"Sure. Sorry I brought it up. Don't know what I was thinking. Why don't you spend the night? It's getting late."

"I think I'd like that," Cary assured her.

And with that, Hank gave her one more passionate kiss on the mouth and drifted off to sleep. Cary's mind raced as she tried to get some rest. When she heard a beautiful woman like Hank say she was open to being with a man or a woman, a fifty/fifty kind of thing, it upset her. Because as much as Cary had struggled with the part of her that could respond to certain men sexually, she knew it wasn't the same thing as what Hank just described. Cary had to be with a woman emotionally. She had to be with a woman, period. And so, Hank had just slid by her on the Kinsey scale.

The list of issues this admission of Hank's could potentially cause in their developing relationship started to add up in Cary's head. She was already desperately insecure, and this would only make matters a million times worse. Cary couldn't compete with the whole world, with a *man*. If part of Hank could fall in love with one, where did that leave her?

She watched Hank as she slept. She looked radiant. And then Cary decided if she was indeed competing with the entire world, she wasn't doing half bad. Hank could get anyone she wanted, and apparently, that could be *anybody*. But at the moment, that person was Cary. She wondered how long she'd be able to hold on to a woman like Hank. Cary figured men must hit on her all the time. She didn't want to be one of those psychotically jealous girlfriends, but she felt she was well on her way.

As Cary continued to watch Hank, she felt an overwhelming urge to wake her up and pick a fight. *Yes, let's waste no time driving her away*, Cary reprimanded herself. So she opted for sleep instead, wishing she hadn't taken Hank up on her offer to spend the night. It would be awkward in the morning. Cary feared breakfast conversation would turn to something like, "We're still seeing other people, right?"

Cary also thought she might do something stupid, like grab Hank's phone while she was in the shower and start looking at her texts or, even worse, her photos. She was dying to see what Rose looked like. *I mean, that's normal*, Cary told herself. Anyone would be curious about their new girlfriend's ex, assuming they were girlfriends. She just better not get caught.

Cary woke up to the noise of water running and a note next to her on Hank's pillow that read: *Hey sleepyhead, why don't you join me?* Cary guessed she wouldn't be going through Hank's phone any time soon. It turned out to be the most sensuous shower Cary had ever taken. Hank was an animal. After they got dressed, having worked up an appetite, Hank made them pancakes for breakfast. The rest of the world was starting to seem irrelevant to Cary. All that mattered was Hank. Cary was hooked.

As Cary headed home to change her clothes, she turned on the radio. "Just a Little" by the Young Rascals played in the background. Cary knew she was falling for Hank and hard. She'd never find someone like this again. There'd be no coming back from a breakup with a woman like Hank. So Cary thought she needed to get her head on straight, and what better way to do that than to spend a little time with Obi?

As soon as Cary pulled up in front of her sister's house, she heard him barking. It was Obi's way of greeting her. When she came inside and picked up his leash, his excitement was apparent. So she got Obi into the back of her sister's Sequoia, where he would have a bit more room, and headed for the dog park. But as Cary turned the key in the ignition, the car failed to respond. With over two hundred thousand miles on it, the vehicle was on life support. Cary got Obi out of the back and brought him into the yard. They could play ball there. Besides, Cary was tired from lack of sleep and all that sex with Hank the night before. Not that she was complaining.

As she continued to toss the ball around, a text popped up on Cary's phone. It was from Vito and Anna. *So did you tell Hank?* it read. *Jesus. What a mess I've gotten myself into*, Cary lamented. Her first instinct was to ignore the message, but just as she was deciding, another text came in. This one was from Hank. *How 'bout pizza and a movie at my place tonight?*

Sure, Cary answered back, like a moth to the flame. Cary feared she would fuck the whole thing up eventually anyway, so why not enjoy it while it lasted: pizza, a movie, and more mind-blowing sex with Hank, a triumvirate of guilty pleasures. She could put a pin in the heartache that was likely to come, at least for now.

Cary spent the rest of the day running some overdue errands and fantasizing about what lay ahead for the evening. She stuck with her decision to pretend she never got Vito's and Anna's text message; it could wait. She could fend them off for a bit, at least until tomorrow. And so, as Cary headed over to Hank's place, she wondered what else she might find out about her tonight. Hopefully, nothing too devastating.

When Hank opened the door, before either of them could make a move, Barry intervened, giving Cary her first kiss of the evening. Hank laughed with joy.

"Hey, Cary," she began. "Now it's my turn."

And with that, Hank ran her fingers sensuously over Cary's lips, sending a chill up her spine. Then she used her tongue to gently part Cary's mouth. Cary couldn't help thinking if Hank was half as good a detective as she was a kisser, every bad guy east of the Mississippi would be behind bars. She thought the pizza could wait. But Hank, ever the gracious host, insisted they eat, proudly displaying a couple of Pepe's signature pies on the kitchen counter.

"I know you don't eat meat, so I got the spinach and goat cheese and a triple meat combo for myself. Hope that's okay," Hank said.

"Of course," Cary answered. "Looks yummy."

Animal rennet didn't seem to be high on Hank's list of priorities, but Cary would eat the pizza, gambling on Pepe's benevolent nature. As they sat down to eat, Hank turned on Netflix and started going through movie options.

"Okay, so what's your favorite movie, Cary?" she asked.

"Don't laugh, but to be honest, I'd have to say *Bonnie and Clyde*. I've seen it like a million times."

"Hmmm...a young Warren Beatty versus a young Faye Dunaway.... Now *that's* a hard choice," Hank sighed.

Not for me, thought Cary. Well, now that Hank had unwittingly succeeded in ruining her favorite movie, Cary couldn't help wondering what would be next: chocolate, perhaps?

"On second thought, why don't we go for something more recent?" Cary suggested.

"Fine by me. How 'bout *Nocturnal Animals*? I know it's been out for a while, but I've been meaning to watch it. Sound good?" Hank suggested.

"Sure," Cary said in response. "It's actually a really good movie. I don't mind seeing it again." They could both crush on Amy Adams. That would hurt a lot less.

"You're sure?" Hank asked.

"Yeah. It's fine," Cary replied. "Really."

"I have an idea," Hank said with a seductive smile. "Why don't we take the pizza into the bedroom and watch in there? It'll be a lot more comfortable."

If there was one thing Cary was OCD about, it was watching movies: every credit to the bitter end. But she'd already seen this one, so if they somehow got a bit distracted, it wouldn't be a problem, at least not for her. She was beginning to get the feeling Hank wasn't that invested in whatever movie they were about to watch after all.

"No worries. I've already seen it anyway," Cary repeated.

"What's *that* supposed to mean?" Hank asked with a suggestive look in her eyes.

They both knew the answer. So they got into bed, on top of the covers for the time being, and continued to consume the pizza while pretending to be engrossed in the film.

After a few minutes, Hank seemed restless. "I'm gonna go grab some wine if that's okay with you. Should I get two glasses?"

Cary didn't normally drink, and wine, in particular, gave her a headache. But for whatever reason, tonight, she went for it.

"You know what? That sounds like a great idea," she responded.

And so, before they knew it, two bottles were empty, and the movie was muted.

"I have an idea," said Hank. "Why don't we play Would You Rather?"

Cary had never seen this playful side of Hank before. Sure, she could be funny, but this was altogether different. *Why not?* thought Cary, but she wasn't sure what she was actually getting herself into.

"Let me explain. We throw out names of famous people, and the other one has to answer who they'd rather sleep with. I know it sounds a bit adolescent...."

"Ya think?" Cary said sarcastically.

Hank pretended to pout and nudged Cary's leg with her foot. After a couple of rounds, they concluded that Julie Christie, in her prime, was hotter than Olivia Wilde, and to Cary's relief, women seemed to win out over men *most* of the time with Hank. Only Sean

Connery seemed to pose a bit of a problem, but Cary put it out of her head. She was dying to ask Hank if, when it came down to it, she preferred women or men. But she'd get around to it in time. Right now, she knew the answer would be something like: "I like you. Isn't that enough?" Cary herself was in no rush to point out how hot *she* thought Thomas Jane and Jeff Bridges were. Their relationship was complicated enough for the time being.

Tonight they fell asleep without having sex. Cary was overcome with emotion just lying beside Hank. She hadn't felt this comfortable with or close to anyone in a long time. Barry joined them at the foot of the bed. All Cary could think as she dozed off was what a lovely evening it had been. The only thing missing was Obelus.

SIXTEEN

Cary had managed to avoid Vito and Anna by telling them she had been called back to work and was doing crazy hours. As long as they thought she wasn't going to be on air, they wouldn't be the wiser. Cary hated the deception, but she told herself it was just a white lie and, in her book, a necessary one until she could figure out the best way to handle the situation with Hank. And so, for the past several weeks, Cary had spent most of her time holed up with Hank, at least when Hank wasn't working her regular detective gig or following up on leads in their joint investigation.

But today began with a text from Vito and Anna insisting on meeting to discuss their next moves with *both* of them. So Cary caved and told them that, as coincidence would have it, she was free later this afternoon. She would have a lot of juggling to do. Vito and Anna were still in the dark regarding her failure to tell Hank about the deer. Cary obviously couldn't get into it with them in front of Hank. In addition, she wasn't ready to tell Vito and Anna about what was going on with her and Hank. She needed to get them each separately to explain things, but how?

Cary decided to text Hank to see if she could meet with the three of them around five or six to see where they were with the investigation.

Hank answered within minutes with a simple: *K*. Their relationship had gotten pretty intense, and Cary wasn't sure the best way to tell Hank she wanted to keep it a secret from Vito and Anna. She texted Hank back: *Can you talk for a sec?* A few minutes later, her phone rang.

"What's up?" Hank asked. "I'm sort of in the middle of something."

"No, that's okay if you can't talk now...." Cary replied, having second thoughts about doing this over the phone.

"Cary, I called you back. What do you want?" Hank said, sounding a bit annoyed.

"Nothing, it's just...it's Vito and Anna...and us...I'm not sure..." Cary began.

"You don't want them to know...to know about us. Am I right?" Hank said rather matter-of-factly. She was a detective, after all.

"Yeah, is that all right...okay with you? I just think it could mess things up...." Cary continued, somewhat relieved.

"It's fine, Cary. I get it. No problem. When it's the right time, we'll know. Gotta go."

"Thanks, Hank, for understanding. I'll pick you up around five."

"Roger that," Hank said.

One problem solved, Cary told herself. *Now onto the next*. Since her phone had just gotten her out of a potentially problematic situation with Hank, Cary decided to use the same method on Vito and Anna. So she sent them a straightforward message: *I haven't said anything to Hank yet. See you between five and six. We'll meet at your place.* Anna texted back a disappointed: *Caryyyyy*. Cary knew what that meant, but two bullets dodged, at least for the time being.

Cary felt like blowing Hank away tonight, so she stuck with her best-fitting jeans but decided on a more revealing top. Not that Hank hadn't already seen all there was to see, but Cary wanted to look extra hot. She hoped Anna and Vito wouldn't pick up on anything.

As she headed over to Hank's place, Cary couldn't help thinking about everything she had learned about her over the past several weeks. Cary had known early on that she came from a family of cops and had decided to follow in their footsteps. Vito had told her that. But she didn't know that Hank's mother had died when Hank was only four years old and that she had been raised by her father and older brother. Cary thought it must have been a difficult way to grow up, not having a female role model. Maybe losing her mom at such a young age had actually made Hank stronger and more self-reliant. *Having* a mother had made Cary less of both. Hank had no mother; Cary had a bad one. There had to be irony there. As far as their fathers went, it appeared Hank had fared far better. She worshipped her dad and credited him with making her the woman she was today.

As Cary pulled up to Hank's house, she honked the horn and waited for her to come outside. When Cary spotted her, she looked beautiful. Cary was in love with Hank, she just hadn't told her yet.

"Hey, come here," Hank said as she pulled Cary toward her.

They kissed and drove off in silence, listening to and then singing along with Brian Hyland's "Gypsy Woman" on the radio.

"God, I love that song," Hank declared. Cary did too.

"So you're cool playing it straight tonight?" Cary turned toward Hank, lowering the volume.

"Straight?" Hank asked, knowing full well what Cary meant.

"I didn't mean it that way.... I only meant..." Cary continued, trying to explain.

"I'm just messing with you. Yes, I'm cool with being professional women on a mission to catch a killer, if that's what you mean. Vito and Anna will never know." And with that, Hank laughed.

When they pulled up to the cottage, Cary felt apprehensive. Hank only knew half the story. The other half could demolish their relationship, and it would be all Cary's fault. She put her Jeep in gear, and the two of them made their way to the front door and knocked. It was Vito who answered.

"Well, where the hell have you two been? Never mind, come on in," Vito said, giving Hank a kiss on the cheek while glaring subtly at Cary. *Great*, Cary said to herself, *and Anna is probably even more ticked off at me*. Cary decided that pointing out that they had arrived on time would serve no purpose. Vito was just needling her.

"Hey, Vito. So good to see you," Hank replied, returning the kiss.

"Hi," Cary chimed in.

"Anna will be back shortly. You're gonna love her, Hank. Don't believe you guys have met. I sent her out to pick up Chinese since delivery takes forever at this hour. Can't catch a killer on an empty stomach." And glancing once again in Cary's direction, he added, "Don't worry, there'll be something for *everyone* to eat."

Another dig: Jesus, when was it going to stop? Cary asked herself. Apparently, no time soon, as Anna, upon entering the guesthouse with their dinner, took the opportunity to stare Cary down. The only consolation at the moment was that it appeared Hank wasn't picking up on any of it. Vito graciously introduced Anna and Hank, and they all began to eat.

The upshot of the evening was that Hank had the card they found in Kim's car in her possession, and Vito and Anna offered to see if they could locate any more. And despite some more dirty looks from Vito and Anna, Cary stayed silent regarding the deer and the card found at that scene. She couldn't wait for the evening to end. When they had wrapped things up, Vito took one last parting shot at her with the following remark, "So if *anyone* thinks of *anything* they may have left out, forgotten about, make sure to let us all know." *Point taken*, Cary thought.

On the ride back to Hank's, Cary almost told her everything. But something held her back. As they pulled into Hank's driveway, a text came in on Cary's phone.

"Go ahead, check it," Hank told her. "It could be something important."

Hank was right. The text was from Vito. It read: *You've put us in a very difficult position and are jeopardizing the entire investigation. If you don't tell her, we will.*

Fuck was the only word that came to Cary's mind.

Cary was almost ready to have it out then and there, but she thought better of it. To fend off Vito's threats, she texted him back: *I'll do it tomorrow. Promise.* That would buy her a little more time. So they went to sleep with Hank clueless as to what was to come.

✳ ✳ ✳

When Cary woke up, Hank was already gone. Truth be told, Cary was thankful. Hank left a note in the kitchen: *See you tonight?* Cary had to figure out the best place to deliver the bad news. There was something to be said for doing it in the privacy of your own home, but a public place like a restaurant would make it harder for Hank to cause a scene if she reacted particularly badly to the revelation. The Seafood Shack it would be. So Cary sent Hank a text asking her to meet her there at seven since it was halfway between Hank's home and the station. Hank messaged back: *Sounds lovely.*

Oh God, Cary thought. *How do I get myself into these situations?*

Cary got there first, and Jon showed her to their favorite table in the corner. Then Hank arrived. Cary didn't think she had ever been this unhinged in her entire life. She barely gave Hank the chance to sit down before blurting out, "There's something I've been keeping from you." Cary couldn't read Hank's face. She seemed to have absolutely no idea what Cary was talking about, yet Cary sensed she understood it was important. Exactly how important, probably not, not yet.

"I did a terrible thing. A thing I regret with all my heart, but there's no undoing it," Cary began in a rambling manner.

"Does this have anything to do with the investigation?" Hank inquired.

There's that question again, Cary thought.

So Cary took it from the beginning, from that awful night that would plague her forever, the night she encountered the "Deer Killer." Cary explained that she had run out late that evening to feed her sugar addiction and told Hank what she saw the as-yet-unidentified man do: intentionally hit the deer with his car. It was even worse than that Cary decided. Analyzing it, he set a trap for the fawns by turning off his headlights. It was sadistic and twisted and evil. *If only I had gone to the police*. That decision would torment Cary for the rest of her life.

At first, Hank didn't say anything. And then the floodgates opened.

"*Legally*," she began, "no one is required to go to the aid of a person in danger, no less an animal. But not reporting something like this.... You witnessed a crime, a crime that obviously had dire consequences. You've put me in a very awkward position, Cary."

Cary wasn't exactly sure what that meant, but Hank had obviously put it all together: that it had all started with the "Deer Killer," that he was the same person who ran down the Wooster girls and killed everybody else, including the two dogs. As Cary tried to think of an intelligent response, fortunately for her, Jon came to the rescue.

"Hope you ladies enjoy your dinner. I'll be back in a moment to take your order," he said with a smile, glancing at Hank.

The interruption regrettably only bought Cary a few minutes to collect her thoughts. She was getting a very bad vibe from Hank. The fun-loving, playful side was decidedly gone. Confessing to being the unreported witness to a crime was definitely a buzzkill. And then, before Cary was able to apologize again for keeping the news from Hank, she shot her down.

"You know, Cary," Hank began. "not reporting what you saw to the police isn't the only thing at play here. You *lied* to me."

And there it was, the phrase Cary had dreaded hearing all night: *you lied to me.* Cary couldn't help wondering if she had Rose to thank for Hank's zero-tolerance policy regarding lies by omission. She doubted Hank would cut her a break over the distinction.

As Cary headed home, she thought it had easily been the worst night of her life. They had finished their dinner in awkward silence, and when the check came, Hank simply got up from the table without a word and left. She was punishing Cary already, but Cary thought she deserved it.

Legally, Hank had said. *Legally what?* It was time to do a little research to see where she really stood. But Cary already figured she couldn't face charges for not reporting what she had seen to the police. She just thought she should. So, the first thing Cary did when she got home was take out her laptop and start googling. As far as Cary could tell, there were only three potential laws that could apply to her type of situation: Good Samaritan, Duty to Rescue, and Failure to Report a Crime. In general, it was a grey area of the law that varied significantly from country to country and state to state. So she decided to start with one at a time.

Good Samaritan laws had been enacted to encourage people to do the right thing by protecting them from lawsuits should something go wrong while they were trying to help. Cary didn't see how this type of law could apply to her because we were talking about deer here, and at the time, she had assumed the deer were dead as the result of the crash. But the more she thought about it, Cary decided she should have called for help to try to save the deer. Hard as it was to believe, that thought had never crossed her mind until now. Cary had been more focused on the fact that she failed to call the police so that they could search for the man responsible.

The rationale behind Duty to Rescue laws was similar. But as far as Cary could tell, none applied to situations involving animals. That left Failure to Report a Crime. It appeared in most states that not reporting a crime wasn't considered a crime in itself, but there were some exceptions, such as Texas and Ohio. And when it came to child abuse, there were widespread state statutes that required mandatory reporting. There was also a Federal Failure to Report law, but the underlying felony had to be a federal offense. Cary had had enough for one night. She was pretty sure she hadn't crossed any legal lines, but moral ones were a whole other story.

Cary slept uneasily that night and woke up with the craziest thought. Hank's reaction was so bad that she had forgotten to tell her the most important part: that she had found another "ODD JOBS?" card in the vicinity of where the deer were killed. How was she going to tell her now? Cary decided to take the coward's way out and text her. Hank had to know. After all, that card was the X factor that had led Cary to confess in the first place.

As Cary took out her phone, she knew that this latest revelation wasn't going to go over well. Hank wasn't stupid. She would understand that the only reason Cary finally came forward was because of the card—well the card and Vito's threats, but Hank didn't know about that. Finding the card at one of the crime scenes, albeit the one Hank had known nothing about, was critical information. Cary had had no choice but to share it with Hank.

And so, Cary sent a rather cryptic text, one with no emotion: *Forgot to tell you last night that I found an "ODD JOBS?" card at the deer-killing scene.* Cary guessed she would learn nothing more about Hank. They were done. It only took a few minutes for Hank to respond: *So that's the only reason you told me. I want to see it and now.*

They were on the same page, Cary thought. How unfortunate that their relationship wasn't going to go any further.

SEVENTEEN

When Cary drove through the streets of Wooster these days, she got a wave of nausea every time she passed a deer. They were everywhere, a constant reminder. The town was overrun with them, and sadly, it was not uncommon to see one lying still by the side of the road, the victim of a passing car. But unlike the poor fawns, Cary assumed they hadn't been hit intentionally. Once she had seen three deer right outside her mother's condo, eating their dinner from a bush that was getting progressively smaller. To Cary, the deceased fawns represented every innocent murder victim. And so, any deer sighting, living or dead, conjured up that horrendous night, the night that had changed everything.

Cary wished there was a way she could get the card to Hank without having to see her, but she knew it had to be done discreetly and in person. Being around her was starting to hurt. She was full up on pain at the moment. Cary wanted it to be quick. They decided to meet at Hank's place, so Cary headed in that direction. She would console herself later.

When she pulled up to Hank's house, Cary had to stop for a moment and collect herself. *I can be such an ass sometimes. How did I let all this happen?* Cary longed for Hank's touch, but she knew she'd never feel it again. Cary got out of the car with a tightness in her stomach and made her way to the side door that entered directly into the kitchen. As she peeked inside, she caught a glimpse of Hank's dog lying by the fireplace. When Barry heard the knock on the door, he got up and ran over to investigate. The familiar scent caused his tail to wag vigorously, and he began to scratch at the door. Then Cary noticed Hank in the kitchen getting something out of the fridge. She seemed in no hurry to let her inside.

Cary knocked one more time, and Hank looked up. She put down a large bowl of what appeared to be grapes and walked over to open the door—but only a crack.

"I brought it," Cary began. "Can I come in?"

"This isn't a good time," Hank answered back. "I'll take it from here."

And with that, she reached out and took the card out of Cary's hand, just touching it slightly. The contact was, sadly, enough to excite Cary. But she knew it wouldn't go any further this time. Hank treated her like she had never seen her before. It was unnerving.

The complete about-face was difficult for Cary to process. Hank was taking it all so personally when it had nothing to do with her. Cary had decided not to go to the police well before she ever laid eyes on Hank. The whole situation just got out of hand, as lies always do. Cary desperately tried to think of a way to salvage the relationship, but nothing came to mind. And then Hank ended the interaction with a simple, "Will that be all?"

Will that be all? Cary thought.

"Jesus fucking Christ, I think I'm in love with you, and that's all you can—" The words came out of Cary's mouth before she knew what she was saying. Hank's eyes revealed a sadness she was trying hard to hide.

"Cary, I can't do this right now. I think you better leave. Just go," Hank pleaded.

Although Cary thought Hank seemed somewhat conflicted, she sensed she was not the forgive-and-forget type. Cary had blown it, period, end of story. It was time to head over to her sister's and get the self-loathing started.

As soon as Cary got back in her car, she lost all control, bursting into tears. She started to get that sick, panicky feeling, the only sensation that ever made her lose her appetite. *Oh, God, what have I done?* Cary cried. She couldn't go through this again. It was unbearable. Cary sat for a moment cursing the "Deer Killer" to hell. But regrettably, in the moment, she knew it was more for what he had cost her emotionally than what he had done to his victims. She needed a big Obi hug, and she needed it now. Cary turned her Jeep around and headed for her sister's.

It was early afternoon, and Cary knew her sister would still be at work. She collected Obi and drove to the dog park. She needed to think. When they got there, Cary kept Obi close to her side and chose her favorite bench to sit on. It was isolated from the rest of the park and would give her a chance to reflect on the mess that was her life. She considered what she should be worried about most at the moment: her failed relationship with Hank or the fact that there was a serial killer on the loose. Yet she had also found crucial evidence to help Hank with the investigation: another "ODD JOBS?" card. That had to count for something.

After about an hour, Cary was restless, so she got Obi up and headed back to her Jeep. It was no easy task getting him inside, but he seemed a bit better today and maneuvered his way into the back seat almost on his own. She didn't know what she'd do without her precious Obelus. As Cary headed back to her sister's place, she texted Anna that she needed to talk to her. In addition to helping out with the investigation, Anna was always working on some project or other, so Cary was pretty sure she'd be home when she got there. She was right.

As Cary pulled up to the guesthouse, turned off her car, and put it in gear, she had a thought. Although she had been wrong to keep Hank in the dark about the deer incident, she had valid reasons for doing so. Kicking off a relationship with a lie, however, a big lie in this case, always backfired; yet somehow, Cary thought she could make it all work out. She was wrong. Then it occurred to her that she wasn't the only culprit. Vito and Anna had kept the same information from Hank, even though it was on her behalf. *How would Ms. Perfect react when she realized that?* Cary wondered. Hank was a hard-ass. Who needed to go out with someone like that? She was done with her—as if she had a choice.

Out of deference to Anna, Cary knocked on the door to the guest-house instead of just barging in. Anna opened the door and gave Cary a big hug. She gave Obi a hug too. She must have sensed something was wrong. Anna had good instincts. Cary knew she would comfort her with her rooibos iced tea and signature brownies. Anna's reper-toire was limited, but her heart was big. Cary would need all the sympathy she could get today. Obi loved Anna. She was one of the few people who could tolerate the issues that came with a Newfie: mainly drool. As they settled in for a session of *what I did* versus *what I should have done*, Cary started to fall apart.

"It's okay, Cary. Everything will be all right. Talk to me," Anna began.

Anna only called Cary, *Cary,* when she knew something was terribly wrong. It actually made Cary feel worse.

"I told Hank. I gave her the card. She hates me. It's over," Cary went on.

"It's over? What's over?" Anna didn't have a clue.

And then Cary remembered that it had all happened so fast that she had never even told Vito about what had gone on between her and Hank, no less Anna. She had a lot of explaining to do. And so, Cary finally told Anna what had transpired between her and Hank.

That they had begun an affair which ended when Cary confessed that she hadn't been completely forthcoming about certain events related to the investigation: namely, the deer. Anna had pretty much stayed out of that decision, deferring to Vito and Cary on whether or not to tell Hank about the incident. That was uncharacteristic of Anna, who always let you know where she stood. Cary could see she was starting to blame herself.

So Cary said, preemptively, "It's not your fault, Anna. Vito and I decided it was best to hold back that piece of information until we were sure how Hank would handle things. As soon as we slept together, I should have told her, but something stopped me," she continued. "This is all on me."

Then Anna went into DA mode and asked Cary one question: "Where are the cards now?"

"I told you, I gave it to Hank. Hank has them, both of them," Cary answered. She thought Anna was distracted these days because of Vito. She needed to pay more attention.

"Right," said Anna. "What do you think she's going to do with them?"

"I don't know, Anna, I really don't. She was supposed to try to lift prints off the one we found in Kim's car.... But now that she has the other one...the deer...she's in a rage.... I'm afraid she's gonna do something crazy like bring them both to her boss and tell him everything. Oh, God."

Then Anna had an idea.

"Why don't the four of us get together and try to fix this mess?" she suggested.

The four of us? Cary felt ill. She couldn't imagine even being in the same room with Hank, but her options were dwindling. So she told Anna to set it up and let her know the details. If Vito agreed, that is. After all, Hank was his friend. It was his call.

Cary beat herself up all night. Every time she fucked up, there was a domino effect that made things a thousand times worse. It appeared this instance would be no different. As she tried to get some sleep, Cary tried to remember when she first learned the difference between a mass murderer and a serial killer. She hoped it would take her mind off the pain she was feeling. She thought it might have been when she heard about the University of Texas shooting. Charles Whitman had climbed to the top of the campus tower in Austin and fired several weapons until he managed to kill sixteen people, including an unborn child, and injure at least thirty-one others. A surviving victim died years later as a result of complications from his injuries.

The other mass murder that traumatized Cary as a child was of the Chicago student nurses. She had seen a book about it when she was about ten years old, and it had a profound effect on her. Richard Speck stabbed and strangled eight student nurses to death. A ninth managed to survive by hiding under a bed. Speck was allowed to live out his life in prison, where he reportedly transitioned to a pseudo woman, occasionally wearing women's underwear. That just didn't seem like justice to Cary. Both mass murders happened in 1966. That had always struck her as odd.

Serial killers were different. They spread the pain around slowly. Danny Rolling, who had brutally murdered five students in Gainesville, Florida in the late summer of 1990, spent a little less than a week terrorizing the campus. Others, like Dennis Rader, a.k.a. "BTK," or Joseph DeAngelo, the "Golden State Killer," spent decades murdering people while otherwise living what appeared to be normal lives. Mass murderers seemed to blow all of a sudden; serial killers, on the other hand, had bouts of rage. It was all demonic as far as Cary was concerned. No one had the right to steal someone's life away from them.

The next thing Cary knew, her phone rang. It was eight o'clock in the morning. *Some people count sheep, others count killers*, she thought.

At any rate, Cary had gotten a good night's sleep and was ready to face the day. Cary missed the call, so without getting out of bed, she grabbed her phone from the nightstand to see who it was: Anna. She left a message: "Vito's on board. Meet us at The Shack in Roton tonight at seven." *Dear lord*, Cary moaned. *Can I get a fucking break?* She didn't think she could eat any more scallops. She didn't think she could face Hank either, no less in the same setting. *That damn Jon better have the night off*, Cary groaned.

This time, Cary didn't give a shit what she looked like. Under normal circumstances, after a breakup, she would have wanted to make the other person regret it. But this was different. She just wanted to die.

* * *

It took every ounce of courage Cary had left to get into her Jeep and drive to that restaurant. But she knew she had no choice. It would likely be the most awkward, unpredictable, and miserable night Cary would ever spend. She got there nearly half an hour early but didn't get out of her car until about ten after seven. She hadn't been this nervous since she took the SATs back in high school. The feeling everyone had when the test started at eight in the morning and you couldn't imagine being alive at noon when it would be over. Yes, *that* feeling.

Cary was intentionally late for dinner even though she had arrived early. She waited long enough to go inside until she was relatively certain that everyone else was already there. Cary couldn't take the chance of being left alone with Hank. When she finally got up the nerve to go in, the first familiar face she spotted was Jon's. Cary decided it was good tonight to see *any* face that wasn't Hank's, even his. When he saw her, Jon came over and said, "I think they're waiting for you in the back. Good to see you again." Cary thought she had been too hard on him. It wasn't his fault that Hank was charming and took a liking to him and had broken her heart. No, that was *her* doing.

Cary made her way through the main dining room until she saw the three of them at a corner table in the back facing the water. She actually thought she was going to throw up. Vito's face also made it clear that Anna had brought him up to speed on things, and so, the gentleman that he was, he did his best to diffuse the situation. "Have a seat, Cary. Good to see you," he bellowed.

Anna had saved the seat next to her for Cary, and Vito and Hank were sitting next to each other on the other side. *Their first double date,* Cary joked to herself. At a square table for four, Cary decided there was no seating arrangement that could offset the humiliation she was about to endure. Hank wasn't exactly looking *at* her; she was looking *through* her. Cary thought there wasn't enough liquor in the world to get her through the night.

"I've taken the liberty of ordering a pitcher of sangria and a raw platter to get us started. It's one of their specialties," Vito continued. "Shrimp, littlenecks, oysters. Hopefully, you'll find something you can eat, Cary."

"No worries," she answered in a quiet tone.

Cary looked up just barely enough to catch a glimpse of Hank's face. It was like stone. Cary thought she was going to implode. And then, right on cue, Jon came over, platter in tow. Cary didn't see how the night could possibly get any more awkward. As he put the dish down in the center of the table, Hank grabbed his hand and said, "Thanks, sweetie. You're the best."

Thanks, sweetie. You're the best? Cary repeated to herself. She was starting to hate Hank with a passion. And why did Hank have to give his hand her sensuous touch? Cary didn't normally drink, but when the sangria came, she poured herself a tall glass. Hank noticed, but

Cary didn't care. *Anything* to get through this spectacle of a dinner. *Never mix business with pleasure. Don't shit where you eat.* Why hadn't she taken those expressions more seriously? Cary was stuck with Hank until the "Deer Killer" was caught. The situation would likely just keep getting worse. It was quite possible Cary would be a full-blown alcoholic by then.

Jon returned to take their dinner orders. Anna and Vito chose the same thing: the eight-ounce filet mignon and a hearts of romaine salad they intended to share. Hank ordered the double-cut pork chops, and Cary went with the clams with linguini. *Clams didn't even have a face,* she reasoned. Cary was surrounded by die-hard carnivores, so why in God's name did they have to go to a seafood place? Maybe Hank had suggested it, she considered, just to stick it to her. The way she was acting tonight, Cary wouldn't be the least bit surprised.

Cary had already lost count of how many glasses of sangria she had had to drink when Vito got down to business. But his opening comment took her by surprise.

"You should be just as mad at me as Cary," he began. "I knew about the deer incident too."

Cary took another big gulp of sangria and decided she wanted tonight to be a blur when she woke up in the morning. She had no clue how Hank was going to respond.

"I'm not *angry*," she replied, clearly lying. "I just want to see justice done."

Evidently, there was no winning tonight. They just needed to make a plan so the police could officially be brought in on the investigation and the killer could be caught. That's what this was all about in the end: catching a killer. After this fiasco with Hank, Cary saw no future in dating women. She preferred to be left alone, to hang out with her precious Obelus, who never judged her, never betrayed her, and never made her feel anything but loved.

"So, where are we with the cards?" Vito asked, his voice disrupting Cary's melancholy thoughts.

Hank explained that she had already given the card they found in Kim's car to her colleague in fingerprinting—he owed her a favor—and she was going to check with him in the morning to see what, if anything, he gleaned from it. Now that she had the other card, she would put it through the same analysis. She'd let them know the results as soon as she knew anything. They all agreed that prints or no prints, the same cards, discovered at two of the crime scenes, bolstered their theory enough to go to the police. However, they were also in agreement that the more evidence they had, the stronger their case would be when they approached Hank's boss, Sgt. Joseph O'Malley, a legend on the force.

By the time they finished dinner, Cary was adequately trashed. She had always been a lightweight when it came to alcohol, and she had really overdone it tonight. Normally Cary never mixed alcohol with her real addiction, sugar, but tonight was different. She needed every crutch known to man to sit across from the woman she thought she loved who seemed to delight in torturing her with disinterest. So Anna and she decided to split their favorite dessert: the molten chocolate cake. The Shack's version was mouthwatering. Cary realized, as the night came to an end, that the cake would be the only titillation she would experience that evening.

Too wasted to drive even an automatic home, Vito and Anna poured Cary into Vito's car and told the valet someone would be back the next day to collect the Jeep. Vito gave the guy a generous tip, and they headed back to Gayle's house. Vito and Anna spent the night as usual in the cottage; Cary slept at her sister's, with Obelus on the floor right next to her. As she fell asleep, Cary tried to remember how many times she came the first time she slept with Hank. It was better than counting sheep.

EIGHTEEN

Cary predictably woke up with the mother of all headaches. She hadn't been this hungover since she was in college. *I'm too old for this shit*, she sighed. For a moment, Cary was disoriented and forgot where she was. She looked at the clock: 6:00 a.m. Then she saw Obi still sound asleep on the floor next to where she lay on the couch, and she remembered everything. *Well, at least the cake was good*, Cary quipped. Her first mission of the day was to find some Excedrin Migraine. Cary's sister always had it in the kitchen. Not wanting to disturb Obi, she carefully made her way around his rather large frame and headed in search of some relief.

Her sister never had any food in the house, but Cary knew Anna would, so she poured herself a glass of water, took several pills, and jumped in the shower to wake herself up. Then the plan was to text Anna and scrounge up something to eat. Obi was a late sleeper, so he didn't even realize she was there until he spotted her coming out of the bathroom. His tail wagged ferociously. He loved her. His breathing was labored today. The laryngeal paralysis was getting worse. Cary was worried sick about him, but there was nothing she could do.

When Cary was done getting ready, she called to Obelus and let him outside to do his business. Then the two of them made their way down to the guesthouse. Cary remembered that they left her car at the restaurant, so after she ate, she needed to figure out who would be able to take her to pick it up. Anna volunteered. They decided to go early to avoid the traffic. Vito had taken the train back to Stamford just so Anna would have a car to help Cary out, as Gayle's truck was currently out of commission. Cary decided she was truly blessed to have the two of them in her life. They had become her support system.

Cary and Anna got into Vito's car and made their way to Roton, at first in silence. Then Anna began to grill Cary on her relationship with Hank—at least it *felt* that way to Cary. She knew instinctively that Anna would think it was a bit unethical or at least stupid of Cary to have gotten involved romantically with their inside "man," a detective no less. Then Anna surprised Cary with the words: "I'm so sorry things didn't work out with you and Hank. You deserve to be happy." Anna, more than anyone, knew how difficult it was for Cary to open up to people, to women. She had watched as Cary struggled to have a healthy relationship, often pursuing straight women who Anna thought sent her misleading signals.

"Thanks, Anna. That means a lot. 1 just fucked it all up," Cary responded.

"Well, God knows I've made more than my share of mistakes when it comes to men," Anna began. "But if I've learned anything about relationships, it's that in the end, it all comes down to one thing: trust."

Anna's pep talk of sorts wasn't making Cary feel any better. It was actually making her believe even more that it was all her fault. But she knew that wasn't Anna's intention. And then Cary turned her head and stared out the window, trying to hide the tears that were beginning to well up in her eyes. Anna noticed.

"Cary. What is it? You can tell me anything," Anna said, trying to console her.

"Sorry, Anna. You don't get it. I'm in love with her. I'm *in love* with her. Oh, God. What have I done?"

And with those words, tears began to stream down Cary's face.

"Oh, Cary, I'm so sorry. I don't know what to say. It'll all work out. We'll all get through this nightmare, and Hank will come around."

"You don't know that, Anna. I blew it. I'm the biggest idiot who ever lived," Cary answered despondently.

"Don't say that, Cary. Things just got complicated. Vito and I, we're here for you. I promise.... Everything will be okay."

When they finally got to The Seefood Shack, Cary collected herself, thanked Anna, and said she'd call her later. They kissed goodbye. The valet on duty fetched Cary's Jeep and opened the door for her with a smile. Cary knew that meant she needed to give him a tip, so she handed him a five-dollar bill. That seemed like enough as Vito had been generous the night before, and Cary was sure they pooled their tips. As she drove away, it only took a few minutes until Cary noticed something stuck to her windshield. She pulled over the first chance she got and took out a card from underneath the driver's side wiper. It read, "ODD JOBS?" "Holy fucking shit," Cary let out a scream. She texted Anna: *On my way back. I need to talk to you now.*

Cary was so rattled by the time she got back to Anna's that she was literally shaking. This time, she barged in.

"Cary, what's going on? You're stressing me out." Anna said in a concerned voice.

Cary took out the card she had just found on her windshield and handed it to Anna.

"Where did you get this?" Anna continued.

"It was on my windshield...under the wipers.... I was driving away and noticed something.... I pulled over to see what it was. It was the card," Cary continued to explain.

Anna didn't want to freak Cary out, but she was pretty sure she already knew what the worst-case scenario was.

"You know what this means, Cary?" she began.

"Yeah. He knows *who* I am and *where* I am," Cary answered.

Cary's nightmare was coming true.

"We better call Vito," Anna said with a worried look on her face. "You stay here."

Cary sat on the couch, clutching her hands, wondering where all of this would lead. They had to get this guy before he killed anybody else, including her. She could hear Anna from the bedroom talking to Vito. From her end of the conversation, it sounded like he was on his way. *Small comfort*, Cary thought. *I'm being stalked by a madman.* Time was of the essence. The sooner they got the police involved *officially*, the better.

* * *

Hank knew she was supposed to report back this morning with the fingerprint results. So she headed straight to the station to talk to Max Craven, her trusted friend and colleague. Max was in his late twenties, a bit overweight, and his lifelong dream was to be an evidence technician. He had reached his goal. He owed her, and he knew it, so Hank was fairly certain no one would find out what she had been up to—at least not from him. His office was in the basement of the building, adjacent to the evidence room. No one would see her there, not at this hour.

Hank knocked on the door, but no one answered. The office appeared dark and empty. Then she heard a voice from behind.

"Hey, Hank," Max said in a friendly tone. "Didn't expect you here this early. Come on in."

Hank was filled with trepidation. They needed a break to catch this guy; they needed help from the police, an *official* investigation.

The four of them couldn't do it alone. It was time to find out how useful the cards might be in cracking the case.

"So, Max, what did you find out?" Hank asked.

"The second card you gave me was too degraded to test for prints, or anything else for that matter," he began. Max saw the disappointment in Hank's eyes.

Then he continued: "But the first card, the first card was different," he said in an authoritative tone. And with that Max took out the card they had discovered stuffed in between the seats of Kim's car and turned it over so that the blank side faced up.

Although it wasn't really necessary, Max dimmed the lights for dramatic effect. He then took out a special penlight and pointed it at the card. If you looked closely, the blue light revealed the slightest imprint on the back.

"Partial prints were found on the card. Probably from the woman.... We can run tests if you want," he continued. "But do you see that?"

Hank wasn't sure if she was seeing what he wanted her to see, but she answered as best she could. "It looks like a paw print," she said, taking in the import of what that meant.

"Exactly," Max said.

Hank knew this guy was fucking around with them, and she hadn't even heard yet about what happened to Cary earlier that morning. She took the cards out of Max's hands and thanked him with an "I owe *you* now." Then Hank went to her car to call Vito.

A few minutes after Anna got off the call with Vito, her phone rang. It was Hank. Cary wondered why Hank was calling Anna. Cary knew she'd never reach out to her unless she had no other choice, but why Anna? Why not Vito? And then, from Anna's end of the conversation, it was clear she had called Anna because Vito hadn't picked up. After all, he had been on the phone with Anna and was probably on his way.

Cary tried to figure out what Hank was telling Anna from listening to her end of the conversation, but it was difficult. She decided Anna would tell her everything when she got off the phone. She was right. As Anna hung up, she came over to Cary and tried to say in as soothing a manner as possible, "Cary, I think you should sit down."

Then Anna filled Cary in on the print results. They both agreed the only reasonable conclusion was that the killer was taunting them. *He is one sick fuck,* Cary thought. It was time to go to the authorities and launch a formal investigation. Hank would have to arrange a meeting with the four of them and Sgt. O'Malley. It would be another torture session for Cary but a necessary one. They were all in his crosshairs— at least Cary was. She resolved to keep a better stash of sugar around in the future *if* she lived through this nightmare.

* * *

The O'Malley meeting was scheduled for the following day at two o'clock in the afternoon. Cary crashed on the guesthouse couch the night before with Anna and Vito in the next room; it seemed like the safest option. Cary just couldn't sleep alone at her place knowing this guy had been following her. Cary let Anna and Vito use the shower first, and then she got ready for the meeting.

Cary decided she should look a bit more professional for her first encounter with the sergeant, so instead of going home and trying to piece together something appropriate, Anna lent her one of her pant-suits. They were close enough in size, and it would spare her the trip. When Cary checked herself in the mirror, she couldn't help thinking, *I could be Hillary Clinton's body double*. She laughed. Pantsuits weren't exactly Cary's look. Even at her old job, the most formal thing they wore was jeans and a tee shirt.

As Hank was already at the station for the day, the three of them decided to meet her there an hour before the meeting was set to begin to get their stories straight. Cary knew that meant to decide how to handle her involvement in the case—this is, that she never reported the deer killings to the police. With this lunatic on her tail, she figured she might be safer in a jail cell after all, but she knew that wasn't going to happen.

They took Vito's car and headed to police headquarters near Stamford, the main precinct in the area. They pulled into the visitor's parking lot, and Vito sent Hank a text. They waited across the street in front of a small coffee house for her to come out. Cary's stomach was in knots. Between her feelings for Hank, her guilt over keeping information from the police, and being stalked by a madman, she just wanted to disappear into the ground.

Cary spotted Hank as she was crossing the street heading straight toward them. She looked hot. *Damn*, Cary thought. As Hank got closer, Cary saw she was wearing her standard cool detective outfit: jeans, leather belt, tight blouse accentuated by a badge, and a gun. *Of course*, Cary thought. *What an ass I am. I didn't have to get all dressed up to meet with a bunch of cops*. She felt and looked self-conscious, and she knew Hank would pick up on it. What a disadvantage that put her at. Suddenly Cary's appearance trumped all her other problems.

When Hank finally made it to their side of the street, Vito gave her a big hello.

"Hey, gorgeous," he began, pouring salt on Cary's wound. "Let's go inside and grab a table."

So the motley four sat down in the back where they'd have more privacy and ordered three cappuccinos and one hot chocolate. Cary was beginning to feel like a child at a grown-ups' dinner party. Cary began to wonder what Hank had ever seen in her anyway. *But that was her mother's negativity talking*, she tried to convince herself. This day couldn't end soon enough.

The consensus for the meeting was simple and straightforward: to tell O'Malley *everything*. That worried Cary, but there was no other way to play it, especially now that her life was in jeopardy. It was no longer just her decision; the killer had a part to play as well. One of these days, Cary was going to strap a feedbag of peanut M&Ms to her head; it might just save her life.

When they got inside the station, Hank took charge. "This way," she told them as they headed down a long hallway to the sergeant's office. Several male cops made flirtatious remarks and gestures to Hank as she walked by. She could have anyone she wanted, male or female, Cary decided. Even if she hadn't fucked it all up, the odds of her holding on to someone like Hank were slim to none. It didn't make Cary feel any better.

O'Malley wasn't quite what Cary had been expecting. He was model-handsome, Cary guessed early forties, and full of personality. As he gave Hank a hug and kiss on the cheek, Cary felt one thing: rage. She couldn't help wondering if anything had gone on between them. O'Malley seemed overly attentive as far as Hank was concerned. Cary tried to put her suspicions out of her head. After all, she and Hank weren't even together anymore. It turned out that just like Hank, *this* Joe O'Malley was a legend because of his father. Apparently, the older generation of cops had produced picture-perfect offspring, the next incarnation of law enforcement: gorgeous, charismatic crime-busters. Cary would have killed to get Hank back, but first, she would have to save her own life.

Overall, Cary thought the meeting went well. O'Malley green-lighted an official police investigation after hearing Hank out. The only cryptic remark he made, of course, was aimed at *her*. When the "Deer Killer" incident came up and Hank, Cary thought, rather gleefully explained Cary's involvement, O'Malley stared Cary down. "We're not going to take it any further," he began. "It's something you'll have to live with. But I hear a Failure to Report law is pending in the legislature," O'Malley informed her, with a hint of satisfaction on his face. Cary decided that even her mother in her worst moments never made her feel as guilty and low as young Joe O'Malley had just managed to do. And in front of Hank, no less.

Today would rank among the five worst days of Cary's life. Of that, there was no doubt. But now they had to catch a serial killer who knew *who* Cary was and *where* she was. The police could be so useless in these situations. Cary hadn't even bothered asking O'Malley for protection because she knew what the answer would be: "Has he threatened you yet? Then there's nothing we can do." Cary wondered how many people had lost their lives to that logic. It would have been the perfect time to have a detective for a girlfriend, but that wasn't going to happen either. Cary was on her own.

Cary wasn't sure how much longer she could impose on Anna and Vito. The guesthouse was small, and having her underfoot would get old fast. But she didn't want to drag her sister into this, nor endanger her and Obi, so she couldn't or rather didn't think it was wise to stay there unless Vito gave her a gun. Cary had gone to the shooting range enough times that she felt confident she knew how to handle a firearm. She'd just have to ask him. So, for the time being, probably another week, Cary would make the couch her home and then approach Vito about the gun. *Sounds like a plan*, she told herself. As long as no more of those creepy cards showed up, she might even get some sleep.

* * *

For the next several days, things seemed relatively quiet. Cary spent most of her time either hanging out in the guesthouse while Anna worked on her laptop or visiting Obi at her sister's while she was at work. She felt irrationally safe during the daytime. At night, the only reason she could rest was because Vito was one door over with his .45. He was an expert shot. Good luck to the person who crossed him.

Tonight, Cary planned to run the gun idea past Vito. Anna was in the mood to cook, so the two of them went to the market in town and got enough food for a small army. Anna thought she'd make her favorite pasta dish: tagliatelle with olive oil, peas, and grilled shrimp. They also bought some fresh bread from the French bakery in Fairview and Vito's favorite dessert: the regular guy cake from Billy's in the center of Wooster. Cary texted her sister to join them when she got home. It was the nicest afternoon Cary had spent in some time. It was almost as if all her problems had suddenly disappeared overnight.

Vito had picked up wine on the way home as usual but was pleasantly surprised at the feast that awaited him. They all needed to chill out. What better way to do that than with food and drink? Her sister was the last to arrive, as always, but still managed to get there before they had begun to eat. Vito was always happy to see her. They had a strong bond. As Anna and Cary set the table and brought out the food, Vito turned on the television. Cary found it unnerving to have it on during dinner, but she wasn't exactly in any position to question Vito's habits. Then, all of a sudden, she heard Eve's voice in the background. She was showing a clip from an earlier press conference starring none other than Sgt. Joseph O'Malley. The case had been blown wide open.

"God damnit," said Vito.

None of them had expected the case to hit the news without any warning. They were all startled. Her sister didn't even know the whole story yet.

"That son of a bitch should have given us a heads up," Vito groaned.

Cary had never seen Vito so angry. And then the phone rang; it was Hank. Vito answered. From the sound of it, it appeared Hank was trying to apologize on Joe's behalf. Vito wasn't having it.

"We just thought the police would start working the case," he began. "No one told us it would be all over the news."

Cary knew the part he was leaving out was the effect the publicity might have on the killer. That was the wild card, and it could have dire consequences for all of them, especially Cary. When Vito got off the phone, all he said was, "Hank's on her way." Their peaceful dinner was over.

There was so much she hadn't told her sister yet, but Cary thought by the time the night was over, she would have it all figured out on her own. When Hank arrived, the only person she required an introduction to was Gayle. *Dear lord*, thought Cary. It was Vito who took the bull by the horns.

"Hank, this is Dr. Gayle Mackin, Cary's sister. I don't believe you two have ever met."

As it turned out, that wasn't exactly true.

"Oh my God," Hank shrieked uncharacteristically. "You're my dermatologist."

Cary was well aware that her sister had thousands of patients all over Fairview County, but what were the odds? It took her sister only a minute to place her.

"What a funny coincidence," Gayle began. "How are you?"

The only thing that could make the evening any worse, Cary thought, was if Hank and her sister actually *liked* each other. Within minutes, that became self-evident.

It appeared there would now be five for dinner, not including Obelus. Cary went to get him as they were anticipating a late night, and she didn't want him to be alone. He liked Hank too, but Cary decided she wouldn't hold that against him. After all, he was just a dog and had no way of knowing what had transpired between them. Had he been in the loop, Cary knew he would have bitten her head off.

So they spent the better part of the evening watching Eve Arora's *Special Report* on the case. The moniker Gene and Eve had settled on for the story was "Deadly Deranged Driver." Cary figured it could have been a lot worse.

Nothing and no one would be spared tonight. Not only did Cary have to deal with Hank, but she was being forced to watch Eve and relive what she perceived was her latest career failure. She was in pain overload. Anna's delicious dinner served as much-needed comfort food. Cary believed people ate more when they were nervous or stressed. She remembered the first thing they did at CrimeTV after the Twin Towers were hit on 9/11 was order enough food to feed them through the winter. Cary would have to eat her way through the coming weeks.

As Cary, Vito, and Anna continued to watch the show, Hank and Gayle cleaned up and brought out the dessert. For a moment, Cary thought she caught Hank looking over at her, but she decided it was probably wishful thinking. As Vito cut the cake, the sound of Eve rattling off the names of the alleged victims caught their attention. When they looked up, they saw a split-screen of Amanda Caldwell and Emily Browne's faces. Next was little Elsie Cooper, who got a screen all to herself, followed by Blair and Dakota Riordan along with their dog, Nelson. Kim's puppy, Andrew, was left out in the cold. *They always mess up something on that show*, Cary bemoaned. *Whenever I'm not there.*

The photos on the television were difficult for Cary to look at. She couldn't help thinking it was all her fault. She had a choice that night, and she made the wrong one. She headed for the wine.

When the show ended, it was ten o'clock. Her sister had to get up early for work, so she headed back to the main house. Obi had fallen asleep, so Cary promised her she would take good care of him and bring him home in the morning. That left her, Vito, Anna, and Hank to make a plan now that the story was all over the news. The "Deadly Deranged Driver" case was now in the hands of the police, but Cary's life was still at stake. She knew the authorities would do their best to apprehend whoever was responsible, but that didn't ease her concern. If need be, Cary was prepared to take matters into her own hands.

They decided one of them had to talk to the valets at The Seefood Shack and find out who was on duty that night or if they saw anything suspicious. They assumed that the killer had followed Cary there and, when they left the car overnight, seized the opportunity to stick the card under the driver's side windshield wiper. Cary volunteered for the assignment. Then Hank caught her totally off guard with the following remark: "I'll go with you." Cary grabbed the bottle of wine. She decided to forego the glass this time.

* * *

The man knew his face would be on the screen one day too. He'd look good on television. *Crime Watch* with Eve Arora was his favorite show. They had taken the bait.

* * *

Cary thought Hank had overreacted to her lack of forthrightness about the deer incident. But the more she thought about it, she realized that wasn't the entire problem. In retrospect, Cary began to think what really bothered Hank was that she hadn't told anyone at the time. *Hank must think I'm a terrible person*, Cary thought. Maybe she was right. Since, for whatever reason, Hank had decided to accompany Cary to question the valets, she decided to try to explain to her why she never went to the police. But this time, Cary cared what she looked like.

Hank wanted Cary to meet her at the station. Cary guessed things were going to be handled in a more professional manner going forward. She left her Jeep in the visitor's parking lot and went inside. But not before checking in the mirror to make sure that she hadn't been followed and that her hair fell properly and that there was nothing stuck in her teeth. *Relationships could turn on a dime*, Cary bemoaned. Hers, however, was dead in the water at the moment. Cary hoped that would change. She *had* to get Hank back.

Hank was waiting for her in the entranceway of the main building. There was no discernible greeting, just, "Let's take my car." *How romantic*, Cary thought. They took the elevator two floors down to the lower level of the parking garage and proceeded to Hank's vehicle. Hank set the GPS to The Shack's address, not wanting to get stuck in traffic, and they drove off in silence except for the radio playing in the background. Like Cary, Hank was a fan of Motown even though it was before her time. She had her car radio tuned to Sirius 49, the Soul Town station.

Traffic was horrendous on I-95 today, so Cary knew it would take them at least another half hour to get there. The GPS had proved unhelpful. Last-minute traffic jams were a bitch. Cary decided someone had to make the first move to break the tension. She gathered it would have to be her as Hank seemed perfectly content to sing along to her favorite songs, ignoring Cary in the process. Cary would have to be her own defense attorney today, but first, she had to find a way to get the conversation started. She went with: "Can you believe what a nightmare 95 has turned into? It's like this all the time."

Brilliant conversationalist, Cary thought, berating herself.

Hank didn't answer. Cary just thought she detected a slight nod of agreement. This was getting unbearable. Cary decided to put her explanation on hold until after they had spoken with the staff at The Shack. She'd save it for the way back.

When they finally arrived, Hank seemed stressed from the drive. Cary thought she had likely only allotted so much time out of her day for this and the traffic on I-95 had messed up her schedule. *Well, that certainly isn't my fault*, Cary told herself. The first thing Hank said as they got out of the car was, "Let's go find the manager." It was around two o'clock, so the lunch crowd was winding down, and the main dining room was almost empty. Hank spotted a man in his late thirties near the bar. Her instincts told her it was him.

"Excuse me. We need to speak with the manager," she began.

"You're looking right at him," the man said with a smile. "Dave, here."

"Are you aware that there may be a serial killer operating in the area?" Hank added.

"You mean that case on the news last night?" Dave answered with a skeptical look on his face.

Hank explained that the police had begun an investigation and identified herself as a detective. She didn't have to flash her badge; it was right there in plain view attached to her belt, as always. Dave just hadn't noticed it yet. Cary thought he was distracted by her striking green eyes.

"So what do you want with me?" he asked nervously.

The police had decided to keep the "ODD JOBS?" cards a secret from the public for the time being. In every case, there was always one critical piece of information that only the killer knew. The "ODD JOBS?" card was that tidbit the police kept to themselves lest they risk compromising the investigation.

"We found something on a car parked in your lot and need to know if you or anyone else...an employee...a customer...may have noticed anything suspicious," Hank continued.

"Can't say that I have," Dave answered. "But you're more than welcome to speak with any of the staff."

"We'll do just that," Hank answered.

She asked him for a list of employees, specifically the valets. Dave said that there was a large turnover but that they did background checks on everyone they hired and had never had a problem. Cary didn't think Hank actually thought one of the valets was the killer; she just needed to see what, if anything, they could tell her that might advance the investigation. Cary thought Hank should have asked for a list of *former* employees as well but knew she would have if she believed a valet was involved. Instead, Hank handed Dave her business card and asked him to call her if he remembered anything else.

After speaking with the valet on duty, they headed back to Hank's car. The valet was a nice kid, eighteen years old, and had been working the night Cary left her car there. That would spare them another trip to Roton. Cary didn't recognize him; she had been too wasted to remember the face of a stranger. But Hank did. The valet couldn't remember seeing anything out of the ordinary that night, however, so speaking with him failed to provide any additional clues.

On the way back to Hank's office, they hit just as much traffic as before. That gave Cary the chance she needed to defend herself and perhaps crack the barrier between them. She started with, "I never realized you saw my sister. That she was your doctor."

"She's the greatest," Hank replied. "All her patients adore her."

That was the longest string of words Hank had directed at her since they broke up. It emboldened Cary.

"Hank, this tension between us...it's just unbearable...can't we talk about it?" Cary continued.

"I'm sorry, Cary, I really am. I'm starting to think maybe it just wasn't such a great idea for us to get involved in the first place...under the circumstances. Didn't mean to come down so hard on you. But right now, I think we need a break. We just have to work together and see what happens with *everything*," Hank replied. And then she added, "Let's just be friends, okay? And concentrate on getting this guy."

Let's just be friends, Cary repeated to herself. *Never ask a question you're not prepared to hear the answer to*. She should have listened to that piece of advice too. Cary was dejected. She saw no point in bringing up the real reason she hadn't gone to the police: that she was *afraid*. And the reason she was afraid was that she had been exposed to too many horrific stories over the years and had always had this feeling that she was going to be murdered. Cary couldn't help thinking that all sounded pretty weird. Hank thought little enough of her already. She didn't need to give her more fodder. Perhaps, Cary thought, they just weren't meant to be. *But those green eyes*. Cary sighed.

* * *

Cary slept at her sister's that evening for the first time since she realized she was being stalked. Her sister usually remembered to set the alarm at night before she went to bed, and Vito was just a short walk down from the main house if needed. He had also agreed to let her keep the gun for now. So, with Obi at her feet and Vito's favorite firearm under the couch, Cary tried to get some sleep. She hadn't told her sister about the gun; she didn't want to cause her further angst, and she wasn't sure how she would react or if she would even allow it in her home.

As she was falling asleep, Cary couldn't help thinking that neither she nor Hank had brought up her other confession as they were driving back to the station. That Cary had told Hank she loved her. But it had to have registered. There was no way to tell from Hank's behavior if she felt the same way, but the more Cary thought about it, her initial harsh reaction might actually be a good sign. If you had no feelings for someone, you wouldn't get that worked up. At least, that was Cary's current theory.

Cary woke up the next morning feeling refreshed from a good night's sleep. They were rare these days. The case may now be in the hands of the police, but that didn't make Cary feel any safer. Vito, Anna, and her sister didn't want her going out alone, so she started taking Obi with her everywhere. Cary felt safe during the day with him at her side. Night was another matter. If it weren't for the gun, she thought she wouldn't sleep again until this nutjob was caught.

Of course, Anna and her sister were clueless about the weapon. It was an extra layer of protection Cary hadn't told anyone about. Only Vito knew. She had promised him she would leave it in a safe place during the day and only keep it with her at night. He would have been furious with her if he knew she was carrying it around. After all, it was registered to Vito, not Cary, so if anything went wrong, it could blow up in his face. But Cary told herself she'd be careful so no one would ever know. It's not like the police were providing her with any protection. She'd have to die first for that to happen.

The day passed uneventfully, but Cary hadn't heard from Anna since the other night, so she decided to stop by the guesthouse to check in. Cary was getting hungry, and it was already around five o'clock. She figured there would be leftovers lying around. Then the three of them could watch Eve's show and catch up on how the media was spinning the latest developments in the case.

When Cary arrived, Anna was nowhere in sight. And neither was Vito's car. Cary made herself at home using the spare key her sister kept under the mat at the front door. *No one would ever think to look there*, Cary laughed. She made a note to remind herself to tell Vito and Anna not to leave it outside any longer.

Safely inside, the first thing Cary did was check the fridge. Thankfully, there was still a good amount of tagliatelle left over, so she grabbed a bowl, filled it to the brim, and popped it in the microwave. Cary poured herself a large glass of wine, took the pasta out of the oven when it was ready, and went to the couch to eat. After she had finished the meal, Cary, as always, went in search of sugar. There was one lonely piece of cake left over from the other night. Cary tried to control herself but rationalized that it was probably on the stale side, and if Anna or Vito had wanted it, they would have eaten it by now. So she finished it off and texted Anna: *Where are you?* Cary then promptly fell asleep.

The sound of a key in the door awakened her. Anna and Vito were surprised to find Cary inside. Since Anna had been staying there, Cary had never come over unannounced. She immediately apologized for her thoughtlessness. She saw Vito and Anna give the empty pot and cake stand a disapproving look, so she apologized for that too. They were cool about it. Vito and Anna had actually just come back from the market and were planning on cooking dinner. Cary got the feeling she should leave, but Anna sensed her discomfort and put a stop to it.

"If you're still hungry," Anna said jokingly, "we were about to make dinner. You're more than welcome to stay and join us."

Vito nodded his approval, so Cary acquiesced.

Tonight's feast would include one of Vito's specialties: eggplant parmesan layered with mushrooms, peas, and ricotta cheese. Vito turned on the television and began cooking. Within minutes Cary heard Eve's voice. She heard *Hank's* too. Cary couldn't believe Hank was already doing interviews. Maybe O'Malley had given her no choice. Maybe O'Malley was her latest romantic interest. *What a mess*, Cary bemoaned.

Eve was questioning Hank about her take on the case and what, if any, progress the police had made up to this point. Tonight, Andrew wasn't forgotten. A full-screen collage of all the victims, animal and human, adorned the set. Hank had broken her heart, and now she was on the scene at her old job. *How in the world has my life gotten to such a low point?* Cary wondered. To make matters worse, Hank looked awesome on television, and Eve was being flirtatious with her.

"If all detectives looked like you, we'd have a lot more cases to cover," Eve joked. Hank's face turned an endearing shade of red. Eve was straight as an arrow but loved to tease attractive gay women. *She must have sniffed Hank out*, Cary thought.

The performance wasn't lost on Vito and Anna. They were concerned that Eve might get either O'Malley or Hank to say something they shouldn't on air. But Cary knew Hank was too smart to fall into a trap. She just couldn't stand looking at her; it was too painful. Cary decided Hank would end up being the unintended star of the "Deadly Deranged Driver" case. But Cary couldn't help wondering why they hadn't called *her* back to the show for the story.

They ate dinner at the nook in the kitchen area; it barely held three. But Vito had outdone himself. Cary thought she would be as big as a house by the time she was murdered. She knew the joke was in bad taste, but she only told it to herself. She had to do something to keep her morale up. It was ten o'clock when they finished eating. Anna suggested they take a drive to The Creamery for some ice cream. Cary was game. They piled into Vito's car and headed for Newtown, the place that to Cary represented her two greatest obsessions: sugar and murder.

The trio arrived only a half-hour before closing, so the line was long, but the wait would give them a chance to talk and catch up on the case. Vito told them that he had spoken with Hank and that she had confided in him that the police were in the process of compiling a description of the suspect from eyewitness accounts. Cary knew that meant speaking with Kim, the dead puppy's owner, and possibly Tim Shaw, who may have been with Amanda and Emily the night they were killed. There had never been any indication that Tom Cooper, the little girl's uncle, had caught a glimpse of the man.

When they got to the front of the line, the three of them placed their orders. Vito went with Mocha Madness, and Anna followed suit. Cary feared they were becoming one of those couples who always ordered the same thing. She got a chocolate ice cream soda with her favorite flavor: Lost in Paradise. In addition to her chocolate obsession, Cary was a huge fan of coconut, and this flavor had the best of both. They left feeling satisfied.

* * *

It had been a long drive in the dark just to get some ice cream. But he had to admit that coconut went really well in a chocolate soda. Who knew? These people sure liked to eat. *Not to worry*, he told himself. *If I ever get arrested, I'll lose the weight in prison.* He laughed and drove off into the night.

NINETEEN

They didn't get back to the guesthouse until well after eleven, so Cary decided it made more sense for her to crash on the couch than head to her sister's. She didn't think Anna and Vito would mind. She could have remotely deactivated her sister's alarm with her phone, but Cary feared if she snuck into her sister's house in the middle of the night, Obi would bark loud enough to wake the entire neighborhood.

As Cary lay on the couch, she wondered when the killer might surface again. It was unnerving. She had left Vito's gun at her sister's house in the piano bench. The odds of her finding it were nil as no one had played the piano in the family for years. It was just one of those hopeful investments that parents made for their children before they knew what their interests really were. Cary's nieces and nephew had their share of lessons like most kids, but in time, they abandoned the piano in favor of other interests.

Cary thought she should move the gun tomorrow. God forbid her sister found it. *What a stupid thing to leave it there.* Cary knew guns were supposed to be locked up, but she couldn't find any appropriate place at her sister's to store it. That's one reason she had been carrying it with her during the day, though the primary justification was for protection. But today, Cary hadn't gone anywhere, so she had left it in the bench. She would fix things in the morning.

When Cary had trouble falling asleep, which was most nights these days, she thought about crime-related things. She pondered that she associated almost everything with murder. If someone mentioned a place, say Chicago, it was the student nurse victims; Wichita conjured up the Carr Brothers' killing spree and Dennis Rader; Indianapolis, the murders of seven members of the same family spanning three generations; and Knoxville, Channon Christian and Christopher Newsom. If she met someone from Seattle, the Space Needle didn't come to mind, only Gary Ridgway. What a warped view of the world she had.

And whenever Cary saw a front door left open, she always remembered what happened to the Harvey family in their own home near Richmond, Virginia, on New Year's Day of 2006. The family of four included parents Kathryn, thirty-nine, and Bryan, forty-nine, and their two young daughters Stella, nine, and Ruby, four. Killers Ricky Gray and his nephew Ray Dandridge beat the Harvey family to death with a claw hammer and slit their throats. They picked the Harvey house because the front door was open.

It took the jury a half-hour to sentence Gray to death for the murders of the little girls. Cary guessed they spent twenty-nine of those thirty minutes filling out paperwork. Gray received a life sentence for the deaths of their parents. Cary failed to see the distinction, but it was a moot point as Gray was executed on January 18, 2017. Dandridge pleaded guilty to killing their accomplice, Ashley Baskerville, and her parents a few days later, receiving a life sentence.

Cary was haunted by one particularly heartbreaking aspect of the case. Stella had been at a sleepover the night before and wasn't home when the killers initially entered the home. But when her friend's mother dropped Stella off at the Harvey house that fateful day, her *own* mother made a fatal decision. Having been warned by the killers to stay silent, Kathy, appearing pale and shaky, fended off the other mother and her daughter telling them she wasn't feeling well. Stella, however, stayed in the house with her mother.

Lost opportunities like that seemed to happen all the time during brutal murders. Killers giving their doomed victims false hope if they cooperated, knowing they had no intention of honoring their end of the bargain. Cary couldn't help wondering what would have happened if Kathy had run out of the house with Stella instead; if the victims of the Carr Brothers had fought back; or if Jennifer Hawke-Petit hadn't gotten back in the car with her killer, Steven Hayes, returning to her home after telling a bank teller what was happening there. But Cary knew they were just trying to save each other.

While Cary fell asleep to these morose thoughts, she awoke to something entirely different: the smell of pancakes. *Now that was the way to start the day.* Vito and Anna were becoming surrogate parents; Cary was getting used to it. The three of them ate first, and then Cary waited for her turn to use the bathroom. Vito got priority this morning because he was on his way to help with the composite drawing of the "Deer Killer." He and Hank were going to tag along with the police sketch artist as he questioned Kim, a couple of Tom Cooper's neighbors, and Tim Shaw, who had yet to admit if he had seen anyone suspicious the night the girls were killed. Cary herself hadn't gotten a very good look at the man. With Hank and Vito gone for the day, Cary and Anna would have a chance to talk.

As Cary was brushing her teeth, however, she heard a text alert on her phone. It was from Gene. They wanted her back on the show temporarily to help produce segments on the "Deadly Deranged Driver" case. *About fucking time*, thought Cary. She got a short-lived reprieve, however, because they didn't need her until tomorrow. That gave Cary a chance to ease into the idea of working again. It had been a while. She knew she couldn't miss the show tonight, though. She would have to be up on the latest news. The idea of working in the city again was intimidating. It made Cary realize what a recluse she had become. Well, at least she wouldn't have to dress up. Television was the last bastion of slovenliness known to the professional world.

When Vito got home that night, Anna and Cary already had the news on. In a *Special Report*, Eve was introducing the "Deer Killer's" likeness to the world. Plastered all over the screen was the sketch the police artist had created from the various descriptions he had gleaned that very day. Cary stared at the screen, trying to conjure up what the real-life killer actually looked like.

* * *

As the man ate his dinner, he tried to assess the drawing on the television in front of him. *Not bad*, he said to himself. He surmised that a neighbor or two must have spotted him in the little girl's driveway. They got the nose and chin pretty good. But his hair was longer now, and he planned on growing a goatee in the very near future. Still, it had been a valiant effort on the police's part. And yet, he was much better looking than that. The man contemplated that the handsomest killers he could think of were Cary Stayner, Ted Bundy, and Scott Peterson. But they had nothing on him, and they all got caught. He found it amusing how people somehow expected murderers to be homely or awkward. They were always looking in the wrong direction. *Handsome men like him could never hurt anyone*. Yes, his looks had always worked to his advantage. *People can be so superficial*.

And yet, seeing his likeness on television like that didn't give him the rush many would assume. Fame wasn't now and never had been his goal. He was better than that. He didn't give a rat's ass if anyone knew who he was—quite the opposite. His plan was simply to get away with it all. Taunting the police and a couple of potential future victims just added to the fun. Life could get pretty boring unless you shook things up. And *that's* what he was good at.

* * *

Cary gambled and purchased a monthly train pass, guessing they would need her for at least that long. She decided it would take a while for the "Deer Killer" to be found, arrested, and charged. On the train ride into the city, she tried to go over recent events in her head. She figured the only thing she couldn't share with Gene, Eve, or the rest of the staff was the initial incident she had the misfortune of witnessing that awful June night. Well, that and the fact that she had slept with the lead detective on the case. It seemed like a lifetime ago.

Telling Gene and Eve about her personal involvement in the case would serve no one's interests. Still, she felt funny about withholding information from them. But that was the only way she could play it at the moment. *Oh, what a tangled web we weave when first we practice to deceive.* More advice she should have heeded. It was one of her grandfather's favorite expressions; he used to say it all the time. Cary guessed she should have taken it more seriously.

When Cary arrived at work, she headed straight for the Wafels & Dinges truck, reliably parked out front. Known to New Yorkers as the "waffle truck," it had gotten Cary through many a stressful day on Eve's show. Cary had no idea if she would make it out of the building again before dark, so she took the opportunity to stock up on her favorite speculoos ice cream covered in a hard chocolate shell and then dusted with a sprinkling of powdered sugar. It gave her a rush every time. She would stick it in the freezer in the break room to be consumed as soon as her stress level reached maximum overload.

After enduring the standard security scrutiny afforded to free-lancers who were routinely kicked out the door and brought back at various intervals, Cary made her way to the eighth floor. The first person she bumped into was Brooke, Gene's number two.

"Well, what in God's name are *you* doing here?" she asked.

Cary knew instantly that Gene, as usual, had forgotten to tell Brooke he was bringing her back. It always made for an awkward beginning. But before Cary had the chance to respond, Brooke interrupted.

"Don't tell me. Gene brought you back for the 'Deadly Driver' case," she said.

No shit, Sherlock, Cary said to herself. But out loud, she only mumbled, "Yes."

Things got somewhat better when Cary got to her usual cubicle. She would be sitting one desk down from Eve's office, adjacent to Ellyn Joseph followed by Lee Snow and Todd Zeff. Their job was to make sure the staff got the facts straight. But before she had a chance to settle in, Cary spotted a box of Little Schoolboy cookies. They were from Eve.

Throughout their years at CrimeTV, Eve had routinely brought her boxes of them. She always signed the outside with the following: *To My Spanish Rose, Love EA*. Because Eve did the show from Los Angeles and was rarely in New York, she had asked an intern to write the greeting on a yellow sticky note and attach it to the box. *Fair enough*, thought Cary. Only Eve would take the time to do something like that on Cary's first day back. She was touched by the gesture. But now that Cary thought about it, she couldn't remember how and when Eve started calling her *Spanish Rose*, but it had stuck.

Cary's first task was to read through the stack of articles related to the "Deadly Deranged Driver" case that had been left on her desk. She thought she could have written them herself. After poring over most of them, Cary was pleasantly surprised at the lack of inaccuracies. The most current article was always on top. Today it described the latest development as being the police artist sketch of the suspect. Cary had seen him in person. She just hadn't gotten a very good look. But it sent a chill up her spine just knowing how close she had been to him.

Next, she would have to make her way to the conference room at ten o'clock for the daily staff meeting. But she had plenty of time. As always, Cary had gotten in before almost everyone else, so she had yet to bump into her friends on the show. She started writing the four sets of questions for Eve to ask the show guests. That job was usually assigned to Cary for each case: Prosecutor, Defense Attorney, Cop, and Latest Developments. Maybe she'd ask Hank if they were ever getting back together.

Normally Cary would never have started working on tonight's case until later in the day. She had learned the hard way that stories rarely stuck and that most work done before four o'clock in the afternoon ended up in the trash can—the perils of working in live TV. But she knew *this* story would stick. As Cary tried to think of interesting questions for Eve to ask the guests, she couldn't help remembering two things Eve had done for her during her tenure on the show—two things she would never forget.

The first was donating five hundred dollars to the mother of a nine-year-old girl who had been brutally murdered. The money was being raised so that she would be able to make the pilgrimage to witness the execution of her daughter's killer. Cary had contributed three hundred dollars herself, but Eve was the only one Cary had asked for money who came through. Eve had a big heart. They were soul mates.

The other thing Eve had done for Cary was to devote an entire show to a case she was obsessed with: the January 2007 heinous murders of Channon Christian and her boyfriend Christopher Newsom in Knoxville, Tennessee. Robbed of their lives, ignored by the media, let down by the legal system, the case had troubled Cary since she first heard about it. Cary had been a guest on the show along with Channon's father, Gary, and the usual talking heads. Of all the innocents they had covered over the years, Channon Christian stood out. Held for days, gang-raped and tortured after her boyfriend was also raped, then murdered and set on fire, *she* had really suffered. Of her nearly twenty years covering murder cases, Cary was most proud of the show she and Eve had done on the case. It was, in Cary's opinion, Eve's finest hour, literally.

Cary's thoughts were interrupted by the ringing of a phone. It was Clyde calling from LA. He was Eve's right hand and arm and everything else, and he had always been good to Cary, so it was a nice way to kick off the day.

"Hey, Cary. So glad to have you back. We can really use the help," he began.

"Thanks, Clyde. It's good to be back. I've missed you guys." Cary responded sincerely.

"Gene wants you to start working on the questions for tonight's show. I think the 'Deadly Driver' case is gonna stick," he continued.

"Yeah, I figured as much, so I already got a jump on them," Cary said, trying to sound in command of her duties.

"Fantastic. You're the greatest. I'll see you on the call later," Clyde replied. And then he added, "Did you get the cookies? Eve was asking."

Damn, thought Cary. She had forgotten to email her.

"Yes, please thank her for me and tell her I was just about to—" Cary said, trying to deflect from her negligence. But Clyde cut her off.

"No worries. All good," Clyde assured her. "Just glad to have you back."

That was a line Cary was prepared to hear a lot today. But she knew they all meant it. So stress aside, it *was* good to be back. They were her work family after all, and Eve's show was as close as she was ever going to get again to being back at CrimeTV.

The time was now nearly 9:30 a.m., and Cary knew that meant the onslaught would soon begin. Usually, when they did the show live in the evening, the "in" time wasn't until noon. But the "Deer Killer" case was different. They were breaking into regular programming throughout the day, and the staff needed all the time they could get to come up with creative ways of covering the latest developments. The "Deadly Deranged Driver" case had taken on a life of its own. Cary wondered how much it bothered Todd that he lost the moniker battle this time. Zeff fashioned himself an old school Walter Cronkite-like journalist, but underneath it all, he had a flair for the dramatic, albeit in a *National Enquirer* sort of way.

Cary thought now would be a good time to use the restroom before the meeting was set to begin. There was usually a post-mortem in Gene's office afterward. No one knew who would make the cut each day. It kept the staff in suspense and off guard. As Cary headed to the bathroom, she bumped into Ellyn and Lee coming off the elevator. Unlike Brooke, they weren't surprised to see her. Gene had selective communication skills.

"Oh my God. How are you?" they said in tandem, each giving her a big hug and kiss on the cheek. "We've missed you so much."

Cary had missed them too. The weirdest part about working on Eve's show was the combination of former CrimeTV people with others who had only worked at LNN. Whereas everyone at her old job knew she was gay, she hadn't told any of the people she had met on Eve's show. So Cary never really had a handle on who knew what. Of course, Cary knew she had oversimplified her orientation to the CrimeTV people to begin with, so she guessed everyone was in the dark about her one way or another.

Cary freshened up in the restroom and headed back to her desk to grab a pen, pad of paper, and the articles. She wanted to be prepared for the meeting in case anyone asked her questions. Ellyn, Lee, and

Todd were now at their cubicles as well, getting settled in for what would undoubtedly be a very long day.

"Let's go. Can't be late," Ellyn said to the three of them. "Eve's gonna conference herself in."

While they always had a late-afternoon call with Eve from LA to make sure they were all on the same page about the upcoming show, Eve rarely, if ever, participated in the morning meeting. Brooke was going to oversee it today. Gene was running late, but Brooke assured the staff he would be there momentarily, which always meant *after* the meeting was over. It fell to Todd to get Eve on the phone. When he dialed, it was Clyde who picked up.

"Hey, guys. Eve will be here in a minute," Clyde began. "How's everything going over there?"

"*Fine*," they all said in unison.

Then they heard Eve's voice on the other end. "Is Cary Mackin there?" she asked in a firm yet provocative voice. The hazing had begun. It wasn't bad enough that freelancers had the job security of coal miners, they had to be treated as if they were last-minute invitees to a sixth-grade birthday party too. But Cary had been through all this before, so she took it all in stride. She knew Eve adored her, and the feeling was more than mutual. Cary had stuck her neck out for Eve when she was just getting started in television, and to her credit, Eve never forgot it. They had a special bond as a result. So Cary could put up with a little kidding from her.

"I hope you haven't eaten all those cookies yet," Eve continued.

"Not a one," Cary answered her, embarrassment setting in.

Cary sensed the regular staff, many of whom were her friends and former colleagues, were getting impatient with Eve's whole *welcome back* routine. But there wasn't much Cary could do about it. Brooke, however, was another matter.

"Okay, everyone. Can you hear us all right out there in LA?" Brooke asked, interrupting Eve.

Clyde and Eve said, "Yes," simultaneously.

"Good. So, Todd, give us the latest."

"Well, we have the police artist's sketch of the suspect, which we already aired last night," he began.

"Exactly," Brooke responded. "We need something new for tonight. Who are we having on, Annie?"

Annie Cline was the head of booking. She was based in LA, but Brooke and Gene wanted her in New York for the case. Cary thought Annie had the most stressful job in the world. But even at the worst moments, Cline always managed to pull it off.

"Well, we haven't heard back from any of the players yet, but we're still trying to reach Kimberly Hunter and Tom Cooper. Siobhan Browne and Richard Riordan aren't returning our calls at the moment." *Why in God's name would they?* Cary asked herself rhetorically.

"But we did get Hank Nowak to agree to do the show again this evening and possibly O'Malley if he can work out his schedule."

Eve cut her off. "Let's put Cary on for some color," she suggested.

Damn, thought Cary. It was bad enough that she would have to deal with Hank tonight, but she didn't think Eve would throw her to the wolves on her first day back. But there was nothing she could say to get out of it. Her best attempt was: "I wish I had known I would have worn something more appropriate...."

"That's okay, Cary," Eve continued, "you can just do a phoner."

Truth be told, in all of Cary's now dozen-plus appearances on the show, she had never gone on in person. The one thing Gene and Eve were pretty good about was letting staffers wimp out and do phone interviews instead of being on camera. It took all the pressure off. Doing a phoner meant Cary could skip makeup and spend time prepping up to the last minute. She could even refer to her notes during the show. Eve would likely throw her some softball questions tonight anyway, just to get her warmed up. She'd handle it one way or the other. Cary thought she'd head straight for the freezer as soon as the meeting was over, however, just to be on the safe side.

As Cary took out the bag containing her favorite frozen concoction, she heard Brooke's voice in the background. "I'll go get her," she said. Cary knew that meant she was being summoned to Gene's office. So she rushed back to her desk and put the bag down. Cary thought it would only take a couple of minutes for Gene to go through his *you're back* routine, so she wasn't worried that the ice cream would melt.

"Cary," he proclaimed in his booming Scottish voice. "Glad you're back. We could really use the help."

Cary thought if she had a penny for every time Gene had said those words to her she'd own a private island.

"Glad to be back, Gene. Thanks for thinking of me," Cary replied, and she meant it. That concluded the obligatory meeting, so Cary made her way back to her cubicle to start thinking about what light she could shed on the case tonight. She knew she could have given Eve her bombshell, but she'd more likely take it to her death. As Cary sat down to write more questions for the guests who were already booked, she took out the plastic dish of ice cream and started to throw the bag away. As she did so, something fell out. It was an "ODD JOBS?" card. Cary felt dizzy.

Her first impulse was to run to the bathroom so she could think. Cary locked herself in a stall and thought she was going to have a panic attack. *Breathe, breathe*, she told herself. She didn't know how she was going to make it through the day. The security at WorldWideCommunications was airtight. Or so it seemed. Cary didn't think there was any way a random stranger could have made his way up to the eighth floor undetected. But the card fell out of the bag. What did that tell her? That someone could have slipped it inside at any point after she had purchased the ice cream. Her nickname at her old job had been the *sugar slut*. Cary wondered if it would be her death sentence.

Cary's instincts told her not to breathe a word of it to Gene, Eve, or anyone else on the show. She needed to speak with Vito first and right away. Cary feared her appearance tonight would be a debacle—if she lived that long. She collected herself, had the presence of mind to hold the card by the edges, and headed back to her desk. *Nothing could happen to her here*, she decided. The lunatic was just messing with her. To what end, Cary wasn't sure. *Sick fuck*. Cary sat down, took one look at the "soup" that was supposed to have been her saving grace for the day, and threw it in the garbage. *Money well spent*, she chided herself. Cary wished she was in her sister's yard with Obi and that she had never agreed to come back to work. But she didn't see any way out of this mess—not unless this guy was caught and soon.

Anna and Vito were heading to their favorite lunch place when a joint text came in on their phones. It was from Cary. *I need to talk to you NOW*, it read. The two of them were alarmed, so they pulled over to call her. When her phone rang, Cary picked up immediately.

"Cary, it's us. Are you all right?" Vito asked in a concerned tone.

"Heading downstairs. If I lose you guys, I'll call you right back," Cary answered, trying to sound calm.

The call dropped as soon as she got inside the elevator. But it didn't matter. The square box provided no privacy for a conversation such as this. Cary would have to wait until she got outside to find a spot where she could talk. When she exited the building, it dawned on her that this guy could be *anywhere*. He could be stalking her right now. So she would have to find a place to talk that, while secluded, would afford her the opportunity to get away should he decide to try and corner her. Cary's nerves were shot, and she still had the show to deal with.

As Cary rounded the corner outside the WorldWideCommunications building, a recessed doorway caught her eye. *The perfect spot*, Cary concluded. She parked herself there and took out her phone to call Vito and Anna back. The call went straight to voicemail. *Fuck*, Cary groaned. She wondered how many people had lost their lives to bad cell phone reception. But before she had the chance to try again, her phone rang. Cary picked it up on one ring.

"Vito?" she asked. "Can you hear me?"

"Yeah, what's going on?"

"I bought i...cream from the waf...truck and...get it out of... fr--zer...was a car..." she tried to explain.

"What?" they said in unison. "You're breaking up."

When the call dropped again, Cary decided that a text was more likely to save her life. So, typing frenetically, she wrote: *He left an "ODD JOBS?" card in the bag my ice cream was in. On the eighth floor. WTF.*

Her phone rang instantly. This time it was Anna's voice on the other end.

"Oh my God. Where are you now?" she asked in a frantic tone.

"Outside," Cary replied.

Simultaneously, they said: "Go inside, NOW."

Cary knew they were giving her the right advice, but she still needed a plan to get through the rest of the day. As she made her way carefully out of the doorway, looking for any suspicious face, Vito came back on the line.

"Cary, listen to what I'm telling you. Go inside. Now, where is the card?"

"Don't worry. I have it," Cary answered.

"We'll be there as soon as we can. Traffic shouldn't be too bad this time of day," Vito continued. "Hank's on the show tonight, so we'll all brainstorm once we get there. But don't tell anyone about this, okay?" he said in an insistent tone. "Not until we get there."

"Roger that," Cary answered.

Cary was away from her desk longer than she had expected. She hoped Gene hadn't been looking for her. She had to stay calm. It was nearly lunchtime now, and as they were doing the show live tonight, she knew the staff would be heading en masse to the cafeteria on the tenth floor to get their sustenance for the rest of the day. It was the only break they would have until the show was over tonight. Normally she would have sought out Ellyn and Lee to accompany her, but today, she thought it was better if she went alone. *In and out,* she told herself. Then back to her desk to wait for Vito, Anna, and, eventually, Hank.

How Cary wished she had brought Vito's gun with her today. But it never would have made it past the metal detectors at the front of the building. She knew that. When she got to the tenth floor, there was a line outside the sliding curtains. That meant the cafeteria wasn't open for business yet. They were a little late today as it was already five minutes after twelve. And then Cary heard the familiar sound as the doors opened. It was like the parting of the Red Sea. These people were animals when it came to food.

Cary recognized some of the cafeteria workers. She had grown quite fond of them. Their faces were a small comfort considering what she was up against today, but they somehow gave her strength. The first positive sign of the day turned out to be the menu. They had her favorite dish. It was the grilled flatbread salad. You were allowed to select several toppings at the reasonable price of $5.99 plus tax. The food at the cafeteria was discounted for the employees. It was one of the only benefits freelancers were allowed to partake in. Cary got hers with spinach, goat cheese, peas, and those tiny shrimp. She loved the way Hector added the dressing, closed the container, and shook the greens vigorously before carefully placing the flatbread on top. Mixing a salad that way was the most useful thing Cary had learned from her entire time working there.

The first non-Eve employee she bumped into who had previously worked at CrimeTV was Doug Frist. He gave her a big hello. "Cary, Cary, Cary. How are you?" he bellowed. Doug was a good guy. He worked in operations, which meant he was responsible for keeping the technical stuff up and running. But although Cary was happy to see Doug, she didn't have time for this today. She made an abrupt getaway and headed back down to the eighth floor to wait for Vito and Anna.

* * *

The flatbread wasn't that exciting. The lettuce was a bit wilted and the chicken dry. *What some people are willing to settle for*, he lamented. How easy it had been for him to make his way around the supposedly impenetrable building. Yes, looks could get you far in life. His mother had always instilled that in him. That and clothes make the man. He didn't doubt that several of these would-be journalists thought he was there for a job interview. He certainly looked the part. *Maybe in another life*, he joked.

* * *

When Cary got back to her desk, she was glad to see Ellyn, Lee, and Todd in place. The last thing Cary wanted was to be left alone. Her desk was at the end of an L-shaped corridor, all the way in the corner. How many lonely late nights she had spent there over the past several years. But she never felt vulnerable until now. Cary thought it would take Vito and Anna at least a couple of hours to get there, depending on how much of a nightmare I-95 was today. And they probably had to go home and change before heading in. Either one of them, or both, could be snagged as guests at the eleventh hour, depending on who else Annie had been able to corral for tonight's show. Cary knew if she just stayed put, she'd be all right until they got there. Vito and Anna knew that too.

Cary couldn't help wondering if the killer was still in the building or if he had ever been there. Now that she thought about it, Cary remembered putting the bag with the ice cream in it down on a bench in the lobby while she dug out her driver's license for the security guard. She had stupidly left her stuff on one of the cushioned benches along the wall. He could have slipped the card in then when she wasn't looking. Making his move in the lobby made sense. Anyone could hang around the main entrance pretending to be waiting for someone without showing any identification. *Yes*, Cary told herself, *that's how it must've happened.*

"How are the questions coming?" Ellyn asked, interrupting Cary's thoughts.

"Oh, fine. I'll have them ready in an hour," she responded.

"No worries," Ellyn replied. "You just seemed distracted. Everything okay?"

"Yeah, yeah, all good," Cary said, trying to sound as normal as possible under the circumstances.

Then Todd chimed in, "Great, Cary, 'cause when you're finished with the questions, I could use a little help."

Cary knew that meant he needed her to do some research on the law. Looking up statutes had become the bane of Cary's existence on the show. At CrimeTV, she had been on the executive level. While she occasionally wrote and always proofed the writing of others, she had never had to do any research. It reminded her of law school in a PTSD sort of way.

"Hey, Todd, I've got some time now. What do you need?" asked Lee. Although Todd must have sensed what was going on, he had no choice but to accept Lee's offer. Both Lee and Ellyn knew how phobic

Cary was about the law, so they always gave her a break. Todd, on the other hand, enjoyed pushing them to their limits. He rather liked pushing their buttons too.

Cary gave particular thought to the questions she would write for the cop, knowing that tonight that cop would be Hank. She thought she'd go with the standard, "Bring us up on all the latest, will you, Detective Nowak?" That was always an easy one. But she wasn't sure how much detail she wanted to solicit from her regarding the "Deadly Deranged Driver" case. The only real development had been the sketch, so Cary mused that she could ask Hank more of a generic question, instead of a case-specific one: maybe something along the lines of, "How reliable are composite drawings of suspects?" Or possibly get into crime stats by asking her, "How often do these types of sketches lead to the apprehension and conviction of killers?" *Not bad*, Cary thought. After all, it was her first day back on the job.

As Cary was finishing up, she heard Gene's voice calling to her. "Cary, get your *arse* in here now," he yelled. *Ah, it was good to be back.* When she got to his office, just a short walk from her cubicle, Vito and Anna were waiting inside. *Shit*, Cary said to herself. She hadn't thought it all through, what the staff would make of them showing up unexpectedly. They all knew Anna and Vito from CrimeTV, so maybe she was being a bit paranoid. Her colleagues would just think Gene or Annie or Brooke had called them in to discuss the case. But what Vito planned on telling Gene was what worried her.

"Have a seat, Cary. Vito already filled me in," Gene said uneasily.

"Vito," Cary began.

"Relax, beautiful. Gene wants to help." Vito rarely called Cary *beautiful* as a term of endearment, so she decided he must be really worried about her safety. Cary also couldn't help noticing that both Vito and Anna were in sweats. They wasted no time rescuing her.

"We had to tell him what's been going on. No one wants to freak the staff out, but in fairness to Gene, we had to tell him," Anna added.

"The guy's long gone. I'm sure of it," Gene said. "He probably never made it past the lobby."

"Cary, I need the card," Vito interrupted.

The *card*. Yes, they would need to give the card to the police. "It's right here," she said as she handed it to him.

"Good. So here's what we're gonna do," Vito continued. "You're supposed to go on tonight, right, Cary?"

"Yeah," she answered hesitantly.

"Okay, so, Anna and I will stay with you the whole time. When Hank gets here, I'll turn this over to her. But don't ask her any questions about it. Got that?" Vito warned. "Oh, and building security has been alerted, and they're patrolling the building, discreetly, of course."

"Yeah, I got it," Cary answered.

"He's just messing with you," Vito continued. "We'll get this sick fuck. Don't you worry, Cary. Until then, let's keep what happened here today under wraps. It was only fair to loop Gene in. But so far, aside from the police, we're the only ones who know about the cards, and I'd like to keep it that way."

"Got it," Cary said.

Vito and Anna accompanied Cary back to her desk. She felt like she was in kindergarten and had just had an accident on the floor. The pair received a warm greeting from the staff, especially Ellyn, who knew them best. Gene provided good cover, so from Cary's vantage point, she didn't think anyone thought anything out of the ordinary was going on. But Cary knew better.

As Cary was getting ready for the show, Vito and Anna decided, with Gene's permission, to position themselves in Eve's office. It had a glass wall with blinds that could be tilted to hide the fact that they were watching Cary's every move. Cary couldn't help thinking Gene was being a real mensch about all this, but her life was in danger, so she decided he had no choice. Gene said he wouldn't even tell Brooke. Cary figured that could only mean one thing: he was terrified.

It was nearly six o'clock, and the show call with Eve and the staff would get started around seven. Cary had written all the guest questions she was responsible for and was ready to go on the show as a phoner. She no longer needed to prepare for this case. Cary was *living* it.

Cary was getting hungry as the only thing she had eaten all day was the flatbread for lunch. And she hadn't had any sugar. It was a rare day when late afternoon rolled around and no sweet substance had entered Cary's body. She was getting withdrawal. She decided sugar, as always, would help to alleviate her stress. Cary peeked into Eve's office only to find Vito standing guard while Anna sat at Eve's computer.

"Hey, guys," she began. "I need sugar bad. Wanna go grab something to drink and get a snack? I have about an hour before the call." Cary said.

"Sure," Vito and Anna said together.

"Let's just go to seven if it's okay with you," Cary continued. "I need a hot chocolate and some of those *bouchons*."

They gladly deferred to her wishes. After all, Cary's life was the one at stake at the moment. They could pick the food once she was safe. Bouchon was a French bakery located on the seventh floor of the building. The little cylinder-shaped brownies Cary had referred to were an addiction she had developed from working there. Every time she was called back, they got her through the day. Tonight, she would need a stash.

When they got to the counter, Cary ordered her usual hot chocolate with simple syrup. She often bemoaned the fact the French didn't seem to realize hot chocolate was supposed to be sweet. Cary also requested a bag of a dozen *bouchons* as she always gave some to Lee, the other resident chocoholic on the show. Anna and Vito got the sandwich special prepared on croissants. Vito paid. *God*, Cary thought. *It's awesome how people treated you when they thought you were going to die.*

They got back to Cary's desk at a quarter to seven, just in time for her to get organized for the pre-show conference call. Hopefully, tonight she would be spared and only have to listen in. Cary had learned a long time ago not to interject herself into the conversation. Tonight, she put her phone on speaker so Anna and Vito could hear Eve and Clyde on the other end. One of the bookers always made the rounds right before the call, passing out the night's Guest Sheet. It was a list of the evening's talking heads and how they were supposed to be fonted and so on. As Cary looked it over, she saw that next to her name it said: *in studio. Dear lord*, she lamented. Cary knew she had to say something, but she felt like she was walking into a trap. And so, she waited for just the right moment to do what she had told herself a million times *not* to do: speak on the call, *unsolicited*.

"Um, Cary here. I think there's been a mistake. I was supposed to do a phoner tonight...." she said rather meekly.

It was Annie who answered first. "So sorry. Let me see...." but Eve cut her off.

"*Now*, Cary Mackin," she began, "are you an Ameri-CAN or an Ameri-CAN'T?"

Eve had never used that line on her before. It took Cary aback. She almost laughed, it struck her so funny. But she knew there was only one answer.

"An Ameri-CAN," Cary replied. "*But...*"

Eve had no intention of actually making Cary go on air from the studio tonight. She was just initiating her back into the show. But when she rescinded the offer, Cary was almost afraid Gene had spilled the beans to her.

"*Spanish Rose*," Eve began, "would I do that to you? Just stay by your phone, and I'll get to you often, I promise."

"Thanks, Eve," Cary said. "Appreciate it. If it had been any other time…"

And that concluded the call. Cary could never tell if it had gone well or not. It could be hard to read Eve, especially over the phone. The only definitive thing Eve did that indicated to everyone that she was none too pleased, was when during a commercial break, she turned her back to the staff, albeit on the internal feed, the frame sync. *That* was never a good sign. But Eve was loyal like a dog and Cary loved her. Eve was and always would be her guardian angel. They had a special connection.

The show would go live in about an hour. Cary had just sent Brooke a more recent picture of herself to use as cover during her phoner. As she waited at her desk for the show to begin, the same booker came by distributing a corrected Guest Sheet. It read: *Cary Mackin, Special Correspondent, New York, NY*. An additional note on the side said: **phoner*. Eve had kept her promise. But they had never referred to her as a correspondent before, just a senior producer. Cary thought it was probably a mistake, but she'd let it go. Sometimes life worked in your favor.

Cary started switching stations to see all the guests in their respective studios on the frame syncs. As she did so, Hank appeared on the screen. She looked gorgeous, as usual. Then Anna and Vito came into the shot. *God knows what they were telling her*, Cary thought. The pair had left Cary alone at her desk as they were sure she would be all right without them during the show. Ellyn, Lee, and Todd weren't going to be on tonight, so they would all be just a few feet away. And then Cary had a horrible thought. *What if the killer saw her on television?*

The last thing she wanted to do was say anything that might incite him further. She hoped Eve would behave herself tonight.

It was now ten to nine. Cary decided to make a quick jaunt to the restroom before the show got underway. When she got back to her desk, the phone rang almost immediately. It was Annie from the control room.

"Cary, can you hear me all right?" she asked.

"Yeah. You're coming in loud and clear," Cary answered.

"Great. Just stay on the line. You know the drill," Annie said and hung up the phone.

Cary was getting very nervous for several reasons. She hadn't been on the show in a while, so she wasn't sure how she would sound. In addition, this wasn't any ordinary case. She would have to watch *what* she said and *how* she said it. Third, *he* could be watching. It was all becoming too much for her to handle. As these thoughts were going through her head, she saw the opening graphic come on the screen. The show had begun. Eve went to Cary first to set up the story and started with a background question.

"Cary Mackin. What can you tell us about who may be terrorizing Connecticut?" Eve asked in her usual over-the-top manner. She always called each guest by their full name, even if she went to them multiple times during the show.

"Well, Eve," Cary began, "it's hard to say."

Eve cut her off immediately. That meant she didn't like the way Cary was spinning the story. The next question went to Hank.

"So, Detective Nowak, do you agree it's *hard to say*?" Eve asked. Cary supposed Gene had kept his word and not said anything to Eve about the card and what it meant. Otherwise, Cary was pretty sure Eve would have gone easier on her.

"Hi, Eve. Thanks so much for having me on again," Hank began. *Suck up*, Cary thought.

"Well, I think whoever did this, is doing this, clearly has issues," Hank continued. "But we'll get him. And if you're watching right now, we're asking that you do the right thing and turn yourself in."

If you're watching right now. What the fuck? Cary said to herself. *Are they trying to bait this guy? Bait him at her expense?*

* * *

How thoughtful of her to think of him and reach out. Detectives didn't look like *that* when he was growing up. He had planned on taping the show, but as luck would have it, he arrived home in time to watch it live. Cary Mackin wasn't very good on air tonight. *She seemed nervous*, he thought to himself. It amused him how Eve called each guest by their full name throughout the show no matter how many times they appeared on air: *television for dummies*. The man prided himself on his razor-sharp wit. Maybe he should have gone into stand-up comedy.

TWENTY

When the show was over, Cary was relieved that she would be able to hitch a ride back to Connecticut with Vito and Anna instead of having to take the train home. She'd rather not be in public if she could help it. She hadn't done a very good job tonight. But Eve wouldn't have understood why. *Fuck it,* Cary thought. When all of this was over, she'd get to explain *everything*.

Cary dozed off on the car ride back to Wooster. She was always able to sleep when she felt safe, however infrequently that might be these days. Being in a car with Anna and Vito provided her with that sense of security. When they got back to her sister's, Cary joined Anna and Vito in the guesthouse for a nightcap. For Cary, that meant more hot chocolate. For the adults in the room, it meant brandy. Although Cary had more than her share of alcohol over the past several weeks, she just wasn't a drinker. If this guy wasn't caught soon, however, she feared that could change.

Vito and Anna suggested she stay over, but Cary declined. She thought she'd get a better night's sleep at her sister's, so she gave both of them a hug and kiss, thanked them for everything, and headed to the main house. Vito watched as she made her way up the hill. Then she disappeared from view. When Cary got to the side entrance, which opened into the family room where she usually crashed, a feeling of dread came over her. She checked the app on her phone—*disarmed*. Her sister was truly hopeless. Since her sister's car wasn't in the driveway, Cary figured she must be out. All the more reason these days to set the alarm. Cary knew she was overreacting to everything lately, but the alarm mattered.

As Cary took out her keys to unlock the door, she thought she saw Obi lying near the fireplace. He usually stayed in the mudroom when he was home alone. *What a bad boy, running wild in the house while his mother and aunt weren't there.* No big deal, though; all small details. She needed to relax. Then as Cary went to open the door, she saw that it was already ajar. As she grabbed the handle, something fell to the ground. Cary took out her phone again and turned on the flashlight. An "ODD JOBS?" card lay by the door. When she turned it over, there was a red mark on the back. Cary's face turned white, and she started to shake violently.

Cary panicked. Should she turn on the lights? She wasn't sure. He could be here right now in the house. Cary had always thought she'd be good in a crisis, but at that moment, she knew she had been dead wrong. She had no idea what to do. None. So, using the flashlight on her phone as a guide, Cary made her way to the fireplace. As she bent down, lying before her was her precious Obelus, gasping for breath, covered in blood. The depth of emotion Cary felt at that moment was something she had never experienced before. As tears flooded her face, she cradled him in her arms. Then, panting heavily, Obelus struggled as he tried to reach out to Cary. As he took his final breath, the dog that had meant more to Cary than anything else in the world draped his front paw over her arm as he had done a thousand times before and left this earth.

For a moment, Cary sat there in a ball, frozen, unable to move. It was impossible to take in what had just happened. But fear is man's strongest emotion, and Cary had no idea where the "Deer Killer" was, so like a bolt of lightning, she ran out of the house as fast as she could and didn't stop until she got to the cottage. Vito and Anna awoke to the sound of her pounding on the front door. As Vito unlocked and opened the door, he didn't quite know what to make of the sight in front of him. In all his years on the force and all the time he had spent as a private eye, he had never seen an expression of anguish like the one on Cary's face. And then he noticed the blood.

"For Christ's sake, Cary, come in," he said frantically.

Anna looked like she was going to burst into tears. But over what, she had no idea. Cary hadn't even realized it, but she was still clenching the "ODD JOBS?" card in her hand. Vito gently pried it away from her.

"There's a mark on the back of it," Cary said in a disjointed way.

"It's Obi," she continued, breaking down. "He's dead." And with that, Cary fell to the floor and began to sob. Vito and Anna's eyes welled up with tears. Anna bent down, sat next to Cary, and held her tight. The next thing Vito did was call Hank. When she answered, he simply said, "Hank, it's me. Something terrible has happened. Come quick. We're all at Gayle's...in the cottage."

When Cary heard Vito mention her sister's name, she realized she could be home at any minute and walk in on Obi. Vito picked up on her concern and grabbed his phone to make the next of several calls.

"Gayle?" he asked.

"Yeah, Vito? What's up? It's late," Gayle replied.

"Where are you?" Vito asked.

"Just wrapping up dinner. Heading home."

"Come *now*. But don't go into the house. Come straight to the cottage, okay?" he implored her.

"What happened, Vito? You're scaring me," she said in a worried tone.

"Just get here as soon as you can. We're all in the cottage." And with those words, Vito put down the phone and began to pace. Anna stood up and, with Vito's help, got Cary to her feet. They took her over to the couch, and the three of them sat in silence.

Cary wasn't sure whether Hank or her sister would get there first. She guessed it didn't matter. Her life was in shambles. Destroyed by an anonymous madman she had never even met. The image of Obi lying on the floor, drenched in his own blood, barely able to breathe. Cary couldn't process what was happening.

Just then, they heard a car pull up. It was Hank. When she walked in and saw the three of them on the couch, she knew there was indeed something terribly wrong. The expression on Cary's face was the most heartbreaking thing she had ever seen. And then there was the blood. Vito was the first to stand up and make his way over to Hank.

"Thank God you're here," he said, glancing directly at Cary. Then, holding it by the edges, Vito handed Hank the latest "ODD JOBS?" card with the trace of a bloody paw print on the back. As Hank turned it over, she thought she understood what had happened.

"Cary," she began, holding back tears. "I'm so sorry."

Then, to Vito, in a low tone, Hank asked matter-of-factly, "Where is he?"

"In the main house, the family room," Vito said. "I haven't called it in officially yet. I wanted you here first."

"Let's step outside for a minute, Vito," Hank responded. "I'm gonna grab some gloves from my car for us."

They closed the door behind them as they exited the guesthouse, leaving Anna alone with Cary.

"That's better," Hank said. "Cary doesn't need to hear this."

"Gayle should be here any minute," Vito told Hank. "She doesn't know what happened, only that there's some kind of emergency. I told her to come directly to the guesthouse. Don't want her walking in on the dog," Vito explained.

"Got it," Hank answered him. "When she gets here, Vito, you know we're going to have to cordon off the house as a crime scene."

"Yeah, but let's take it slow. She's going to be devastated," Vito declared.

And with that, they heard the sound of a car driving a little too fast for the narrow dirt path it was traveling on. It was Gayle.

"What's going on?" she asked them, as she got out of the car almost before it had come to a full stop.

"Gayle, I think we better go inside. I'll explain," Vito answered her, taking her arm.

The three of them went back into the guesthouse. As Gayle looked Cary up and down, she let out a scream and ran over to hug her.

"Oh my God, are you okay?" she asked her, bordering on hysteria.

Cary couldn't seem to find the right words to answer, so Hank intervened.

"It's Obi," she began. "He's dead."

Gayle didn't seem to understand what Hank was trying to tell her, but the blood all over her sister spoke volumes.

"What happened?" Gayle continued. "Where is he?"

"We have to call it in," Vito started to explain. "We have every reason to believe the killer we've been tracking is responsible for this."

And then, wearing gloves, Vito held up the card for Gayle, turning it over so she could see the back side with the bloody paw print.

"Oh, no," Gayle began to wail. "Oh, no."

Vito took her in his arms and held her. And then he said, "It's time to call crime scene."

Vito picked up his phone and placed the call. The authorities would be there soon.

"Hank and I will go up to the house to meet them," Vito declared. "Anna, stay here with Gayle and Cary, okay?"

Then, as if awakened from a coma, Cary spoke. "I'm coming with you." Gayle echoed her sentiment. So the five of them made their way up the hill to the house, uncertain of what would come next.

When they got there, the door was wide open and the lights were off. Cary had made a hasty escape. Vito, Hank, and Anna all understood they were about to enter a crime scene, so with that in mind, Vito delicately instructed Cary and Gayle on what to do when they got inside. "Just follow me," he began. "And don't touch anything."

Using a pen, Vito flipped on the light switch. There was blood everywhere, more than he could have imagined. The rug in front of the fireplace was soaked through with it.

And then they spotted Obi.

"Anna, take them outside," Vito pleaded.

"No," Cary interrupted. "I have to do this."

Gayle showed no signs of going anywhere either. The two of them squatted down and touched their beloved Obelus's head, flooding the rug with teardrops on top of the blood.

"Cary, please," Anna implored her.

And then the sound of sirens approaching filled the air. Vito and Hank went outside to greet the police.

"In here," Vito said, directing his comment to Officer Bill Crenshaw, an old friend.

"What the hell's going on?" Bill asked him.

"You'll see," was all Vito was able to say.

As he walked Crenshaw inside, the other officers began processing the area, putting up the all too familiar yellow crime scene tape around the perimeter of the house. When Crenshaw got inside, he was taken aback by all the blood.

"Jesus," he said. "What the hell?"

And then he saw Obelus. Vito showed him the card, and he understood what they were dealing with. Vito knew they'd have to question

Cary. He just wasn't sure if she was up to it yet. But Vito also knew the killer could be close by, and the sooner they started looking, the better. He had the sense that they wouldn't find any prints at the scene. This guy knew what he was doing, and he had a plan. They needed to catch him before he ruined any more lives. Vito was just at a loss as to exactly how.

"Vito," Bill said. "Can I have a moment?"

Vito knew what he was going to ask him.

"Can I speak with the woman who found the dog?"

"Sure, just give me a minute, okay?" Vito said.

Vito made his way over to where Cary, Gayle, and Anna were standing. He pulled Anna aside.

"The police...they need to ask Cary some questions. Do you think she can handle it?" Vito asked her.

"Not sure. Let me go feel her out," Anna answered.

So Anna went over to Cary and touched her gently on the arm.

"Cary, the police, they want to know if you'd be willing to talk to them, clear a couple of things up," Anna asked her.

"Of course," Cary answered in a shaky voice. "I'll do anything to catch that monster. *Anything*."

And so, Cary sat down with Officer Crenshaw, Vito by her side. She told him as precisely as she could recall what had happened.

"When I went to open the door, I had a bad feeling," Cary began. "Then I saw Obi. I thought he was asleep. The room was dark. I was afraid to turn on the lights, so I used my phone."

And then she started gasping for breath.

"Take your time, Cary," Vito tried to comfort her. "It's okay."

He went to get her a glass of water. Seeing Cary like this tore Vito up inside. He had a deep affection for her. She didn't deserve what was happening to her. Cary took a sip of water and regained her composure.

"He couldn't breathe," she continued. "He was covered in blood. I didn't know what to do, so I ran...ran out of the house to Vito and Anna."

Cary told them that she hadn't seen the man. There had been no sign of him. It was all a blur.

"That's good, Cary. That's good. That'll help," Vito told her.

Vito knew the next step was to remove the body. He didn't think Cary would want to witness that scene. But she was already back by Obi's side. Vito needed Anna's help.

"Anna, can you come over here?" he asked her.

"Sure," she replied.

"They're going to want to take Obi," Vito began to explain. "It's up to Cary or, I guess, Gayle if they want to do a necropsy, but under the circumstances, it might not be a bad idea."

"Let's go talk to them," Anna suggested. "This is too much for me."

So Vito and Anna walked over to Gayle and Cary, unsure of the best way to approach the subject.

"Gayle, Cary, it's time for the police..." Anna began. "Vito, can you explain?"

"They need to remove...take Obi...." Vito continued. "They're going to want to do some tests...."

Gayle and Cary looked at each other and understood what Vito was trying to say. It was Gayle who answered first. "Do what you have to, Vito. We want this guy caught." And then she added, "Vito, think we can have Obi's regular veterinarian do it?"

"Sure...of course...whatever you guys want," Vito responded.

And so, the police picked up Obi's lifeless body and placed it on a stretcher. As they covered him with a white sheet that started to turn a light shade of pink, Cary broke down. And then, as they loaded Obelus's tattered corpse into one of the emergency vehicles, Cary came to a stark realization: the *alarm*. She turned to her sister, standing only a few feet away, right next to Vito and Anna, and blurted out: "It's all your fault. What the fuck is wrong with you? I'll never forgive you. *Never*," Cary shouted. And Gayle, with a stunned look on her face, simply stood there in silence.

TWENTY-ONE

Cary spent the night in the cottage, but she didn't get much sleep, only dozing off for a couple of minutes here and there out of sheer exhaustion. Vito and Anna were up most of the night as well. Cary had heard them talking in the early morning hours but hadn't been able to make out what they were saying. Gayle couldn't stay in the house after all that had happened, including the tongue-lashing she had received from her sister. So she decided her best option was to crash at their mother's. Whereas Cary had steered more or less clear of Felicia, lately, Gayle had seen her more regularly. But Gayle wouldn't tell their mother why she had to stay with her, not just yet.

As daylight shone through the windows of the cottage, Cary got a sick feeling. She had been so overwhelmed with emotion over Obi that she failed to grasp the larger import of what had transpired only hours before. The killer had been in her sister's *home*. That meant he was keeping a close eye on her, on *them*. She wondered if he had been stalking Anna and Vito too. The attack on Obi had been vicious, excessively bloody. Cary couldn't bear to think about what he must've gone through being chased around the house by an evil madman. She was broken, shattered. There would be no closure, just never-ending heartache. And all her sister had to do to prevent it was to set the *fucking* alarm like Cary had begged her a million times.

Cary heard Vito and Anna moving about in the bedroom. She got up and made a quick run to the bathroom, then returned to the couch. Cary had slept in her clothes, so there was no need to worry that they would walk in on her. She was getting used to having little to no privacy these days anyway. Cary knew she wouldn't be able to return to her own home anytime soon. She couldn't be alone, especially at night.

Vito was the first to emerge from the bedroom. He appeared exhausted and worried. Cary wasn't sure what the plan was concerning Obi, if the police intended to go public with the information or keep it quiet for the time being. She needed to know. But she'd save it for after breakfast, not that she had any appetite on this awful morning.

"Hey, Cary. You get any sleep?" Vito asked, knowing full well what the answer would be.

"A little," she replied.

"When Anna comes out, why don't we all go get some breakfast? It's important to eat, keep your strength up," Vito continued.

Cary's first instinct was to say no, but she decided she always felt safe around Vito and Anna, and this guy wouldn't dare try anything in broad daylight—not after what he did last night. Any vaguely normal serial killer would lay low after a stunt like that.

When Anna was ready, they all got into Vito's car and headed for the diner. They decided to get takeout and go straight back to the guesthouse. No reason to tempt fate, and they were emotionally and physically drained. Vito went inside to place the order, leaving Cary and Anna behind in a *locked* car. Cary had to remember to get Vito's gun from her sister's house. She had left it there in the usual place when she got called back to work. She wondered if the police had discovered it while they were processing the crime scene. *Shit,* she hoped not. The last thing she wanted was to get Vito in any sort of trouble.

After about fifteen minutes, Vito returned to the car carrying a tray of hot drinks, two coffees and a hot chocolate, as well as a bag containing three egg sandwiches. Cary wasn't sure she could eat, but Vito insisted she at least try. As they drove back to the cottage, a wave of sadness came over Cary. It was all starting to sink in. She didn't think she could go on without Obelus. How he had struggled to overcome his illness. How she had cared for him. He was the sweetest boy. How blessed she had been to have him in her life; how she loved him and he her. How terrified he must have been, not understanding any of what was happening to him. Just wishing she was there to save him. Tears began to stream down Cary's face. If it was the last thing she ever did, she was going to get this guy and make him suffer the way Obi had. Even more, in fact.

When they got home, the three of them went inside to eat. Cary took a bite but couldn't keep anything down. Vito and Anna, however, were starving. They couldn't remember the last time they had eaten. Cary decided that instead of dragging Vito and Anna into the potential gun debacle, she would wait until they left for police headquarters in Stamford and go to the house herself to look for it.

As Cary walked up the hill, she was filled with anxiety. The first thing she took note of was a cop sitting in his car apparently guarding the scene. The police must not have finished processing it yet. *Shit. How am I going to get the gun?* Then squatting in the brush, trying to remain undetected, Cary watched as the cop got out of his car and found a bush to pee in. But Cary knew that wouldn't give her enough time. So she waited for him to return to the car to see what would happen. Fortunately, a nap seemed to be his next priority. Cary figured he must have pulled an all-nighter and was probably going to be relieved soon. She had to make her move.

So Cary ducked underneath the police tape, opened the door carefully, and went inside, careful not to disturb anything. The room had a stench Cary thought might be a combination of the blood and Obi's decomposing body, since enough time had passed before the police had removed it. She was overcome with emotion. Cary needed to make this quick. It was unbearable to be in the same room where he had died. And the cop could wake up at any minute. As she made her way to the piano, Cary prayed the gun would be inside the bench where she had left it. When Cary finally got up the nerve to take a peek, she saw a shiny reflection of light as she opened the top. It was the gun: undisturbed, exactly where she had left it. Cary picked it up, stuck it between her jeans and lower back, and ran out of the house.

As Cary headed back to the cottage, she couldn't help thinking that most people would be shocked the police hadn't discovered the gun—at a crime scene, no less. But Cary knew better. It reminded her of the Entwistle case in Massachusetts. Neil Entwistle was convicted of killing his wife and infant daughter on January 20, 2006. But in searching the family's home the following day, police had overlooked the bodies of his wife Rachel and little Lillian, lying underneath a pile of blankets in the master bedroom. *You just can't make this stuff up*, Cary told herself.

Time would move slowly from now on, Cary thought. No matter what had gone on in her life for the past five years, Obi had been there to either celebrate her victories or comfort her in her defeats. That would no longer be the case. She couldn't help thinking her current situation was the reverse of so many of the murder victims they had covered over the years. She was alive, but her dog was dead. The countless photographs of victims and their pets continued to haunt her. It saddened Cary to picture the loyal animals patiently waiting by the door for their owners to return, not understanding that they never would. Two teachers, Victoria Soto and Rachel D'Avino, killed in the Newtown, Connecticut massacre, and Channon Christian were three who came to mind.

Meredith Emerson was another. The twenty-four-year-old University of Georgia graduate was last seen alive hiking with her dog, Ella, a lab mix, on Blood Mountain of all places, on New Year's Day, 2008. Gary Michael Hilton held Emerson and her dog captive for several days before murdering her. Hilton said he couldn't bring himself to kill Emerson's dog. Cary couldn't help thinking sparing poor Ella was a ploy on the part of Hilton to gain sympathy. A photograph of Meredith, with Ella by her side, proudly displaying the dog's diploma, presumably from obedience school, was heart-wrenching. After their daughter's murder, Emerson's parents adopted Ella and brought her to live with them in Colorado.

Hilton, dubbed the "National Forest Serial Killer," agreed to take police to Emerson's body in order to avoid the death penalty; instead, he got a life sentence with the possibility of parole after thirty years. As part of his plea agreement, Hilton made arrangements for his dog Dandy to be placed in a home. Cary couldn't help but feel sorry for the golden retriever who had the misfortune of being owned by a sociopath. Hilton told investigators how hard Emerson had fought for her life, struggling to overpower him until the bitter end. His version of empathy was to decapitate her.

If not for the police connecting him to a string of other homicides, Hilton would have succeeded in cheating justice. Fortunately, he was tried, convicted, and sentenced to death in Florida for the murder of a forty-six-year-old nurse named Cheryl Dunlap. There was a reason Cary and her colleagues at CrimeTV had nicknamed Florida *the try 'em and fry 'em state*. In Cary's opinion, Florida delivered justice. *What a fucked-up world we live in*, she often lamented.

When she got back to the guesthouse, Cary was surprised to see an unfamiliar car parked outside. Her heart started to race. Then before she knew what to do, a man lowered the driver's side window slightly and nodded, holding up a badge. A gun was visible on the dashboard.

"Ma'am, I'm Jake. I'll be here for a while," the man called out in a cordial yet friendly tone. Cary detected a hint of a southern accent.

Vito was truly a blessing. Cary wasn't sure what strings he had to pull to provide her with her own personal security guard, but she was deeply grateful.

As Cary took a closer look at the car, it appeared to be an undercover vehicle, mostly used to give police the advantage in pulling over wayward drivers. Undercover cop cars were a sore spot for Cary. She had long been conflicted about their use. They had enabled killers like cousins Kenneth Bianchi and Angelo Buono, known as the Hillside Stranglers, to abduct and then rape, torture, and murder their victims. All they had to do was flash a fake police badge and tell their prey that they were undercover detectives in an unmarked car. But for the time being, Cary was cool with one being parked outside her sister's home.

When Cary got inside, there was a note from Anna saying she had run out to do a couple of errands but would return shortly. Cary hadn't noticed it lying there earlier. *I guess she didn't go with Vito after all*, Cary decided. She deduced that whenever Anna and Vito feared she would be left alone, Jake or another willing participant would come to her rescue. Cary thought it wasn't such a bad idea. Knowing Jake was right outside, Cary was able to lie down on the couch and get some badly needed sleep. The familiar sound of a text coming in disrupted her slumber, however. It was from her sister. *Please, Cary, I'm just as devastated as you. Come over. Mom wants to see you. We'll all talk.*

Cary didn't know what to say. She loved her sister more than anything in the world, but her incredible negligence had cost Obi his life. Gayle never listened to her—*never*. It was exasperating. But this, this was a whole other matter. Cary needed time.

I can't. Not yet. Just give me a few days.

Her sister answered back: *K* with a sad emoji face, shedding a tear. Somehow, that just didn't seem adequate under the circumstances, but Cary knew it was her way of trying.

Cary checked the time. It was almost five. She had slept longer than she planned, but there was no sign of Anna yet. After a few minutes, however, she heard a car drive up. Gayle had lent Anna her old F-150 truck that she had won in a raffle several years ago. It only had about a thousand miles on it and had just been repaired. Anna looked out of place sitting in the front seat. She opened the door with her key and entered the cottage carrying a bag of groceries.

"Hey, Cary. I'll be right back. I just have to get the rest of the bags from the truck," she said. "I drove up to that farmer's market near Holton. They have the freshest fruits and veggies. I even bought some honey and jam. We'll have a nice dinner when Vito gets home."

Cary insisted on helping her with the bags, so she got up off the couch, and the two of them went outside. There was no sign of Jake. Cary thought he must've left as soon as he saw Anna drive up. She guessed the sound of the two cars blended together.

They put the groceries away in silence. Anna thought Cary looked awful. She hadn't showered and, from the looks of it, hadn't slept much either. Vito and she would fix her a good meal; hopefully, Cary would eat it. As Anna started the preparations, Cary headed for the couch.

"Sorry, Anna," she began. "Just need to lie down for a minute."

"No worries, peanut," Anna answered gently. "Good idea. I can handle dinner."

And so, Cary dozed off to the sounds and smells of cooking in the background. Not long after, the screech of tires woke her up. Vito was home.

"Something smells good," he said as he walked through the door. Then glancing in Cary's direction, Vito gave her a concerned look.

"I'm okay, Vito," Cary said. "Really, I am." But she knew it was a lie. Vito knew it was a lie too.

"Thanks for sending that guy Jake to watch over me this afternoon," Cary said, trying to show her gratitude.

"Jake?" Vito answered her, confused. "Who the hell is *Jake*?"

"The cop.... I just assumed.... You mean you're not the one who sent him to keep an eye on me?" Cary continued.

"I don't know any Jake. There is no *Jake* on the force," Vito said in an agitated tone.

The three of them exchanged worried looks.

"Oh my God, it was him.... It was *him*," Cary said in a frantic voice.

"Cary. *Think*. What did this guy look like?" Vito questioned her pointedly.

"I don't know. I don't know.... He had sunglasses on...a baseball cap.... I wasn't really paying attention. He didn't even get out of the car. Oh, God," she continued.

"It's okay, it's okay, Cary. He's just playing with you," Vito added. "We'll get him. I swear to God. We'll get him."

And with those words, Vito stepped outside abruptly, returning just minutes later holding another dreaded "ODD JOBS?" card. If they needed any further confirmation of who had been *protecting* Cary that afternoon, Vito held it in his hand.

"Dinner's almost ready," Anna said, interrupting. "Hope you guys are okay with linguini and fresh clams. I went heavy on the garlic, but it's so much better that way," Anna rambled on, not knowing what to say as she tried to lighten the mood.

"Anna, what the fuck? He was here," Cary replied. "Don't you get what that means?"

"I'm sorry, Cary," Anna began. "I...uh..."

"We're *all* in danger, I'm afraid," Vito interjected, trying to diffuse Cary's anger.

Cary wasn't sure she'd be able to eat anything, but she'd try. They gathered around the small kitchen table and loaded their plates with the pasta, a salad Anna had prepared with sliced grilled peaches and buttermilk dressing, and fresh bread and butter purchased at the market. *She really knocked herself out tonight*, Cary thought. As Cary took her first forkful of food, Vito started to bring them up to date on the latest developments in the case.

"You mind if we put on Eve's show?" he asked them.

"All right with me. Cary?" Anna turned to her.

Cary wanted to block the whole thing out. She wanted life to go back to before that night, before the "Deer Killer" had entered their lives. But Cary knew that was impossible. He was still out there, and for Obi's sake and the sake of every other life he had destroyed, she knew she had to help no matter how much it hurt.

So Cary simply answered, "Sure."

O'Malley and Hank were on set tonight with Eve. She had come to New York to cover the case. Eve seemed to be reviewing the same points over and over again, occasionally flashing the perp sketch and victims' photos on the screen. Cary couldn't help thinking Gene was soaking this case for all it was worth. There was new information, of course, Cary was painfully aware of that, but fortunately, the police weren't releasing what happened at her sister's house to the public—at least not yet.

"Cary," Vito said, turning to her. "The tests from Obi...we'll have the results in a couple of days...maybe even tomorrow."

Cary put her head down on the table for a moment. Then she stood up and asked in a quiet tone, "Does anyone want some wine?"

Vito opened a bottle and poured three glasses. Cary finished hers first.

"I don't know what we were thinking," Vito began. "I guess we weren't. But Anna and I should never have left you alone today," he continued, clearly blaming himself for what had happened earlier that afternoon. "Not even for a minute."

"I...uh..." Cary tried answering him, unable to find the right words.

"We'll figure something out. I promise," he assured her.

And with those words, Vito, Anna, and Cary retired for the evening, an uneasiness settling over them.

As she tried to fall asleep later that night, Cary wondered how often they were planning to use her on Eve's show for the case. Cary didn't think she was anywhere near up to returning. She'd deal with it if they contacted her again. Tossing and turning, she tried to picture the man's face she had encountered that afternoon. It was a blank. Now that she thought about it, the badge could have been a fake. And, in retrospect, there was no clear indication the car was a police vehicle, unmarked or not. *Damn*, Cary thought. And she cursed Bianchi and Buono to hell, once again. Meanwhile, her plan was to hole up and stay away from everything and everyone, except Anna and Vito, of course. Cary didn't know what in the world she would do without them.

And then there was the situation with her sister. She would deal with that tomorrow. Cary thought that Gayle must be in a great deal of pain on top of the guilt she was undoubtedly feeling. *Life could get so messed up*, Cary lamented. One misstep and you were done. Cary's mistake was running out that night in search of sugar. How absurd that sounded, yet it was true. One Snickers bar hidden in a drawer might have saved Obi's life. Reporting what she had seen to the police could have prevented all the death and heartache that had taken place since that evening. And being honest with Hank could have saved their relationship. But there was no fixing things now. Cary would have to live with the consequences of her actions.

* * *

The first thing Cary did when she woke up the next day was text her sister. Gayle answered almost immediately: *Took the day off. Can you meet me at Mom's around noon?* Cary wrote back: *Sure.* It was already close to ten; Cary had overslept. But she wondered if you could really oversleep when you had no place to go. Vito and Anna were already gone. Cary guessed they must've snuck out of the cottage quietly so as not to disturb her. Usually a light sleeper, Cary had indulged in a couple of glasses of wine before bed, which is probably why she hadn't heard them leave. *What a lightweight I am*, she thought. *There would be no Jake today to protect her*, Cary joked to herself nervously. Cary figured Vito could only do so much. That's why she needed the gun. Cary had slept with it by her side all night. She would carry it all day too. It freaked her out that she had been that close to him, if only for a brief moment. *Sick fuck.*

The thought of seeing her mother again was daunting. They had been at a standoff. Neither had been willing to make the first move. The only sign of life to Cary that her mother had shown recently was a curt text she sent her after Cary appeared on Eve's show. *My star daughter*, it had read. Cary had forgotten to answer it in all the chaos that had followed. She decided to jump in the shower before she headed over to her mother's. *Why give her another issue to pick on*, Cary thought. As she made her way to the bathroom, her head began to pound. *Hungover from a little wine*, Cary groaned. *I'm pathetic.*

And then she spotted the note. *We got someone to look after you. Name is Cliff. He'll be outside when you wake up. We'll stay until he gets here. You're in good hands.* It was signed V & A.

Cary finished showering and got dressed. She threw on her usual jeans and a tee shirt. Winter was her favorite season, but fall was a close second. When Cary stuck her head out the window to check the weather, there was a briskness in the air. It was refreshing. She thought she'd need her leather jacket too. Cary had considered getting rid of all things leather in her life now that she had become borderline vegan, but she had ultimately decided it would just be a waste. Therefore, she continued to wear her favorite bomber jacket, guilt-inducing though it was.

The last thing Cary did before heading out of the cottage was grab Vito's gun. She checked to make sure the safety was on and that it was fully loaded. Her sister and mother didn't need to know she was carrying it. Cary would keep it sandwiched between her jeans and back as usual.

As Cary walked toward her Jeep, she noticed a rather tall man leaning against the side of his car: a little Fiat convertible he looked like he could barely fit into. The contrast struck Cary as comical, but the situation she found herself in these days was anything but. Before Cary had the chance to go over to him and introduce herself, however, the man approached her, a concerned look on his face.

"Cary?" he began, sticking out his hand to reassure her. "I'm Cliff. Cliff Danjuma. I'm a friend of Anna's *and* Vito's, I guess," he answered, laughing slightly. "I'm here to watch over you for the time being."

"Yes, I know who you are," Cary began. "They left me a note. So nice to meet you."

"Reverse traffic helps," Cliff continued, explaining his presence. "I got here as soon as I could after my wake-up call from Anna this morning," he said with a smile.

Cary was warming up to Cliff. He had a kind yet strong face that matched his muscular body. The man before her was well upwards of six feet tall, clearly hit the gym regularly, and had a British accent. He appeared to be of mixed race. Cary sensed there was a story there but decided to steer clear of any drama at least until she spoke to Anna and Vito.

"I was actually on my way to see my sister," Cary began. "She's been staying at my mother's since...well since her dog was killed. I don't know if they filled you in...." Cary said uncertainly.

"Just briefly," Cliff answered. "But Anna gave me the big picture. I'm so sorry," he said with genuine empathy.

"Why don't you get into your Jeep, and I'll follow you," Cliff suggested.

"Sure. That'll be nice.... I mean...it's a comfort to have someone like you around," Cary said somewhat awkwardly.

It was about a twenty-minute drive from her sister's house to her mother's condo. It felt good to be out, to be heading somewhere, even if it was to see her mother. And so, with Cliff in her rearview mirror, Cary put her Jeep in gear and stepped on the accelerator. She was still angry with her sister, but she didn't need a war right now, with anyone. She had no idea how she would feel when she saw her, however. The drive through some of Wooster's most beautiful and winding roads was relaxing. It really was a lovely town, Cary decided, when no serial killer was terrorizing its inhabitants.

When she got to her mother's complex, Cary pulled into her usual parking space, right next to her sister's car. Cliff stayed in his vehicle, discreetly watching her. As Cary got out of her Jeep, a text popped up on her phone. It was from Anna: *Did you see our note? We sent someone to look after you. Name is Cliff. He's right outside.* The timestamp read 8:11 a.m. *Damn cell phones*, groaned Cary. *Good thing I saw the note.* She texted Anna back, *Sorry just saw this. We're good.*

This was going to be a tough afternoon, Cary concluded, but at times like these, people needed their family, even a dysfunctional one like hers. Cary had a key to her mother's but decided to ring the doorbell instead. Somehow it seemed a bit presumptuous for her to just barge in like she owned the place. After about a minute, her sister came to the door. She looked sickly, drained.

"Cary, Mom's in the living room. Let's go outside for a minute," she said.

Cary didn't know how to interact with her or what to say. It was the most awkward interaction she had ever had with her twin.

"I just wanted to say," Gayle began, "I never meant for any of this to happen. I can't live with myself.... I'm—" But Cary interrupted her.

"I'm so sorry. None of this is your fault. I mean...I don't know. I should never have said any of those things. I just...I don't think I can live without him." And Cary broke down in tears.

"Cary, before we go back inside, I need to tell you something," Gayle continued. "Mom doesn't know what happened to Obi. She just knows he's dea...I mean, he's not with us anymore. I don't want to frighten her. I don't see the point."

Cary agreed.

"There's one more thing, Cary," her sister went on. "I was just wondering when I could return to the house. Just to get a few things. I don't think I can stay there, not just yet. Not after what happened." And her voice began to shake.

"I'll see what Vito thinks," Cary answered. "They're still running some tests too. On Obi, processing the scene.... I'll talk to him tonight about everything."

"Thanks, Cary. We need to get each other through this. And we need to get this monster caught—soon."

And with that, Gayle grabbed Cary and hugged her, holding on tight. She was a mess. They proceeded to open the door and go inside. As they did so, their mother's voice could be heard in the background yelling at the television. For seventy-eight, their mother was in good shape and didn't exactly keep her opinions to herself, even if the television couldn't answer her.

"Mom, Cary's here," Gayle began.

Her mother looked up, assessing the situation. The first thing she said to Cary was: "Is *that* what you've been wearing to work?" The disdain on her face was evident. Granted, Cary told herself, her mother didn't know *how* Obi died, but she knew that he *had* died. Yet all she could think about was how her daughter was dressed. Cary almost walked out, but Gayle intervened.

"Cary hasn't been working," Gayle began. "Not since—"

Their mother cut her off. "That dog was a nuisance. For heaven's sake, you didn't give *birth* to him. He was something that your sister bought, and there's nothing to be upset about. It's a relief. Nobody lives with an animal that size in their own home. He belonged in a barn...." she went on and on, only making matters worse.

Cary thought if there was ever a case for justifiable homicide, this was it. She grabbed her car keys, held back tears, and ran out of the condo. At that moment, Cary didn't care if she ever saw her mother again. As Cary got into her Jeep, Gayle called out to her. "Cary, please. Don't go. She didn't mean anything.... She doesn't know what happened."

"I can't be around her. Not now. She knows he's *gone*, isn't that enough? What the fuck is wrong with her? It's amazing we can walk and talk being raised by an egomaniac like that," Cary declared.

"She's a nightmare. I'm not arguing. Just hold on a minute. I'll get my coat, and we can go grab lunch. I need to get out of here anyway," her sister told her.

And so, the two of them drove to Frankie's, a lovely little restaurant on the water, to try to chill out and assess where their lives were at the moment and where they were heading. Cliff followed circumspectly. Cary saw no reason to alarm her sister, and Cliff seemed like-minded. Lunch turned out to be a welcome distraction under the circumstances. When Cary dropped her sister back off at their mother's, they kissed goodbye, and Cary said she would let her know what Vito thought. Gayle left Cary with these words: "Be *careful*."

"You too," she replied.

By the time she got back to the cottage, Cary was emotionally drained. Every time she gave in and agreed to see their mother, this was how it ended. There was no sign of Vito and Anna yet, so Cary decided to pour herself a large glass of wine and take a nap before they returned. She thought maybe tonight they should get takeout. The two of them had been doting on Cary since Obi had died. She was feeling a little guilty about it. Tonight, Cary thought dinner should be on her. She'd text them and see what they were in the mood for. But first, Cary thought she should check on Cliff and thank him. She found him outside in the driver's seat of his car, checking his phone.

"Thanks so much for everything," Cary began. "Actually, I'm about to order dinner for all of us...Anna...Vito.... Wanna stick around?"

"Well, 1 guess.... If it's not too much trouble, sure," Cliff replied, somewhat hesitantly. "It'll be good to catch up, and they can bring me up to speed on everything regarding this maniac."

"Great," Cary answered. "See you in a bit." And she went back inside.

Anna and Vito were up for anything. *You decide*, they texted back. Cary grabbed her laptop and started searching for a place that delivered. She was wiped and had been drinking, so she didn't want to venture out again with Cliff no doubt on her tail. He had done enough for one day. Cary settled on Antonio's, a family-favorite Italian landmark in the area. She ordered several pasta dishes, their world-famous gorgonzola salad, and plenty of breadsticks. Cary thought that maybe after dinner, they could go out for ice cream. The Creamery closed in a couple of weeks, and she always got a winter stash to tide her over until the spring.

The sound of the doorbell woke Cary out of a deep sleep, the disorienting kind of late afternoon nap that always made you feel groggy. It was the delivery boy. Cary straightened herself out and answered the door, gun tucked behind her back.

"What do I owe you?" she asked him.

Cary rarely carried cash but fortunately had just enough on her tonight to pay him, including a decent tip. She had forgotten to give the restaurant her credit card over the phone. Cary put the food down on the kitchen counter and set the table for the three, rather, four of them. Vito and Anna should be home soon. Cary was hungrier than she had realized, so she started picking at one of the dishes. But just as she went to take another forkful, she heard the sound of Vito's car. *Perfect*, Cary thought. It would be good to see them after what her mother had put her through this afternoon.

Vito gave her a hug and kiss on the cheek and put down his keys and wallet. Anna did the same. "What a thoughtful thing to do," she said to Cary. "We're starving."

They took their seats at the table and began to eat. Cary knew she looked terrible. But they were too worried about her to say anything. She was sure Vito and Anna didn't want her to think they had noticed. After a minute, Cary addressed the pair.

"Is it okay with you guys if we skip Eve tonight?" she asked. They nodded in agreement.

"Oh my God, I almost forgot. I asked Cliff to join us. He must still be outside.... Did you guys see him?" Cary asked.

Vito and Anna exchanged looks. Cary wasn't sure what to make of it.

Then Anna simply answered: "Um...turns out he had to head back to the city for something, but don't worry, peanut. He'll be here to watch out for you during the day.... I mean, when you aren't with us."

"No worries," Cary began, curiosity getting the better of her. "How did you guys meet anyway?"

"I'm gonna step outside for a minute," Vito said, as his phone began to vibrate. "Have to take this call."

"Well, that was good timing," Anna continued.

"Meaning?" Cary asked suspiciously.

"Nothing. It's nothing, Cary. I met Cliff at a trial in LA—that music producer who killed his ex-wife. Cliff does freelance security. He's...he's a bodyguard, I guess you could say. Anyway, it went on for six months, I think. The trial, I mean. Vito and I were sort of on a break.... It got complicated. We...uh...Cliff and me...we...um...got involved, but it ended as soon as the case wrapped up. I'm not sure how Vito took it," Anna continued to explain.

"That's okay, I get it," Cary said in a comforting tone. "Vito's not holding it against you now, is he? I mean he's not jealous of Cliff?"

"No, no. It's just we needed his help with all that's been going on.... Cliff's help...and I'm not entirely convinced Vito's okay with it, but it is what it is," Anna answered Cary, as if that settled the matter.

As Cary was about to dig deeper, Vito came back into the cottage, a concerned look on his face.

"Cary," Vito began. "The results of the necropsy came back."

Cary froze. She wasn't ready to hear this. Anna took her hand.

"Why don't you sit down?" he began. "Um, it looks like the cause of death was severe blood loss. No surprise there. But that's not all...."

"Go on," Cary said. "I need to know. I need to know *everything*."

"Well, it seems...I mean," he began, trying to find the right words. "It appears his skull was fractured, and Obi had several broken bones. In fact, all four of his legs were—"

Cary stood up and started pacing around the room.

"Enough," she cried out. "When is this nightmare going to end?" Vito and Anna had no answer.

As Cary poured herself a large glass of wine, she remembered that she had promised her sister that she would ask Vito about the state of her house and when she might return to get her things. He told her that the police had finished processing the crime scene, but it hadn't been cleaned up yet. That would be taken care of in the next couple of days. The police had found several sets of prints, so the authorities were hoping, if they were willing, to fingerprint Cary, her sister, their mother, and anyone else who regularly went to the house. That way, they would be able to match prints to known persons and see if there were any unidentified prints left over.

"Can we leave my mother out of this for the time being?" Cary asked. "Let's see if all the prints can be identified. If not, I guess we'll have no choice but to drag her into this mess. But right now, she's in the dark."

Vito seemed to think that was a reasonable approach, so he acquiesced. Then he had an idea.

"Cary, give me your glass."

He took a napkin from the table and carefully picked it up.

"What has your sister touched of yours recently?" Vito asked her.

"Ah, let me think. She was in my car, so the passenger side door handle," Cary answered, understanding what Vito was up to.

"And your mother?" Vito continued. "Can you get me something from her?"

"Sure. I'll have Gayle do it. My mother and I..." Cary began.

Vito understood. He wanted to spare them the hassle of going down to police headquarters so he thought he could lift their prints off these surfaces and have them run against the ones found at the scene. Vito knew getting prints this way wasn't as good as obtaining them from the person directly, but he thought this might work. If it failed and he was wrong, they would have to make the trip down to Stamford.

They were all too tired to make the drive to Newtown for ice cream, so Cary went to bed sugar-deprived. She opted for more wine instead. As she lay there trying to fall asleep, Cary tried not to picture the room where Obi had died. Cary thought Vito's estimate of several days for the clean-up was on the low side. They would probably have to discard all the rugs and repaint the walls. Cary didn't think she could ever bear to be in her sister's house again. It always astounded her when people sought to buy what crime aficionados referred to as "murder houses." *People were so demented*, Cary mused. *Human beings could learn a thing or two from animals.*

Cary slept well due to her newfound consumption of alcohol. The first thing she did when she got up was hide the gun under the couch before Vito or Anna saw it. Vito seemed to have forgotten all about it. In all fairness, he was distracted these days. Since Obi had been killed, Vito had sort of lost track of things. While Cary was staying at her sister's house, she had told Vito the gun was locked in a safe location during the day. Apparently, since Cary had been crashing at the guesthouse again, he hadn't thought about where she was stashing the gun. She hoped he wouldn't think to ask.

After Vito and Anna left for the day, Cary decided to make herself some breakfast and then call her sister. The call went straight to voicemail. "Gayle, call me," is all Cary said. The phone rang within minutes. "Cary, what's up? I'm late for work."

Cary didn't realize Gayle had gone back to work already. She hadn't really thought about it.

"Oh, sorry. Can you talk for a second?" Cary asked her.

"Yeah, sure. But make it quick."

"I spoke to Vito. He thinks the house will be ready in a few days. And we may have to go to Stamford to get printed, but I'll let you know. Vito thinks he may have come up with another way," Cary added.

"Okay. Thanks for letting me know. Gotta go. Talk to you later...." Gayle replied as she was about to hang up the phone.

"No, wait," Cary said hesitantly. "There's something else. The results from the necropsy...it's bad.... I...uh—" Cary continued but Gayle interrupted her.

"I know. Vito just called me. It's all too much...the thought.... We'll talk later." And the phone went dead.

Cary felt lost. Then she had a morbid thought: *the dog park*. She finished getting ready, collected the gun from under the couch, and headed to her Jeep. She spotted the Fiat with Cliff reliably sitting in the front seat eating a donut. *There's a reason there are stereotypes....* Cary had to laugh. She greeted him warmly and explained where she was heading. Cary would spend the better part of the day in the place Obi loved the most. Cary didn't care if it was crazy or weird or fucked up. She had to do something to make the pain go away. Anything was worth a try.

As Cary drove through Wooster on her way to the park, it dawned on her that Vito hadn't mentioned Obi's remains. What if they had been discarded? It was awful to think about what was left of her precious boy. Cary started to panic. *Oh my God* was all she could think. So Cary texted Vito immediately. *Where is Obi?* He answered: *Don't worry. We have him.* Relief came over her. She would get the details tonight.

As she pulled into the parking lot of the dog park, Cary was overcome with emotion. She had picked up a sandwich and hot chocolate on the way, Cliff watching her every move. Cary had also brought a book with her in case she was able to focus. She wasn't sure how long she'd be there, so she had wanted to be prepared. And, of course, there was the gun, securely placed as always by her back. With her jacket on, she was sure no one would notice, not even Cliff.

Cary was grateful that she didn't recognize any of the regulars among the people there today. She just wanted to be left alone to mourn. Cliff followed behind on foot, giving Cary her space. As Cary made her way to her and Obi's favorite bench, her eyes welled up with tears. Nothing good lasted in this world. But *evil*, evil was hard to get rid of. In spite of Cliff and the gun, Cary felt exposed in an open setting like this. But she didn't care anymore. *Bring it on, madman. Let's see who wins this time.* After a little while, Cary began to get hungry, so she took out her sandwich and began to eat. It was the first time she could taste food since Obi had died. She felt close to him here.

When she got up to throw her garbage away, Cary heard a familiar voice. It was Hank.

"Cary?" she said. "Oh my God. How are you?"

Cary wanted to die. The last thing she needed was to bump into Hank under these circumstances. God knows what she would make of Cary hanging out in the park by herself. But before Cary could figure out an exit strategy, Barry came running over to her. It was the first interaction she had had with a dog since Obi had been killed. She didn't know how to react.

"Barry, come here. Bad boy," reprimanded Hank.

"No, it's okay, really. I don't mind," Cary said.

And with that, Cary returned the greeting, petting Barry on the head and accepting his paw with grace. Tears began to stream down her face.

"I'm so very sorry," Hank said with sadness. "We'll get him, I promise."

And then Hank had an idea. "Why don't you come back to the house with me? I have the day off. We can catch up."

Cary wasn't sure what she was getting herself into, but she accepted the invitation. But first, she had to get rid of Cliff.

"Just give me a minute," Cary said to Hank. "There's something I need to take care of. I'll be back in a sec."

Cary managed to approach Cliff at an angle where Hank couldn't see them and made her case.

"Hey, Cliff. I'm going to head over to this woman's house. She's a detective. I'll be fine. Why don't you take the rest of the day off? Check with Vito if you want. Her name is Hank."

"I don't know, Cary. Vito was very insistent that I not leave you alone," Cliff continued. "Anna too."

"I'm telling you it's okay. I'll text them right now. You'll see," Cary said.

It only took a minute for Anna and Vito to respond. *Tell Cliff he's a free man...just for today*, the text read. Cary turned her phone to Cliff, somewhat satisfied, so he could read it.

"Got it," Cliff responded. "But if you need anything, you just call me, okay?" And with that, he gave her a card with his number on it.

"Sure thing," Cary answered. "You've been great, Cliff. You really have."

Cary doubted things would end the way they had in the past once they got to Hank's place. But she was too distraught to even think about romance. Cary was broken, just like Obi. She didn't think she would ever smile or laugh again. What a morose partner she would make.

Cary followed Hank and Barry back to her house. She was having trouble getting her bearings. She was a mess. When Cary pulled up behind Hank's car, she instinctively fixed her hair. *Habit*, Cary thought, even if it was for no purpose. It felt odd being in Hank's house again after all that had happened between them. She didn't know where to put herself. Hank let Barry out the rear door and then made her way over to Cary.

"Eve ditched the story," Hank began. "No new developments, so they put it on hold for the time being. Too bad. We were hoping the publicity might help smoke this guy out."

So that's why Cary hadn't heard from Gene. Not that she would have gone on the show again with things the way they were, but in a weird way, it made her feel a little better. And he didn't deserve the attention.

"Cary," Hank continued, "the way things ended between us. I want you to know—"

"It's okay, Hank. I get it, I do. There's really nothing to say," Cary replied.

"What you said that night. You aren't alone," Hank tried to explain.

Cary wasn't sure what Hank was getting at, but she wasn't sure she even cared. She felt dead inside. Nothing and no one could fix her life. She would just have to run out the clock like so many broken people do, the ones who don't have the nerve to take matters into their own hands.

"I'm not sure what you're getting at," is all Cary said in response.

"I...I...um...what I'm trying to say," Hank continued, "is the feelings weren't one-sided. You meant a lot to me."

Cary was taken aback. Although she had tried to convince herself that it was more than just physical for Hank, part of her wouldn't allow herself to believe it because if she was wrong, it would hurt all the more. And now this confession. Cary was at a loss.

"I don't know what to say," Cary answered uncertainly.

And with that, Hank reached over and stroked Cary's hair, touched the back of her neck, and gently kissed her on the mouth with her usual expertise. Normally, Cary would have been all in, but at the moment, she didn't know how much more she could handle. Her emotions were raw, and she felt unstable. Before Cary had the chance to pull away, however, Hank's hands made their way down her back. But this time, they came to a roadblock: Vito's gun.

"Oh my God, Cary. What the hell are you thinking carrying this around with you?" Hank admonished her. And then, taking the gun from Cary, she asked, "Where did you get this thing?"

Cary was afraid to tell Hank the truth, but lying before had ruined their relationship, so she saw no reason to repeat the mistake. Vito didn't even know she was carrying it concealed, though, so how could she tell Hank? But Cary knew she had no choice. She'd fess up now and tell Vito tomorrow and then suffer the repercussions from both of them.

"Vito lent it to me so I could protect myself, God forbid, if I needed to, under the circumstances," Cary began to explain. "He showed me how to use it at the shooting range. Vito seems to think I'm a natural."

"A natural what?" Hank responded. *"Ass?"*

Hank had never spoken like that to her before. *I guess she does have feelings for me after all*, Cary pondered.

"I'm sorry," Hank began to apologize. "It's just that you could blow your own foot off with that thing, maybe worse."

Cary's nerves were fried. She needed to have that gun at her side, or she didn't know what she would do. *Why did Hank have to make an issue out of it?* If anyone knew how useless the police were in situations like this, it had to be her. Maybe it was time to have it out with Hank in full. Tell her *everything*. And then if she regretted giving Cary a second chance, so be it.

"Do you know why I chose to cover crime as a journalist instead of something else like politics, entertainment, or whatever?" Cary asked Hank, as she tried to find the right words.

"I don't know. I just assumed—" Hank began, answering her.

"You just assumed what?" Cary asked her. *"What?"* Cary repeated, raising her voice.

"Cary, calm down. What the hell is going on?" Hank responded, confused.

"Nothing, nothing," Cary answered. "Just, why do you think I'm obsessed with victims, with what they go through, have gone through?" Cary continued, afraid of getting to the truth.

"I don't know.... I suppose because you're an empathetic person who—" Hank began.

"Because I think I'm going to be one of them," Cary blurted out.

Hank was stunned. "I'm not sure I know what you're getting at," she answered.

"Since as far back as I can remember," Cary began to explain, "I thought I was...was...going to be murdered." She thought it sounded bizarre when she said it out loud, and Cary could see Hank wasn't exactly getting it.

"Murdered?" she responded. "Why, Cary, that's crazy. Where would you ever get an idea like that?"

"Why does anyone feel anything? Think anything?" Cary replied. "It just *is*."

Cary thought Hank must think she's crazy, and maybe she was. But this one single thought had dictated her entire life. For a brief moment, Cary considered sharing the issues she had with her parents with Hank, her father's beatings, her mother's relentless criticism, but something stopped her. That something was the knowledge that neither had anything to do with her fear. It just existed in her head; it always had, and it always would, and Cary knew searching for a rational explanation was pointless.

"Well, carrying a gun around like that might become a self-fulfilling prophecy," Hank said, somewhat comically. They both let out a nervous laugh. And then Hank took Cary's hand and led her into the bedroom. Cary was more ready than she had thought to pick up where they had left off.

* * *

They stayed in bed until almost six o'clock. What a decadent and strange afternoon it had been. She wasn't sure what Hank made of her confession, but Cary thought she might take pillow talk to a unique level. There was one more thing she needed to explain.

"Hank," she began, "I'm not sure if you understood what I was trying to get at before."

Hank put her finger on Cary's lips and said, "Shssh."

Cary sat up. "The main reason I didn't go to the cops or even tell you about the deer incident was because…"

Then Hank interrupted her, "…was because of your *premonition*," she said. "But Cary," Hank continued, "people feel all sorts of things. Just because someone thinks they're going to die in a plane crash or fall down a flight of stairs or, yes, even be murdered doesn't mean that that's what's going to happen to them. For every person who has a fear of flying…" Cary knew what Hank was going to say next.

So Hank got it, after all, thought Cary.

* * *

It was now nearly eight o'clock at night. Cary had to get back to the cottage. Vito and Anna would be worried about her. Hank insisted on following Cary home. She also tried to dissuade Cary from carrying the gun during the day and from sleeping with it at night but didn't succeed. When they pulled up to her sister's house, Cary left her car slightly down the road from the guesthouse. Hank pulled up behind her and got out of her car.

"I'm worried about you, Cary," she said. "Please don't go and do anything stupid."

"*Never*," Cary assured her, smiling slightly.

And then Hank said the words Cary never thought she'd hear: "*I love you.*"

Cary's heart was heavy, and her eyes welled up with tears. The past few weeks had been filled with so many emotions. There was Obelus, and now this. Cary leaned into Hank and began to sob. Hank held her for a moment and said, "It'll be all right, Cary, I promise. I'm so sorry… sorry about everything."

As Cary fell asleep on the couch that night, Vito's gun lay beside her in its usual place. They would agree to disagree, Cary decided, at least until the "Deer Killer" was caught. And she dozed off for the first time without the aid of alcohol since Obi had died.

* * *

What a long day it had been. The dog park of all places. He hadn't seen that one coming. *Victims loved to throw themselves pity parties*, he decided. What a stroke of luck that the girlfriend had shown up. He knew he hadn't had to follow them all day and well into the night, but he deserved to be rewarded for all his hard work. Such a lovely couple they made. What *normal* man would turn a blind eye to that?

Not that he hadn't had his share of beautiful women over the years. Dating had always come easy to him. More often than not, the women were even the aggressors, unaware of how lucky they were to still be alive. Well, nearly all of them. Letting someone live, few understood the self-control that took and the power that gave someone. *What a rush*.

TWENTY-TWO

The first thing Cary did when she woke up the following morning was check her phone. No word from Hank. *Well, she must be busy, probably already at work*, Cary contemplated. It took about a minute before Cary realized she didn't have a headache. *No more alcohol for me*, she assured herself. Sugar would again be her drug of choice.

Cary hadn't had much of a dinner last night, so she headed for the kitchen in search of something to eat. There was no sign of Vito and Anna, not even a note this morning, so Cary figured she would have the day to herself. After opening a couple of cabinets, she found a box of Anna's favorite fruit granola. Cary grabbed a bowl, filled it just high enough to allow room for the almond milk she would pilfer from Anna, and went to the kitchen table to eat her breakfast.

As Cary glanced through her phone, catching up on all the latest, a text came in. It was from Vito. *We'll be home around three. Hope to have the print results for you. Tell Gayle.* Cary decided Cliff was going to have another short day. Cary's stomach was in knots. For a few brief moments, she had almost felt relaxed but not anymore. Today would be as difficult as all the rest.

Cary wasn't sure who she should text first, her sister or Hank. She opted for Gayle. *Can you come by around three? Vito thinks he'll have *the prints back by then*, was all Cary wrote. She wanted to reach out to Hank but held back. It was still early; there was a chance Hank would get in touch with her. Cary weakened her hand by being the first. She wasn't sure how to pass the time until mid-afternoon when Vito and Anna would return. Then Cary had an idea: *the gun range.*

Cary wasn't sure what would happen if she just showed up there unannounced, without Vito, Cliff in tow. They might let her in, but she didn't want to take the chance. So Cary decided to play it safe and text Vito for permission. She was pleasantly surprised by his response: *Good thinking, Cary. I'll give them a heads up.* Cary got dressed, grabbed Vito's gun, locked the front door, and headed for the range.

"Hey, Cliff," Cary called out. "Feel like following me to the shooting range in New Canaan?"

"Sure, why not?" Cliff replied, a reassuring smile on his face.

Cary thought the drive alone would do her good.

When Cary arrived, she gave the guard her name, and after looking her up and down, he let her through, pointing to the appropriate parking area to leave her Jeep. Cliff parked his Fiat beside it. Cary felt anxious. For all her shenanigans carrying Vito's gun around with her, Cary realized she hadn't fired it in a while. *Slow and steady*, she told herself. Cary took the spare ammo out of her trunk and proceeded to the firing line. The range was more or less deserted this morning. It was nearly lunchtime, so Cary figured people were either taking a break or hadn't arrived yet. It was an upscale kind of place. Cliff, as always, gave Cary her space while never letting her out of his sight.

Cary carefully put on the required goggles and earpiece and took out Vito's gun. She opened it to make sure it was fully loaded. Then she waited for the paper outline of a man to appear before her. As Cary began firing, she felt the usual rush holding a gun gave her. She waited until the weapon was empty to assess her performance: nothing but bullseyes, awesome. Good luck to this guy if he ever crossed her path. Even Cliff looked impressed.

Cary felt better on the drive back home. She hadn't realized how much shooting would boost her confidence. She needed to be able to protect herself. She had done well. When Cary got back to the cottage, she checked her phone. No messages. It was almost two-thirty, not enough time for a shower. She would just rest before Vito, Anna, and, hopefully, her sister arrived.

The sound of the front door being unlocked awakened Cary. It was Vito and Anna, right on time. She started up from the couch.

"Hey, Cary," Vito began. "How'd it go at the range today?"

"Good," Cary answered him. "I hit the mark every time."

"Wow, impressive," chimed in Anna. Cary knew Anna wasn't a big fan of guns and was only being polite, considering the current circumstances. *Fuck it.*

"Is Gayle coming?" Vito inquired.

"Not sure. I think so," Cary replied.

"Mind sending her another text, Cary?" he asked her. "I think she should be here."

Cary texted her sister again, reminding her that Vito and Anna had something to share with them at the cottage and *now*. But before the text went through, they heard the sound of Gayle's car approaching.

"Great," said Vito.

As Gayle made her way inside, Vito gave her a hug and encouraged her to sit on the couch next to Cary. She obliged.

"So," he began, "this probably isn't the result you were hoping for, but the only prints they were able to match were you guys and your mother, of course," Vito said in his best professional voice.

"I'm not sure I follow," Gayle said, not fully understanding the import of what Vito had just told them.

"It means," Anna interrupted, "that whoever did this, whoever was in the house, either wiped things clean or probably wore gloves."

"So where does that leave us?" Gayle asked, knowing the answer.

"Back at square one, I'm afraid," Vito concluded.

Cary didn't think this was the best time to bring up the gun, to tell Vito that she had been carrying it during the day. It could wait. But then Vito said in an ominous tone, "There's something else."

"We have Obi's remains, in the car. Should I bring them in?" Vito asked with great empathy on his face.

Cary and Gayle looked at each other and nodded. The box Vito brought over to them was smaller than Cary would have thought but still quite heavy. Obi had been a big boy. Cary couldn't wrap her brain around the fact that her precious Obelus was inside that container, that all that was left of him was ashes. She started to shake.

"It's okay," Anna began to speak. "It's okay. Everything will be all right."

But Cary knew that would never be the case. Things would never be all right again.

Gayle was still staying at their mother's house, so she didn't want to bring Obi's remains there. They decided for the time being to keep them at the cottage with Cary and company. Going forward, in addition to the gun, Obi would sleep next to Cary. That night, Cary broke her no alcohol rule several times. After her sister left and Vito and Anna retired to the bedroom, Cary lay down on the couch, Obi next to her on the coffee table.

Cary realized she hadn't heard from Hank all day. *I love you, right,* Cary thought to herself. And then a text popped up; the time stamp read 4:34 p.m. *Damn phone,* Cary groaned. She answered it: *Sorry. Just got this. What's up?*

Hank responded: *Thought you might like to stay over tonight.* Cary didn't think it was such a bad idea. But since Cary had been drinking,

Hank agreed to pick her up. Cary left Vito and Anna a note on the kitchen counter, got Vito's gun, bent down to kiss Obelus's remains, and went outside to wait for Hank.

Cary thought spending the night at Hank's was just what she needed. It was even starting to feel like home. Tonight would be special. It would be the first time they would be together since Hank had verbalized her feelings, that they openly knew they were in love with each other. It was late when they got to Hank's house, so, silently, they made their way into the bedroom. The alcohol was starting to wear off, but Cary was fine with that. She would want to remember every minute of the evening.

As they got into bed, Hank gave Cary a knowing look that tore right into her soul. Cary had never felt this close to anyone. She was overwhelmed with emotion. They began to reach for each other. Their bodies were in sync—and their minds. *So this is what it was like when you finally found the right person*, Cary told herself. She sensed that Hank was thinking the same thing. The sex went on for an hour or so, and then before Cary knew it, Hank was sound asleep in her arms.

Cary wondered how Hank could get up so early for work tomorrow after the passionate evening they had just shared. But while Hank slept like a baby, Cary was wired. Trying not to disturb her, Cary slipped out of bed to see what, if any, sugary substances there were lying around the kitchen; she came up empty-handed. *I'm not much of a dessert person*. Wasn't that what Hank had told Vito the first time Cary met her?

Having dozed off for a bit, it was now nearly three o'clock in the morning, and yet, Cary knew she'd never get any sleep if she didn't satisfy her craving. So against her better judgment, Cary put on boots over her pajamas, grabbed her jacket, and headed for the door. *Daylight would be coming soon*, she rationalized. Glancing at the keypad on the wall, Cary saw that the alarm was set. And she was just about to open the door. *Good catch*, she told herself. So she entered the code and was about to reset the alarm to "away," bypassing the motion detectors so that Hank wouldn't set them off if she got up for some reason, when Barry startled her by licking her hand. Cary hadn't noticed him right there beside her in the dark. *No harm in taking him with me for a ride.* But when Cary got outside, she remembered her Jeep wasn't there. So she went back inside to get Hank's keys. After all, Cary didn't think Hank would mind if she borrowed her car. And so, Barry and Cary jumped in Hank's car on a mission.

Cary loved late-night car rides when no one else was around. It helped her unwind and think. These days she chose to think about nothing. She looked over at Barry, curled up comfortably next to her in the passenger seat. The image brought on an overwhelming feeling of sadness. Obi didn't deserve what had happened to him. And it was all her fault, well, her sister's too. She'd never have that kind of unconditional love in her life again. There was something about the bond people shared with their special dog: the innocence. Cary felt distraught. If it weren't for Hank, she didn't know what she would do.

Cary had gotten about half a mile from Hank's home when she realized she had forgotten the gun. She couldn't find her phone either but figured she wasn't about to call anyone at this hour. Barry was now asleep, so he wouldn't make any noise if she went back into the house. Cary turned the car around and headed for Hank's. When she got there, Cary snuck inside and grabbed the revolver from underneath the couch in the den where she had left it for the night. She had learned her lesson. She wasn't going anywhere without that gun. As Cary got back into the car, Barry gave her a glance and went back to sleep.

As she drove away from Hank's house for the second time in ten minutes, Cary turned on the radio. Hank had it set to Sirius 49, the Soul Town station, as usual. Sam Cooke's "Bring It On Home To Me" played in the background. *They both had good taste in music,* Cary decided. What a night they had had. Romy, Kim, and all the rest were irrelevant now. Hank was the here and now and the *future*. Cary finally fit in.

Cary wasn't sure what would be open this time of night. She didn't feel like driving all the way into the center of Fairview to find a gas station, and she was pretty sure the diner and Super Stop 'N Shop only stayed open twenty-four seven on weekends these days. Then she remembered this little place where they held farmers' markets in the fall and spring. It was owned by an elderly couple who often began their workday in the middle of the night. It was worth a shot. As Cary pulled up to the parking lot, she turned off the engine, took out her wallet, placed the gun against her back, and made her way to the front entrance. She thought she saw a light on in the back and began to knock on the door. No answer. *How stupid to go out at all hours of the night like this, especially these days*. Cary hadn't matured since adolescence. *Time to grow up*, she admonished herself.

As Cary walked back to Hank's car, a vehicle appeared, seemingly out of nowhere, headed straight for her, headlights blazing through the dark. Barry woke up and began barking and scratching at the window in the front seat. As the car raced toward her, tires screeching, Cary understood what was happening. She had spent her entire life wondering what went through the mind of someone as they realized they were about to die, to be *murdered*. And now she knew. She had just gotten the details wrong. They were her people, she had always known it, she had always tried to remember them, *all* of them, and now she wondered who would remember her.

EPILOGUE

Cary's shattered body lay still on the ground. She had needed to be taught a lesson. She had looked like a deer in headlights. How ironic. It might be time to get another car. He would figure out the best place to hide the body for the time being, in case Connecticut brought back the death penalty. If there was one thing that he admired about the police, it was that they were men and women of their word. Yes, he couldn't forget about the girlfriend: Detective Hank Nowak. He had Eve to thank for knowing who she was and her full name. She would put up a better fight. It could wait, though. He'd had a busy time of it trailing the four Musketeers. Sometimes he made himself laugh.

ACKNOWLEDGMENTS

Premonition is my heartfelt tribute to all of the murder victims that have come to my attention throughout my life. It is also meant to highlight some particular cases I became obsessed with and to draw attention to what I perceive are failings in our legal system. But without the following people, *Premonition* might never have become a reality. I first want to thank Ana Crespo, who, more than a decade ago, encouraged me to start writing, insisting that she knew I had a "book in me." Apparently, she was right. I owe you so much, Ana, for your wisdom and loyalty.

Next, I have to thank Emi Battaglia, who led me to Anthony Ziccardi and Post Hill Press. Thanks, Anthony, for giving a new author a chance.

To Nancy Grace, my real-life guardian angel, who I have been blessed to know and call a friend for more than twenty years—I love you.

To my friends and test readers—Tim Jennings, Jason Horowitz, Beth Karas, and Rikki Klieman—I so appreciate you taking the time to give me thoughtful and very helpful feedback.

And to my friends and colleagues—Rita Cosby, Jack Ford, Robi Ludwig, Ashleigh Banfield, Gregg Jarrett, Kimberly Guilfoyle, and

Jerry Boyle—thanks for helping *Premonition* reach the largest audience possible. I am deeply grateful.

I want to thank Dennis Baker for his amazing work on the book proposal, which caught the eye of several key players involved with bringing *Premonition* to life.

To Lenore Riegel and Jerome Charyn, you have my unending gratitude for "mentoring" me through the process of getting a book published.

My deepest gratitude to Maddie Sturgeon, Devon Brown, Jessica Vandergriff, and the wonderful team at Post Hill Press. You were a total delight to work with.

To all of my Court TV and *Nancy Grace* friends and colleagues, please know that although you may think you see yourself in the book, each character is unique and complex. Many are composites or totally fictitious. But although I took much of my inspiration for the book from real life, some events have been exaggerated for dramatic effect. Certain situations may seem familiar but the characters in them are fabricated. In no way did I want nor mean to offend anyone, and I hope everyone will appreciate the story in the spirit in which it was intended.

And finally, to Obelus, my best friend, soul mate, and steadfast companion who was by my side every step of the way throughout the entire journey. You are the true hero of *Premonition*.